# THREE KINGS  ONE THRONE

## MICHAEL WILLS

Published in 2013 by the author
using SilverWood Books Empowered Publishing ®
2020 edition independently published

SilverWood Books
www.silverwoodbooks.co.uk

ISBN 9781916392670 (KDP paperback)

British Library Cataloguing in Publication Data
A CIP catalogue record for this book is available from the British Library

Cover from left to right:
The Papal banner flown by William of Normandy at the Battle of Hastings
The raven banner flown by Harald Hardrada at the Battle of Stamford Bridge
The "Fighting Man" banner of King Harold II"

Michael Wills was born on the Isle of Wight and educated at the Priory Boys School and Carisbrooke Grammar. He trained as a teacher at St Peter's College, Saltley, Birmingham, before working at a secondary school in Kent for two years.

After retraining to become a teacher of English as a Foreign Language, he worked in Sweden for thirteen years. During this period, he wrote several English language teaching books. His teaching career has included time working in rural Sweden, a sojourn that first sparked his now enduring interest in Scandinavian history and culture – an interest that, after many years of research, both academic and in the field, led him to write *Finn's Fate* and the sequel novel, *Three Kings, One Throne*.

Today, Michael works part-time as Ombudsman for English UK, the National Association of English Language Providers. Though a lot of his spare time is spent with grandchildren, he also has a wide range of interests including researching for future books, writing, playing the guitar, carpentry and electronics. He spends at least two months a year sailing his boat which is currently in Scandinavia.

For more about Michael Wills and his work, visit his website at www.michaelwills.eu.

# Acknowledgements

In my desire to make this novel as historically accurate as possible, I have read widely on the period covered by the book. I am greatly indebted to the scholarship of others. I have listed the books used as primary source material at the end of the novel.

As ever, I owe a great debt of gratitude to my wife Barbro for her advice on content, and her patience and fortitude in proofreading the developing versions of the book. She has been my companion on long journeys to battle sites, archaeological digs and museums, and has given constant encouragement. I would also like to thank Emma Wills Davies for her helpful suggestions about the story and for her assiduous proofreading.

# Map of Scandinavia

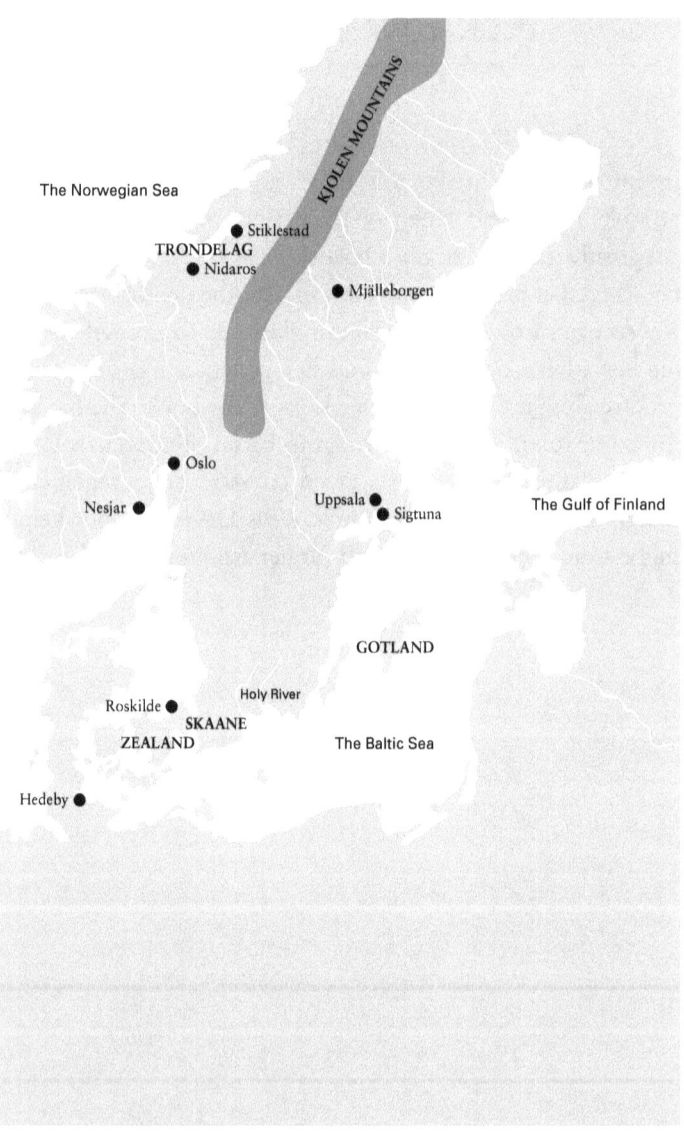

The Norwegian Sea

KJØLEN MOUNTAINS

● Stiklestad
TRONDELAG
● Nidaros

● Mjälleborgen

● Oslo

Nesjar ●

Uppsala ●
● Sigtuna

The Gulf of Finland

GOTLAND

Holy River
Roskilde ●
SKAANE
ZEALAND

The Baltic Sea

Hedeby ●

# Contents

# The Lineage of Two Men – Ivar and Torkil

|            Denmark            |           England            |
| :---------------------------: | :--------------------------: |
|         Finn Arvidsson        |                              |
|     Born in Lapland AD 961    |                              |
|           With Aneca          |          With Hilda          |
|                ↓              |               ↓              |
|         Olav Finnsson         |            Alric             |
|   Born in Roskilde AD 982     |   Born in Selceeflet AD 985  |
|         Died AD 1026          |        Died AD 1052          |
|                ↓              |               ↓              |
|        Ivar Olavsson          |            Edlin             |
|  Born in Roskilde AD 1012     |  Born in Selceeflet AD 1016  |
|                               |               ↓              |
|                               |       Torkil and Emma        |
|                               | Born in Selceeflet AD 1036 and 1037 |

# Introduction

The eleventh century was one of the most exciting periods in the history of the Western world. In England, it was a time of uncertainty, of violence and political turbulence. At a national level, trusted allies frequently changed allegiances and powerful men, motivated by greed, hatred and revenge, determined the course of events. Life for the people of the country was full of uncertainties. Foes could quickly become friends and vice versa. Every sail which approached the shore could bring with it lethal danger. And it was not only the Norsemen's longships which threatened the people of England, for the country had conflicts with the Welsh, the Scots, the French and the Flemish at various times during the century. There were even outbreaks of civil war in the country itself, with devastating results. England was not alone in experiencing a tumult of political upheaval, for Scandinavia and the Continent also suffered from wars, coups and rebellion.

My story relates to the effect of these troubled times on the lives of two men, one born in England and one in Denmark, who are cast around on this sea of historic turbulence until, on one occasion, they meet.

The history of the century is complex, and so I have chosen to describe only those events which shaped the lives and characters of the main players in the story. But one issue of complexity which I could not avoid was that two of the most influential men of the period had very similar names: Harold, Earl of Wessex, and Harald, King of Norway. Where identifying them is not obvious by virtue of the context, I have sought to differentiate between them in a number of ways, most often by mentioning their nationalities or adding the surname 'Sigurdsson' to Harald, the King of Norway's name. Later in the story, he gained the epithet 'hardrada' or 'hard ruler' (though opinions differ about the exact meaning of the title). Thus, ultimately, I have used this epithet to identify him.

Less than a kilometre from my home near Salisbury, runs a track, now sadly much overgrown, known as Green Lane. There are many byways in England with this name as it was the label given to ancient trails and animal droves linking villages, farms and market towns.

As often as time permits, I walk along the path and, as I do so, I am conscious that I am probably following the route of an English king and his entourage when they passed that way in the month of October nearly a thousand years ago. The blackthorn bushes which catch my jacket if I leave the centre of the track, the brambles which a wind may stir to grab at my hat, the disturbed woodpigeons which startle as they noisily flap out of the trees ahead, and the circling raptor which gives up the hunt when his prey takes cover at the sound of approaching feet; these things would have been seen, heard and felt by the royal procession accompanying the King on his journey to his capital after a hunting trip in south Wiltshire.

Conjecture? Yes, perhaps, but this track leads to the River Avon which would have to be crossed by the royal retinue. Green Lane guides the traveller to Britford, the only place where the Avon could be crossed on foot, for this was over one hundred years before Salisbury was founded. The alternative route north would have been through Wilton. To have travelled there would have added to the journey time, and the King was in a hurry. Before he crossed the river, he was met by travellers coming in the opposite direction, men who urgently needed to discuss a matter of national importance with the King. The meeting took place on the bank of the Avon at Britford; a meeting from which came a decision that, ultimately, was to contribute significantly to a calamity for the country.

During a period of just over a hundred years from 950 AD, the Kingdom of England was the most fought over domain in Europe. Violence, theft, blackmail, marriages of convenience, murder and gross disloyalty abounded as rival factions sought the ultimate prize: the crown of the realm.

Michael Wills
Salisbury
March 2012

# Chapter 1

## Trial by Ordeal

The rider coaxed his horse to slowly push its head through the tall reeds. Cautiously, horse and rider approached the shoreline as noiselessly as possible. They stopped, and the young man carefully reached for the hood on his peregrine falcon's head. He gently slid it off and immediately felt the vibrant power of the bird as she anticipated the hunt. The falcon was trembling as it was restrained by jesses[1] knotted to anklets on its legs and dug its claws into the elbow-length leather hawking glove on the rider's arm. One flap of its wings while tethered was enough to startle the flock of richly coloured wigeon feeding on the salt marsh. The male ducks erupted in their characteristic musical whistle, and the females made their abrupt growling call as the flock attempted to flee the imminent danger. As the sky began to fill with the white-bellied birds, the rider released his hawk. The hunter strained with her wing muscles to gain height and speed in pursuit of the quarry as the flock turned and headed over the shore.

The rider on the horse gazed skywards, hoping that the sheer number of ducks in the wheeling flock would not confuse his bird and that the one she chose would be brought down

---

[1]  Jesses – tethers restraining the hawk by the legs

over the land. The falcon was experienced and immediately picked a duck which had been slow to lift itself from the feeding ground. The duck twisted and turned and climbed and dived, but the hawk copied its trajectory flying above it and gained distance. Then the raptor dived down heavily onto the duck and struck it to the ground. There, its claws grabbed the duck and held it.

The rider turned his horse and made his way back through the reeds in the general direction of where he thought the falcon had brought the duck to the ground. As he moved back into the open pasture, he heard the distant sound of another horse's hooves. A horse and rider were cantering towards him, but he paid them no heed; he was intent on recovering the spoils of his hunt.

By the time he had located the falcon holding the duck in the grass, the speeding rider had caught up with him. The young man turned and immediately recognised the horseman as the steward on his grandfather's estate. The youth realised what the steward's message would be: a request from his mother to return home as he had been away for so long. In fact, he had been hunting since dawn.

He leapt from his saddle and put his foot on the duck's head, denying the falcon its expected meal. His priority was to ensure that his valuable hunter was safely tethered on his arm. The bird had been a gift from visitors to his home the previous year: a king and a duke. A properly manned[2] and trained peregrine falcon was enormously valuable, and the bird was the youth's most treasured possession.

"Master Torkil, master, come quick. 'Tis your grandfather; he has become worse. Your mother requests that you attend her and your grandfather," he pleaded. His tortured face betrayed the fact that he had foreseen that his task would be difficult.

---

[2]  Manned – a hunting bird which has become familiar with humans

"Why now? You can see the sport is good today. Grandfather has been ill for some weeks. Can't he wait?"

"Your mother fears that he has not long to live. He is asking for you."

The steward slowly dismounted from his piebald cob[3], his lack of agility betraying his age and indicating the damage sustained to his body in another life, long ago, when he was a warrior. He bent down and grabbed the struggling duck by the neck with both hands. He pulled and twisted the feathered neck as the pink down from the duck's breast flew in a flurry around him and handed the lifeless form to Torkil. The youth tucked the duck into his leather pouch, which was already quite full, and remounted. The steward did likewise, but with more difficulty than the younger man who said sullenly, "Alright, let's go. What a waste of a good afternoon's sport."

The ailing grandfather was propped up on a cot near to the fire in the centre of the room for, although it was nearly summer, he suffered badly from the cold in the stark, stone-floored chamber where he been brought to spend his last days before meeting his Maker. He was lying on a sack mattress which was stuffed with hay; under his head, he had a linen pillow filled with the same material. Normally, the whole family and servants slept in the hall together but, because of his age and infirmity, the invalid was in this room by himself.

Torkil quietly joined his mother in the chamber. She was an elegant and well-dressed woman, her head covered by a black scarf indicating that she was still in mourning for someone who had been close to her. But they were not alone with the old man, for in a corner of the room behind them stood a monk. He was dressed in a black habit and held a cross in one hand. He neither spoke nor stirred.

---

[3]   Cob – a workhorse of indeterminate breed

The old man reached out to the boy who reacted by drawing away. He was frightened. He did not want to watch as death crept up inexorably on his grandfather.

In a surprisingly strong voice, the old man said, "Come, sit beside me, Torkil. Your father is dead, and it falls to me to tell you our family's story. Soon you will be a man and master of this estate. A landed man must know his heritage."

The woman pushed the youth forward and, reluctantly, he sat on the flagstones by the bed.

The old man looked up at the wooden beams as if waiting for divine help with his recollections. "I speak of the time of King Aelthelred. A king in name only to us; we never saw much sign of his damned authority even though we supported his army several times at great cost with men from the estate. Of course, we did see his cursed Shire Reeve[4] when he was tax collecting. The Viking armies roamed the country at will, despite paying them the *geld*[5]. I could tell you many things for, although I do not remember what the weekday is today, I have a clear memory of those times. I want to tell you of your great grandmother and how our family gained lands and status. I was born a peasant, son of a poor couple. I cannot read and I can only write my name, but I can tell you a story even if my speech is sometimes the tongue of an uneducated man. You are lucky, you want for nothing, and you have had an education with that leech of a priest who tries to filch my fortune by demanding favours: money for this and money for that."

The old man was silent for a few seconds. He licked his lips and continued. "In our village we had a Viking raid in November of my sixteenth year. They took my father; he was never seen again. As I said, we were poor, but we had made a

---

[4]  Shire Reeve – local representative of the king, became known as 'sheriff'

[5]  Geld – money paid by the English king to Viking raiders to persuade them to desist from attacks

living in Selceeflet.[6] Father was a clever blacksmith though he had but one eye and a lame leg. Many buildings were burned, but not our house. The little wooden church didn't suffer as much damage as did the church in the next village, Creektown. There the building had been burned to the ground. It was nothing but a heap of black cinders. But, in Selceeflet, in the weeks before Christmas 1001, the villagers had repaired the church roof and replaced the scorched timbers.

"But it was not for a Yuletide service that I was viciously dragged with my hands tied to stand in the church, and I can remember every detail. The memory has burnt itself into my brain. I still get nightmares about what happened."

The old man sat up and spat on the floor. It seemed that he did so not because of a physical need but in an expression of disdain for the tormentors he remembered.

"It was a bitterly cold December day, and the wind was ruffling the cloaks and cowls of the people who had not arrived early and were unable to enter the overcrowded building. As I was dragged in, the people who had been our friends cursed and shouted at me. Yes! These were neighbours I had known all my life, and now they had turned against Mother and me, damn them all! The church was normally big enough to serve the needs of our village, but that day the congregation was swelled by visitors from Creektown and some even from as far away as Eremue[7] down the coast. Oh yes, the bastards came from near and far to see the humiliation and suffering of Mother and me. Perhaps the folk outside were the lucky ones, for there were no open shutters in the church walls and the stench of the farming and fisher folk, crammed into the tiny place, was made worse by the fumes of a log-burning brazier in the narrow aisle."

---

[6]   Selceeflet – Anglo-Saxon name for Shalfleet, Isle of Wight. Literally 'Shallow Creek'

[7]   Eremue – Yarmouth

The old man scratched the stubble on his unshaven chin. His face was sallow and gaunt. The blue veins stood out on the back of his bony hands as he seemed to be easing an irritation through the whiskers. He continued. "My mother, Hilda, was standing by the blazing fire between two ceremonially dressed guards. What was it they called them? Oh yes, 'agents of justice'. Ha, that's a laugh; overpaid pompous fools. She was barefoot and dressed only in a grubby white shift, for she had been locked in a pigsty overnight. Although she was now old, nearly forty, she was still a fine-looking woman. But that day she had not been able to spend time putting her long hair into the customary plait and it hung dishevelled over her shoulders and face, partly obscuring her eyes. But even from where I was held, I could see that those eyes were filled with tears.

"The fat priest who stood at the front was looking at her lustfully while he waited for one of the guards to call for silence. He, the so-called man of God, was comfortable enough while Mother froze. I can see him now: he wore a heavy cloak with a cowl around his shoulders. So capacious was the warm cloak that the cloth hung in folds. His hands were hidden in the long sleeves, but a cross which was in his right hand protruded from that side. The guard bawled at the rowdy congregation and very quickly silence fell. They wanted the show to start. The priest stared at Mother. His face was stern and there was no hint, no, not a trace of the mercy which his church preaches.

"*Hilda, you are accused of being a whore for Viking warriors who visit you in the dead of night. God will decide on your guilt or innocence.*

"The crowd knew what was to happen next and the bastards were all jostling, trying to get a view of one of the guards as he wrapped a wet cloth around the end of an iron rod which was sticking out of the fire basket.

"Then the priest said, and any man could hear that he was enjoying saying this, *You will take the hot iron and walk nine paces*

18

*towards me. Then you may drop the rod to the ground. Your wounds will be dressed and kept covered for three days. If, when the bandages are unbound, the wound is healing then you have been wrongly accused and you are innocent. If they are not healing, then, since we have no proof that your husband is dead, you are sentenced to have your ears and nose removed.*[8]*"*

The old man paused and then said, "You can't imagine how desperate I was. I struggled against the ropes which were binding my wrists and shouted out protesting that she was innocent, but one of the men holding me shoved a cloth into my mouth to keep me quiet."

He stopped to rest and the woman with the black scarf gave him a cup of water to drink from. By then he had the complete attention of his grandson, and the boy was kneeling nearer to catch every word.

"What happened, Grandfather?"

The storyteller waited in silence for a few seconds, still staring at the ceiling beams, and then continued. "The church was completely silent as my mother raised her hands to grasp the red-hot end of the rod. She uttered a gasp and the smell of burnt flesh was added to the foul air. She walked towards the priest; one step, two, three, four, five, and then there was the sound of ringing as the iron rod hit the flagstones of the aisle floor. Mother collapsed in a crumpled heap at the feet of the priest. He was really taken aback and at first didn't know what to do. There was uproar in the congregation as the spectacle had ended early; the mob had not got full value. The priest told my guards to set me free and for me to take Mother home to get her wounds dressed.

"They cut the ropes binding my wrists and I angrily pushed the crowd aside to claim her motionless body. I tried to lift her, but my hands were at first numb from the ropes which had tightly

---

[8]   Later the formalised punishment for a woman's adultery. King Cnut's Law 53: 'If a woman during her husband's life commits adultery with another man, her legal husband is to have all her property and she is to lose her nose and ears.'

bound me. The guards tried to help me, but I spat at them and said that they had done their vile work; I would tend to Mother.

"I carried her out to the cart which was waiting outside and covered her with a coat. She was shaking violently from the cold and the shock. An old woman whom the priest had appointed was going to dress her wounds. She sat next to Mother, and I led the cart home to our little house on the outskirts of the village."

"But, Grandfather, why did they accuse her?"

The boy's mother intervened. "Torkil, let's give Grandfather a rest before he continues."

"No, no, I am alright. I want the boy and you to know. I have much, much more to tell, but, Edlin, give me some more water, my throat is so dry, and then I will explain why my mother was so cruelly treated."

He sipped the water and then continued, speaking slowly and purposefully. "What I am going to tell you now may seem like the imaginings of an old man, but I swear that it is true. I am dying; I have no need to lie. One afternoon I was helping my mother to set up her weaving loom. My father was working in the smithy outside. Suddenly the door was thrown open, it smashed back on the wall, and two heavily armed Viking warriors burst into the room. Fortunately, the ceiling was too low for them to swing a sword at me so one threw me to the ground. I hit the floor with such force that I was winded, but I was conscious enough to see the other man throw Mother onto the table and lift her skirts. I struggled to my feet and jumped onto the back of one of the men, trying to gouge his eyes. It was the only thing I could do; we had no weapons.

"It all happened so quickly. A third man came in and, when I saw him raise his hand axe, I knew that this was the end of my short life. But the blow didn't strike me. Instead, the axe cut through the round helmet in front of me and buried itself in the skull of the man whose back I was riding. He fell to the floor with me on top of him. When I looked up, I saw the man who had used the axe swing his seax[9] and slash the throat of the one interfering with Mother.

"It was utterly unbelievable. There were two dead Vikings and their blood all over the floor. He helped Mother and me to our feet and just stood there looking at us for ages. He then turned, left the building and closed the door. We heard voices and, when we tried to look outside the door, we were pushed back in by two warriors who appeared to be guarding our house."

The old man coughed a deep wracking cough which seemed to come from his belly. His face contorted with the pain from his gut. He wheezed, took several deep breaths and then continued. "Later, the man who had saved us came back and dragged the bodies of the warriors outside."

There was another long pause while the old man winced and fought for breath.

"But why did he save you, Grandfather?"

"I asked him that, but he did not speak our language. He just left with all the other warriors. I went out to see if I could find my father."

"Did you?"

"No, there was blood on the ground in the smithy but no sign of my father, and I never saw him again. Never, ever again. But let me continue."

He tried to do so, but another coughing fit made it impossible. The boy's mother intervened. "Father, you rest now and we will continue this afternoon when you have had a sleep."

The old man indicated with a wave of the hand that he agreed. The woman adjusted his blankets and then ushered the boy out. As they left, the monk came forward and began a chant in Latin.

Later that afternoon, Torkil's mother called him in from the stable yard where he had been sitting watching a farmhand breaking in a new riding horse.

---

[9]   Seax – a large knife carried by both Vikings and Anglo-Saxons

"Grandfather is feeling better and wants to continue to tell you his story."

Torkil enthusiastically ran inside and into the great hall. There, the old man, wrapped in furs, was sitting in a large wooden chair.

"May is a wonderful month, full of the promise of impending summer; my last summer, I fear. First, the hawthorn blossom, and then the elder, and then the hungry months for the poor and the most profitable months for the rich."

Torkil knew what the old man was referring to. In June and July, the fruits of the previous harvest had been used up and the spring crops had not yet matured. The poor were forced to eat whatever scraps and wild herbs they could find. But for those rich enough to have surplus supplies in their barns, this was a good time as their food stocks commanded the highest price of the year.

"But the time I talk of is winter," said the man in the chair. "I told you of the plundering of our village by the Norsemen. Two nights after the raid, soon after dark, when I was sitting by the fire discussing with Mother what would become of us if Father did not return, there was a soft knock on the door. Well, we were both quite nervous after the raid but, in the hope that it might have been Father, I opened the latch."

The old man paused, reliving the moment which changed his life. He shifted his position, drew a deep breath and continued. "The door was pushed open by a broad, well-built man with shoulder-length grey hair whom I immediately recognised as the warrior who had saved us two days before. We were terrified.

"He walked into the room followed by another, taller, but slimmer man. The first man turned to the second and said something in Norse. This second man introduced himself in good Anglo-Saxon as Knut and said that we should not be afraid.

"Well, we were afraid; we had seen what these men were capable of. But Knut reassured us and said that they had come as friends. He asked me my name and I told him that it was Alric. He said that the grey-haired man was Gunnar, chieftain of the Viking force on the island and that they had come to see if Mother and I were alright.

"I asked Knut why they cared about us, and he shocked us both by telling us that Gunnar was my uncle, my father's elder brother! Through Knut, I asked Gunnar how he could know this and if he had seen Father. With some hesitation, he told me that he had seen that I wore a bear's claw necklace, the same as Finn, his brother, had. It didn't make sense: he had killed the man I was on top of before he could have seen the necklace."

"Is that the same necklace you wear now?" asked Torkil.

"Yes, the very one, though now it is in a silver mount and hangs on a chain. My father always said that it was lucky and would protect the wearer from death at the hands of a stranger. His mother had given it to him in the Norselands. You shall have it when I die."

"Was your father from the Norselands?"

"Please, no more questions. Let me tell you my story!"

Torkil sensed the old man's annoyance and noticed his mother shaking her head at him. He let his grandfather continue uninterrupted.

"Mother was still terrified and stayed silent, but I was feeling braver now and asked Gunnar through Knut how he would recognise my father. He confidently told me that my father, Finn, had a limp and a tattoo of the hammer of Thor on his right cheek. He went on to tell me that he had thought that his brother was dead, because he had seen him drowning near to Portland nineteen years before. My father had been taking part in a Viking raid on Dorncester. Gunnar had had to stay on the ship because he had been wounded the day before. He and the crew had had to move the ships out from the shore because Saxon archers were firing at them. Finn was the only warrior to come back from the raid. But when he appeared on the beach, a large number of Saxons were chasing him. Gunnar had tried to save Finn but was unable to pull him onto the Viking ship before it was forced to leave in a hurry. Gunnar was amazed to find that Finn must have escaped from the Saxons.

"I asked him if the Vikings had taken my father as a slave in the raid two days ago. He said no and that he would not have allowed that to happen. I could tell that he was getting irritated by being questioned and, afraid that the mood might change for the worse, I fell silent.

"Gunnar fumbled with his cloak, pulled out a leather pouch, walked across to the table and put the leather bag onto it. He spoke to Knut who then addressed me directly and told me that Gunnar was a rich and powerful man who could help me if we fell on hard times because of my father's absence. Gunnar had brought a gift to assist us through the winter. He pointed to the leather bag and asked Mother to open it. Inside were many pieces of silver. We both stared with amazement at the fortune before us.

"Knut asked if they could sleep on our floor until first light when they would have a better chance of finding their way back through the forest to Werrar.[10] Mother invited them to sit and started to prepare some food for them. Later, they slept on the floor in front of the fire embers for a few hours until the cockerel crowed; then they picked up their weapons and left.

"Our undoing was the fact that Thomas the swineherd was about early, driving his pigs to the forest to eat acorns, and saw the two armed men leaving the house. He ran off towards the village. I thought that they might chase him and kill him, but instead they strode off into the woods. I wish they had killed him."

Torkil's grandfather took several deep breaths, his strained face betraying the pain he felt.

"That was a black day for us. For, not an hour later, the priest

---

[10]   Werrar – on the River Medina on the Isle of Wight. From Old English 'wer' and 'ora': 'the river bank by a weir'

and several village elders arrived at the house and demanded to know who our visitors were. Mother, already grief-stricken on account of Father being missing, broke down and told the interrogators that the warriors had brought us a gift of silver. Then prurient tongues started wagging and, ere long, accusations were made of Mother whoring. The rest of the story you already know. Now I must rest. Come back tomorrow and I will finish my story."

The effort of speaking for so long had drained the old man and he slumped in the chair. Torkil's mother motioned to the monk to help them, and the three of them lifted him onto his bed. As the monk lifted the old man's shoulders, his hood fell back. Torkil noticed that, on the left side of the monk's tonsure, there was an ugly scar on the side of his head and part of his ear was missing.

# Chapter 2

## The Evil Protector

The following day, Torkil was once more called in to join his mother in his grandfather's room. The old man was lying in bed staring at the ceiling. He looked even more frail than the day before.

Edlin pulled a stool up to the bed and whispered, "Father, are you sure you feel well enough to talk to us today?"

He smiled and said, "I fear that if I do not then you may never hear my story. The boy's father never knew how we came to be landowners. He was too busy spending my money and enjoying his sinful ways with that brute Swegen Godwinson to take an interest in our estates. A lot of good it did him. He got his just reward when he was killed in a drunken brawl in Normandy."

The old man's daughter did not need to be reminded of the profligate ways of her late husband. She had spent much of her married life alone in England while he had been forced into exile in Flanders and Denmark with the disgraced eldest son of Earl Godwin of Wessex. There was no doubt that her husband had been party to the murders carried out by Swegen Godwinson. They were both violent men. She knew it. She had accepted that her husband sometimes took his fists to her, but the worst thing was when he beat the boy, and he did not stop at using his hands. The lad had a scar on his forehead from when his father had thrown a drinking horn at him. She had always done her best to protect Torkil, and it had become a habit. Now, even though his father was dead, she continued to shield him from discomfort and worry and worldly affairs. Perhaps the vicissitudes of her life with her late husband had increased her maternal instinct and she wanted to hold on to Torkil as a boy for as long as possible. Or was it that she feared that, provided with the temptations of adulthood, he might go the way of his father?

"Where is the boy, Edlin?" The old man craned round to see if Torkil was in the room. Torkil was a well built youth with a shock of red hair and blue eyes. He had had a comfortable upbringing in material terms, the benefits of the family's wealth. But he was a lonely figure: there were no other boys of his status nearby and so he had no real friends. The village folk had to show respect to him – most of them depended on the landowner for their living – but he was not allowed to socialise with them. He occupied most of his time indulging in the privileges that wealth brought, including education. He had formal lessons with the priest most days but, as soon as he was allowed, he would go to the stables and have his pony saddled to go riding, sometimes hunting with his hawks; and occasionally he was allowed to go out with the fishermen, who owed service to the family, to learn boat handling skills. Nevertheless, he was young for his age. He had been shielded from the violence of the times, partly because the estate was isolated geographically, but also because of the clever way in which his grandfather had furthered the family's interests without making enemies. The wily old man had always been skilful in political matters, had avoided trouble with neighbours, and carefully used his position as vassal to the Earl in Wintoncaestre[11] to gain favour.

Torkil had lived in his grandfather's house all his life, but the old man, although kindly towards him, was a distant figure: he always seemed busy with the estate's affairs and seldom had

---

[11]  Wintoncaestre – Winchester

time for his grandson. In fact, Torkil was somewhat frightened of him, but not the sort of fear that he had had for his father, a father who had had no time for the boy and had never shown any affection. He was ashamed that he did not grieve for his father, but in fact, with him gone now, he felt relief, for he knew that sooner or later he would have had to confront his father physically to defend his mother and himself.

"Come closer, lad, so I don't have to speak loudly. You don't need to fear me. Bring the stool closer."

The boy sat beside his mother and waited for his grandfather to begin.

"Where did I get to?"

"Grandfather, you told us of the visit of the Norsemen to your house and the silver."

"Ah yes, the silver. That silver was a curse on us. The priest took it as evidence but, as you will hear, in the end it was a curse on him." He smiled and, for an instant, seemed to be savouring something in his thoughts.

"We went about our business for several days after the visit of the priest and the elders. Mother was desperately worried about Father, as was I. We had no means of support without Father's income. I had learnt a little about the blacksmith's skills, but not enough to make a living. Despite my urging, Mother did not eat enough and she was growing weak. And then they came to get her.

"*Hilda, wife of Finn the blacksmith, you are to be tried for whoring.*

"I can still hear the priest's words." The old man gave a shudder and paused for a while.

"And I have already told you what happened next. So, I will go on to tell you how I became a fugitive orphan.

"When we returned to the house after the trial, mother's condition worsened every day. The burns hurt her terribly and her arms became very inflamed and swollen. She would not eat and frequently fainted. The woman who had been sent to care for her tried to feed her soup, but with little success. As Mother lay prone on her bed, the woman said to me, *We had better keep her alive or it will be the worse for you!*

"She explained that, if Mother did not survive the trial by ordeal, she would be deemed to have been guilty and, as I had supported her story about how we came by the silver, my sworn testimony would be deemed to be lies. Lies under holy oath! Retribution could be awful."

The old man's voice had got quieter and quieter, and he frequently paused in the telling of the events.

The woman stood and bent over the bed. "Father, would you like to rest now? We can come back tomorrow."

"No!" His voice was suddenly much stronger and he grasped his daughter's arm tightly. "Edlin, don't go. I must tell you this before I die. Please listen!"

The woman sat down again.

"Mother died on the third day, early in the morning before the woman came to the smithy. In the flickering candlelight, I had been wiping her fevered brow when she gasped, a horrible guttural sucking of air, and then exhaled a long breath, before she was permanently silent. I was just sixteen years old, my father had been missing for over a week, my mother had been humiliated, vilified and put to a terrible death, and now I was in mortal danger.

"With difficulty, I dragged Mother out to the edge of the forest to bury her before the priest discovered that she was dead. Once he knew this, my life was in danger. It was already getting light, and I was surprised to see that there was another grave, recently dug, where the forest met the pasture. One of Father's hammers was placed on the grave; it almost looked like a cross. Beside the grave was a wooden spade with an iron digging edge, the sort that Father used to make. I grabbed the spade and worked quickly in fear that the woman would soon arrive at the house to tend to Mother. She would surely tell the priest and the elders of Mother's demise and denounce me."

The old man stopped; he was getting visibly agitated as he recounted the story of his mother's death and had become breathless. The room was silent apart from his heavy breathing as he tried to calm himself.

"It was heavy work but, by the time the sun rose, I was satisfied that the grave was deep enough and I rolled Mother's lifeless body into the hole which I had dug alongside the other grave. She fell onto her back; her open eyes appeared to be focussed on the sky beyond me as I peered down. I thought that I should climb down into the hole and close her eyes, but just then I heard the woman calling into our open door to announce her arrival.

"I dug and scooped and scraped the soil back into the grave as quickly as I could and threw the spade into the bushes. I ran along the forest edge to a partly overgrown path which I knew would lead me south-east into the densest part of the forest."

Once more the old man stopped and paused for breath. He had been getting more and more excited as he relived the terror of that morning. "A drink of water please," he said.

The woman called a servant and asked for a fresh jug of water from the well and, when it arrived, gave her father a drink.

"I was cold, muddy, wet, hungry and very frightened. I fought the overhanging brambles for a long time until I came to a small clearing. The cropped grass betrayed the frequent visits of hares. This was a place where Father and I had sometimes snared them. He was very good at it; he always said that he had learnt hunting skills in an earlier life. In the corner of the clearing was a pond; the trodden path showed that someone often went there to fish or collect water. There were two other paths leading from the grassy space. The one going east had a tangle of undergrowth, indicating that it was not often used. The one striking south was well trodden, but never by us. For along that path lived the hag. I had never seen her, but all of the villagers including the priest were afraid of her reputed powers in the dark arts."

"Witchcraft?" asked Torkil.

"Call it what you will, but you have to remember that Vectis[12] had only been Christian for three hundred years. It was the last part of England to be converted, and that was done by force. So there were many who secretly still clung to the old ways and were very superstitious."

"Were you?"

"My mother was a Christian and I was brought up as a Christian, but my father was a pagan. Nevertheless, we villagers feared the power of the hag. Children who misbehaved were told that they would be given to the hag."

The grandfather groaned and held his hands over his stomach as if to try to ameliorate the pain.

"Another drink, if you please, Edlin."

He grasped the beaker with both hands and held it to his mouth. He gave it back to the woman and then he continued, "Hesitatingly, I walked down the southbound path. In my desperation, I had decided that, since she was hated and feared by the villagers, she might help me. The enemy of my enemy could be my friend. After a little while, I heard a dog barking and, shortly after, I heard a woman shouting. The pathway was awful. There were rotted bird carcasses hanging from the bushes, and here and there the stones on the ground had eyes painted on them with limewash and red ochre. Coming round a corner in the path, I saw a wooden hovel with a turf roof. The dog was tied up outside."

There had been silence in the room throughout the old man's recounting of his story. The monk never stirred and the mother and son had listened with rapt attention. But now the room seemed to become even quieter. The woman and the boy almost froze with the terror they felt about the occult. The storyteller had had their attention all the time, but now they were hanging on every syllable.

---

[12]  Vectis – Isle of Wight

"In the low doorway stood the hag. She wore a rough brown cloak which touched the ground as she stooped under the low door frame. Her tangled grey hair partly covered her face as it fell forward. To my amazement, she was pushed aside by another, younger woman.

"'What do you want?' the younger woman shrieked.

"I told her that I needed her help and, after some time, I managed to persuade her that I meant them no harm, but that I needed to hide. I must have looked awful in my muddy clothes, but they could see that I was young and unlikely to be a threat to them. The old woman pushed the dog aside and bade me enter the house.

"Well, I could tell you much about that house and my time there, the mysterious incantations and the weird ceremonies. But the important thing was that the villagers never found me. Or, at least, if they thought that I was with the hag, they never dared come to get me."

"But where did the other woman come from, Grandfather?"

"That was because of the terrible, unspoken truth about poor villages like ours. If a girl child is born out of wedlock, or if some parents have a new baby and already have too many mouths to feed, babies, usually girls, are put out into the forest for God to take them. The hag knew that she must pass on her skills to another. So, she rescued one of the girl babies and brought her up on goat's milk until she was weaned. She then became the hag's apprentice.

"Yes, terrible things happened in the little hovel which I won't tell you about, but the worst thing was that the women would only take me in and hide me if I agreed to denounce the Christian faith and embrace their customs and beliefs. Well, I was so angry with the priest in our village and the cruel way in which he had treated Mother that I had no difficulty in rejecting the faith I had been born into and instead worshipped the evil one, Beelzebub."

The listeners were aghast.

"Tell me about it, Grandfather!" said the young man.

"No, I will not speak of that shameful time, suffice to say that the hag told me that my life would be successful and I would become wealthy if I did as the dark force required."

He lowered his voice as if speaking to himself and said, "And she was right."

There was a long pause while the old man reflected.

"So you see, I had to tell you my story, for when I die we will never meet again in heaven. My destiny is to go to another place, and I am fearful that no amount of priestly blessings or promises of forgiveness can save me."

Edlin held her hands to her face contemplating that the riches they enjoyed, the privileges they had and the power they wielded came about because of her father selling his soul.

She took a deep breath and said, "So this is why you asked the Bishop for a monk to come to pray for you, to try to save your soul?"

"Yes, but there is little chance of that, I fear. I am beyond redemption. Though why Bishop Stigand, an Anglo-Danish churchman, should send me a Norman monk is beyond understanding. I am the son of a blacksmith. Does he really think I understand Latin? I have paid a fortune to have a holy one here to pray for me and I can't understand a word he says."

The old man stretched his neck to peer round to where the monk stood and looked at him disdainfully.

There was a long silence which was finally broken by Torkil. "So what happened next?"

The old man continued. "It was in the early spring that I decided that the danger of the villagers finding me was passed. I could not stay with the women all my life, and they encouraged me to find others to become disciples of the evil one. I pretended to agree with this, but secretly I had decided to see if I could find my uncle Gunnar. After all, he had caused Mother's death and my exile. Surely he would help me.

"One morning I set off back to the clearing with the pond and fought my way through the overgrown path which led east. After two hours, I reached the river and then walked along it in the direction of the cooking fires. As I came round a bend, I saw several longships at anchor in the river. Slaves were working in the cold river clearing reeds and digging around the landing stage. Foolishly, I walked up to the guards and, in my language, asked for Gunnar. One of them beat me with a stick and shouted some command which I did not understand. One of the slaves, an Anglo-Saxon, shouted to me and told me to help the slaves or I might be badly beaten. Then it dawned on me: I looked terrible, my clothes were filthy and torn, and my hair was tangled and muddy. I looked worse than the slaves!

"The guard hit me again, thinking that I was a slave, and pushed me towards the river. And so began my slavedom. It was hard work in the muddy waters. Our job was to enlarge the landing stage at Werrar so that even the largest transport ships could come alongside with supplies and building materials.

"We slaves lived in huts by the river and worked every day from dawn to dusk. Every time a ship came in, I tried to see if Gunnar was on board, but he never was. Then one day some horsemen came into the settlement from Sweyneston where a village was being built. One of the warriors, an older man than the others, rode past me as we were being marched to the river just after dawn. I saw immediately that it was Gunnar!

"I shouted his name, but that was the last thing I remember as the guard walking behind me must have cudgelled me. When I awoke, I was in a hut, lying on some furs. Gunnar was sitting on a stool looking at me. When he saw that I was conscious, he called out and a woman came in. She stripped off my clothes and washed me before Gunnar brought some clothes of the style which those Norsemen wore. Later, he called in another man who spoke my language. I recognised him as Knut, the man who had been the interpreter when Gunnar had brought the silver to my mother. He asked me why I was here as a slave. I told him the whole story bit by bit as, in between my speaking, he translated for Gunnar.

"After I had told of how Gunnar's silver had destroyed our family and how I had had to take flight, I could see the old warrior getting more and more angry. He growled something at Knut who turned to me and said that my loss would be avenged and that I was to stay at Werrar with him as my mentor until the expected arrival of King Sweyne with his fleet.

"Gunnar's vengeance was as swift as it was cruel, and two days later, when I came ashore from helping Knut with some repairs to one of the ships, a pole had been erected outside the hut I shared with him. On the top of the pole was the priest's head."

The two listeners gasped.

"Oh, Father, what evil has been perpetrated in your name!"

"No, my dear, you see, my father was a Viking, a pagan. I was now amongst pagans. My shame at denouncing my Christian faith was mitigated because it was of no importance to my new family, the Norsemen."

"But weren't they Christian by that time, Grandfather?"

"Oh no, only when it suited them. They were cunning and, as time went on, it suited them more and more when they sought to integrate with and manipulate the Saxons who were very devout Christians. But you have to understand too that the Christian Church is a very clever organisation with a very clear hierarchy, and the administrators are no fools either! The Church is run by literate and able people. This organisation is useful for kings, to strengthen their central authority in a kingdom. Back in Denmark, Sweyne had recognised too that Christianity brought the idea of divinely ordained kingship which would guarantee the succession for his son."

The dying man took a very deep breath and then gasped with pain. He blew the air out slowly, his whole body shaking as he did so.

"And now I am very tired. If I am able to, tomorrow I will finish my story."

With that, the two listeners left the hall, and the monk stepped forward and started to pray aloud in Latin.

Outside, Torkil's mother was wringing her hands, the black headscarf having fallen back on to her shoulders. It was plain to see that she was crying as she sought to comprehend what she considered to be her father's sin. Without speaking to her son, she made off in the direction of the church. As she walked out into the yard, the glare of the sun highlighted her auburn hair which was the colour of a sycamore leaf in autumn and was plaited at the back of her head. The same light made her unwiped tears glisten as they ran from her blue eyes down her cheeks. Her emotions were in turmoil. She had lived in her father's house all her life, never suspecting that their wealth had as its genesis a pact with a pagan. Would the sin of her father blight his descendants? Would retribution be exacted from her and her children? For as well having a son, she also had a daughter, Emma, though she did not live at home. She was a novitiate nun at Wilton Priory. Surely, the sacrifice of her daughter to serve God would atone for her father's sin. Her father's dark secret about having renounced Christianity made the other sin, on which occasion she had been complicit, seem very insignificant. She thought back to that event. One of her husband's creditors, a bestial brute of a man, had visited the Hall to collect what he was owed. He and his henchman had threatened her father and molested her in front of the children. Alric, her father, had shown her how to make poison from deadly nightshade[13] using the most toxic part, the root. At supper, the two men had first had difficulties in breathing and then they started to fall about as they lost balance. Finally, they had delirium and convulsions before they died. Had her praying

---

[13]    Deadly nightshade – solanacaea

36

really atoned for this act? These and many thoughts tormented Edlin as she went to pray.

Torkil had no such concerns. He was fixated by what his grandfather had had to say. It mattered not to the young man that his grandfather had sold his soul. The story was exciting, and he wanted to hear more.

# Chapter 3

## Massacre and Vengeance

*The King gave an order to slay all the Danes that were in England. This was accordingly done on the mass-day of St Brice.*

The Anglo-Saxon Chronicle AD 1002

It was two days before Torkil and his mother were able to hear more of the old man's story. The day after he had told them of his escape from Selceeflet, the wise woman nurse from Eremue had bled him and placed leeches on his stomach to drain the 'bad blood' which was causing his stomach pains. This left him weak and listless but, by the next day, he was once more desperate to tell his story. It was as if the relating of his experiences lifted a weight from his shoulders, shoulders which were no longer strong enough to bear some of the burden of his memories.

When his daughter and grandson were sitting next to his bed, he turned his head towards them and said, "Today you shall know the rest and I shall advise you, Torkil, on how to run your life and the estate."

"Please continue, Grandfather."

"The summer of 1002 was a wonderful time for me. I worked with Knut and sometimes, when we had some spare time, he gave me weapons training. Occasionally, I went riding with Gunnar to Sweyneston, and all the time I had the privilege of being treated with respect by everyone because of my relationship with my uncle. But Gunnar was not well. He seemed to have increasing difficulty in walking and his hands were suffering from stiffness. His energy had diminished in the short time that I had known him.

"Then there was the great day when the Danish King Sweyne's fleet appeared in the river. It was a powerful force, but they did not do much fighting in that year because King Aelthelred sent an Alderman to negotiate a '*geld*'. The Saxons paid us twenty-four thousand pounds in silver to leave the country in peace. Can you imagine that! Twenty-four thousand pounds! Sweyne left at the end of the summer and Gunnar, who had permission from the King to retire from service, left with the fleet. He was my only relative and, although he could be a very difficult man, I was sad to see him go. I tried to persuade him to take me with him, but he said that I would have a better life here.

"A new chieftain was appointed, but the work was almost finished on the harbour so only twenty or so Norsemen remained to guard the port and await the return of the fleet the next year. The new leader, Sverker, had never been to the island before and relied very much on advice from Knut and me. By this time, I had a good working knowledge of Norse language and so we both acted as interpreters. Once again, I retained a privileged position. Everything was going well for me until the beginning of November when rumours started to go round that the English king, Aelthelred, had sent emissaries around the country with a secret message. And then, on 13 November, the contents of the message were revealed."

Once more, the atmosphere in the hall became tense with excitement as the boy and his mother were spellbound by the suspense. The old man had a coughing fit and the woman gave him a cup of water.

Eventually, he was able to continue. "As usual, Knut and

I were ready to start work at first light. As we walked to the river, we were shocked to see a Saxon warship berthing on our dock. We turned and ran for the chieftain's hut to warn him, but we were too late: the hut was surrounded by slaves who were dragging Sverker out and beating him with rocks, sticks and anything which they could find. I pulled Knut's arm and turned him towards the stable. We were spotted by the soldiers who had started to disembark from the warship, but we just had time to lead two horses out and help each other onto them. We kicked the horses and headed up the track as the soldiers started to throw spears at us, but the range was too long and the spears fell short.

"Knut and I left our horses at the forest edge and eventually found the hag's house. We persuaded her to let us build a shelter near her house to spend the winter in hiding. Ha, it wasn't difficult to persuade her that I had a pagan disciple. Knut was a pagan!

"It was a hungry winter, but we survived. In the spring, we returned to Werrar. It was deserted and largely destroyed, but we stayed there until King Sweyne's fleet appeared. We learnt that the massacre of Danes which Aethelred had ordered had not only been carried out in our area but over the whole part of the country which he controlled. Sweyne was furious, especially when he learnt that his sister Gunhilde and her husband Pallig Tokeson had been murdered. He planned a terrible summer of vengeance.

"Sweyne remembered me as a relative of Gunnar's and took Knut and me with him. We sailed to Exeter where the army disembarked, and then the fleet returned to Werrar to await orders. We destroyed Exeter and marched eastward plundering and destroying towns on our way. Sweyne's revenge was thorough and he showed no mercy; that is, apart from once. When we reached Wilton, the ancient capital of Wessex before Wintoncaestre, we sacked the nunnery and burnt the town. The nuns tried to protect the bones of St Edith which were held as holy relics in the church of St Denis. Even though Edith was the half sister of King Aelthelred, Sweyne spared the church and the nuns.

*…then led he his army into Wilton; And they plundered and burned the town. Then went he to Sarum; and thence back to the sea, where he knew his ships were.*

The Anglo-Saxon Chronicle AD 1003

"We moved on to Sarum, but this was the only place which withstood us. The defences were formidable with deep ditches and high earthworks. So, from there, we turned south. Since Knut and I were the only ones who knew Werrar well, we were told to take a troop of warriors and to go ahead of the army to arrange for the ships to meet Sweyne at Hamwic.[14]

"The year after, Sweyne returned again and destroyed Norwich, but this time he did not have things all his own way because a Saxon earl, Ulfkytel, almost defeated his army. But that was the last year that Sweyne plundered England, for the year after there was a terrible famine in the country; the crops failed and many starved to death. Once again, I was lucky. I had returned to Werrar because I remembered that, before he was killed, the chieftain had kept the village funds, the silver we needed for trade and expenses, in a wood-lined pit hidden under the floor of his hut. After Sverker died, only Knut and I knew of this. Sure enough, when I had removed the burnt timbers and had spent an hour scraping around the old floor, there was his hiding place, and inside was the silver.

"As I said, it was the year of the famine. Farms were being deserted and land was cheap. I bought the land around the village of Selceeflet, which I had once been chased out of, and several farms. I had no trouble from the Saxons and they were pleased to get cash for their worthless farms."

---

[14]    Hamwic – Anglo-Saxon name for Southampton

There was silence for a while. The man with a past but no future seemed to be relishing this memory. His face betrayed contentment until his reverie was terminated by a shudder and a gasp as a sharp pain pierced his stomach.

"A drink please, I am nearly finished."

Edlin once more leant forward and helped the old man put the cup to his lips. He paused and took several deep breaths.

"Sweyne charged me with the responsibility of overseeing the rebuilding of the port at Werrar. He and his army continued to rove the country plundering and burning and they used the port as a base for the fleet. In the winter of 1006, Sweyne did not return to Denmark, despite the attempts of Aethelred's army to chase him out of the country. He brought his ships and men to Werrar and overwintered on the island.

*When winter approached, then went the army home; and the enemy retired after Martin Mass to their quarters in the Isle of Wight, and provided themselves everywhere there with what they wanted.*

The Anglo-Saxon Chronicle AD 1006

"In the spring of the next year Aethelred paid thirty thousand pounds in '*geld*' to bribe Sweyne to take his army home. I was now a landowner. I married your grandmother, the daughter of a wealthy neighbour, and my wealth grew as my money and her money made more money. As you know, I don't farm all the land. I let others do that and they pay me rent. I was able to build this house you live in today and with wealth comes power. When I had five hides[15] of land and a church and a mill, my lord Earl Godwin accepted me as a thayne.[16] But here is the real secret of the success of our family. And remember this, Torkil:

---

[15] A hide is 30 "modern" acres of land. It was seen as enough to support one household

[16] Thayne – the owner of at least five hides of land, appointed by the king

42

power has to be wielded very carefully lest you are perceived to be a threat to the higher authority. Thus it was that I provided soldiers to King Aelthelred's army, more than I needed to, and gained his confidence. But when I heard in 1013 that Sweyne was once more on his way to England, there was no doubt where my loyalty should lie. And I was at Werrar to welcome Sweyne and his son Cnut and to place my men at his disposal.

"It was more difficult when Sweyne died the next year and Aelthelred returned from France to drive Cnut out of the country. That was a dangerous time for me but, with a few suitable gifts and promises of loyalty, I survived until Cnut returned and my men helped him crush Aelthelred at the battle of Ashdown.

"And so it went on through this turbulent century, and there were yet more kings until we now have Edward, one of Aelthelred's sons, on the throne. He is the sixth king of England in my lifetime, and even two of them have reigned twice. I have served them all. But King Edward too needs friends, for the real power in the country resides with the landowning families. But the most powerful family in England, the Godwins of Wessex, were driven into exile last year.

"Your father became too entangled with Swegne Godwin, the black sheep of that family. This led to his downfall and death on their so-called pilgrimage to Jerusalem. It is to my shame that a son-in-law of mine was blamed for being an evil influence on the Godwin family heir. But if they return from exile, and I am sure they will, you would do well to offer them your loyalty and maintain good relations with them. But, to sup with the devil, you need a long spoon; always keep a distance between you so that you can bend when winds blow. Never become so enmeshed in one cause that you cannot change and espouse another. For, as we saw last autumn, Duke William of Normandy embraces King Edward like a young brother, a young brother who just waits to inherit."

There was silence in the room as they thought about the drama of last year when the King and the Duke had visited the island to indulge William's great passion for hunting. The choice seemed odd as there were better hunting grounds in the great forest across the water, but William had insisted on the visit. They were honoured to entertain the royal party for two days, but the cost of entertaining him and his entourage had nearly been ruinous.

One of the visitors, Robert d'Evreux, a friend of the Duke's, had shown an unwelcome interest in Torkil's fourteen year-old sister, Emma. She looked older than her years and Robert could see that she was turning into a beauty. So persistent was he with his suit that Edlin had decided that the girl should be sent to Wilton Priory, a Benedictine nunnery, for her protection.

"The Duke's interest in our island was more than about hunting," speculated the old man. "I have seen our harbours used as a base for invasion before."

There was a long silence while the old man contemplated something. He fumbled under his bedclothes and pulled out a roll of vellum.

"Now, Torkil, look at this carefully. If you are clever, you can make this estate grow. This map shows the property of all the thaynes on the island and marks the boundaries of our estate. I have marked the value of their land and the extent of their farms. You can also see the harbours and the main cart tracks."

The old man ran a finger over the area of their estate and then, after they had studied it for a while, he rolled the map up and replaced it under the covers.

Turning his head so that he could look at Torkil directly, face to face, he said, "Now go and think on what I have told you. Goodbye, my boy."

While they had been discussing the map, the Anglo-Saxons had not noticed that the monk, whom they had assumed could not understand their language, had moved forward to eavesdrop.

Darkness falls late in May, but the monk was patient. The room was deserted save for the old man in his bed. The mutton fat candles had not been lit so that he could sleep, and the curfew[17] had been called. Certain that he would not be disturbed, the monk crept in to the room and up to the bed. He pulled the linen pillow from under the old man's head and pressed it firmly over the wizened face. Gradually, the struggle of the recumbent figure diminished until he was quite still. The monk put the pillow back under the grey head and retrieved the vellum roll from under the covers.

Next morning, the old man was discovered cold in his bed and it was clear to all that he had succumbed to his illness.

Thus in AD 1052, Torkil became master of the estate of Selceeflet.

---

[17]  Curfew – in the original sense, the time in the evening when the fires are damped down

# Chapter 4

## Memories of a Warrior

Ivar, the old grey-haired warrior, sat patiently on his horse waiting for three trumpet blasts which would call him to action, but he knew that, though he was in full armour, he might have a long wait before he was required by the commander. He had volunteered to be in the reserve cavalry. All the young bloods wanted to be in the first attack for fame and glory. Fame and glory! He had been in a hundred battles and he knew that a warrior in the first charge will have everything from logs to rocks thrown at him as well as facing the usual weapons: spears and flying arrows. Let the glory seekers soften the enemy up and cull their numbers a bit before the reserve finish the job. He wanted to be alive at the end of the day to collect his mercenary's pay.

From where he sat on his warhorse in the cover of trees, he could not see the battle front though he could hear the characteristic sounds of two armies confronting each other: the ring of metal on metal, the oaths and bellowed threats, the whinnying of horses, and the screams of the wounded. He knew from past experience that the best way to allay anxiety was to occupy his mind. His thoughts started to wander. How did he come to be here? He had given up the mercenary life years ago, so when the Duke's men came to his house in Domfront, in Normandy, recruiting mercenaries, he told them that he was too old for soldiering; in fact he told them that he thought he was more than fifty years old. But they had said that this was not an invitation: it was a command. The Duke needed all the experienced fighters he could find. And so he had had to open the old chest and find his hauberk[18] and his sword. His wife Aveline was not pleased. He had promised her that his fighting days were over. But she knew that bad would come of it if he refused to serve the Duke. They lived very comfortably in the village. Although it was on the disputed border between Normandy and Brittany, they were well protected. The town had a wall surrounding it and a new castle to defend it. It was a busy place as it was on the pilgrim route, and this was good for their business selling grain, for not only did they supply the abbey but also the hostelries where pilgrims stayed.

Sitting on the horse which he had been allocated, he felt his sword hilt for reassurance. It was a weapon which had served him well for over thirty years. He fingered the bear's claw which had been mounted on the pommel of the sword. His father had given it to him when he was a boy. It was on a leather thong then; his father said that it would bring him luck. He remembered when he had first got the sword in Novgorod,[19] or Holmgård as it was called in older times. What memories!

But the adventure had started long before that. It had begun that night when the Norwegian raiders landed in Roskilde and plundered the town. That was in 1026. The Danish king then was Cnut, but he was also king of England. He was away most of the time, and the defences of Zealand had been neglected. Ivar was just thirteen years old when the Norwegians killed his father. His mother had died in childbirth, so he had become an orphan that night. They might have killed him too, but the raiders decided that he could have some value as a slave.

---

[18]  Hauberk – chain mail armour covering the thighs, with long sleeves
[19]  Novgorod – meaning 'new city', called Holmgård by the Norsemen

The old warrior tried to remember life before the Norwegians took him, but the trauma of the aftermath of his capture had chiselled such strong images in his mind that they had blotted out much of the detail of what had happened before he was carried off to slavery. He remembered vividly the sea battle in his first month of captivity, when he was on the Norwegian ship. King Cnut had caught up with the Norwegians and their allies the Swedes. It had gone badly for them and the Norwegian King Olof had been forced to abandon his ships in the Holy River in Skaane.[20] What a journey they had had then! Only a few officers had horses; slaves and warriors had had to walk all the way to King Olof's capital, Nidaros.[21]

But things did get better on the journey. In Denmark, Ivar's wealthy father ensured that he had good tutors, most of them churchmen. They had worked him hard, but his father had got good value for the fees he had paid. On the long journey to Nidaros from Skaane, it had been pointed out to the King that Ivar could read and write, and when the deeply religious King had visited churches on the journey across Sweden, he noticed the red-haired boy speaking Latin to the foreign monks. The King had liberated Ivar from hard, menial jobs and made him one of his servants. An educated boy would be useful to him in his religious crusade. As a young servant, he was soon to see though that, while the King had not been a bad master, he could be cruel, especially when forcing Christianity on non-believers. Then he had often been vicious. People had said that this was the main reason why he had been hated by many in his own country.

On his return to his capital, the King had experienced one disaster after another as his power had been challenged and he had lost support. Eventually, the monarch had been forced into exile in the land of the Rus together with his warriors and servants.

---

[20]  Skaane – a Danish province in what is now southern Sweden
[21]  Nidaros – Trondheim

The Rus were the descendants of the Swedish traders who had settled around Novgorod many years before. They were ruled by Grand Prince Jaroslav, a man of great wealth and formidable power. He had welcomed King Olof to his town and had looked after his visitor generously. But despite the prince's lavish hospitality, the Norwegian had been waiting for an opportunity to return to Nidaros. And he got his chance in 1030 when a messenger arrived to tell King Olof that the jarl[22] whom King Cnut had put in his place to rule Norway had drowned. The deposed King had seen his chance to reclaim his throne and had set off west with two hundred and forty warriors. The Grand Prince had provided all the warriors with weapons and armour. But this army was very small. They were so short of men that Ivar had been enlisted. The King had told him that, as he was then seventeen, he should become a warrior. And so the boy had found himself marching to war in fearsome company, carrying weapons that he did not know how to use.

When they had passed through Sweden, the King of that country, Anund, had added four hundred of his best men to the Norwegian army and had given King Olof permission to recruit more men as they marched through Jaernbaraland[23] over the mountains towards Nidaros.

As they had proceeded, the King had managed to recruit more fighters on the way by making promises of land and plunder, but most of the recruits were farmers and, apart from shields, many did not have proper weapons. However, the army had gained major reinforcement when, near the Norwegian border, they had met up with a large force of seven hundred real warriors which had been brought to serve the King. Remarkably, this fighting band was led by a fifteen year-old boy, Harald Sigurdsson. He was the King's half-brother.

---

[22]  Jarl – earl

[23]  Jaernbaraland – literally, 'iron bearing land', the province of Dalarna

Harald was very tall for his age; in fact he was the tallest warrior in the army. He was also very sure of himself. Ivar had heard him talking to his men to encourage them. The young Norwegian had proclaimed that his mission was to restore his brother to the throne and that he was confident that the army, with the help of God, would succeed in this. In fact, there had been an air of confidence throughout the force now that they were over two thousand strong. That confidence was to be shaken when they reached the hill overlooking Stiklestad. There they had got their first sight of the enemy. Below them there was a huge force formed into three columns, each following a banner. There had been thousands of men, at least three times as many as they were.

But nothing could have daunted the King's resolve, although he did take the precaution of keeping his young brother behind the shield wall. This wall was a compact semi-circle of shields carried by his strongest men to defend him, the King and his skalds.[24] It also protected the King's standard.

Olof's battle plan recognised the numerical weakness of his force in relation to the enemy. He issued orders for his men to spread out on a wide front, to prevent being outflanked, and then to make a charge at the enemy, trying to throw them into confusion. The shield wall was to advance behind the charge.

In the event, Olof's impetuous nature caused the plan to fail. Unable to control his fury at those who opposed him, the King had broken out of the wall brandishing his sword and had charged headlong at the enemy. Soon after he had been killed, (first he had received an axe wound to his thigh and then one of the enemy commanders had speared him), both skalds had been butchered.

It was at about this time when Ivar had noticed Harald being attacked. He had rushed to his aid. Although Ivar was not

---

[24]    Skalds – court poets who were enlisted to record the events of the battle

a trained warrior, he could wield an axe, which he had done to good effect. He had killed two of the attackers by planting his axe in their backs as they had been slashing at Harald in front of them. Ivar had then helped a man who was trying to protect Harald from the onslaught. He recognised the man as one of the warriors who had been with the King in Novgorod. To judge by his decorated helmet, fine neckband and polished chainmail, he was a nobleman. Others gathered round to fend off the attackers for the boy was now helpless with a ghastly gash down his left arm and a cut on his leg. He must have had a blow on the head too for his helmet was missing and there was blood on his scalp. The two of them had bundled the boy on to one of the pack horses, and tied him with his head on one side and his feet on the other. They were very lucky to get away from the fighting and had only managed to do so because of the miracle.[25]

As soon as the King had been killed, it had begun to get dark even though this was in the middle of the August afternoon. There had been confusion as warriors on both sides could not identify their enemies because of the increasing gloom. Some had fallen to the ground to pray in response to this divine intervention, but not the two men with the horse. They wanted to escape the inevitable slaughter of the King's men by a victorious enemy.

Those four years since he had been seized from his home had been packed with remarkable experiences for a young boy, but old Ivar recognised that it was then that a new and even greater adventure had begun, and central to this adventure was to be the unconscious fifteen year-old boy who was lashed to the horse which the nobleman and the slave had hurried from the field of battle.

---

[25] On 31 August 1030, there was a total eclipse of the sun over Norway between 13.40 and 14.53

# Chapter 5

## Escape from Stiklestad

"What's your name, boy?" growled the nobleman breathlessly at his young helper.

"I am Ivar Olavsson from Denmark, sir."

"Well, young Olavsson, we have a big responsibility here. This boy bouncing like a sack on the back of the horse is the next King of Norway. We have to get him to safety."

"Are you his kin, sir?"

"No, I am Rognvald Ulfsson, Jarl of Orkney."

There was a long silence while Ivar considered what illustrious company he was in: a jarl and a future king. He was walking on the side of the horse where the wounded warrior's head and arms were hanging. He saw that blood was dripping onto the flanks of the horse.

"Prince Harald is bleeding badly. We must get help," ventured the young man.

"We can't stop. Unless we can get him away from here quickly, he will be killed anyway. We have to move on."

"Sir, which way are we going?"

"We will go to Sweden, but we can't go back the way we came. The enemy will be chasing the survivors of the battle that way. We go north."

The two men, jarl and slave, were running beside the horse,

but they were slowing down. Rognvald was still in his byrnie,[26] and his heavy sword was in its sheath. Although he had left his shield on the battlefield, he was still carrying a heavy burden and he was getting tired. Ivar still had the bloody axe in his hand. He had never had a byrnie and, apart from the axe, his only weapon was a seax, but he too was in need of a slower pace.

As they entered a forest and had some cover to hide in, they slowed down and walked beside the horse instead. After a while, they stopped when they heard sounds from the wounded warrior. He was regaining consciousness. They untied the ropes binding Harald to the horse and, after some effort, got him to sit astride the horse. The young warrior had difficulty in riding the horse without a saddle and it was clear that he was too weak to stay there without support.

"You go to the other side and hold his left foot to keep him from sliding off. I'll hold the right foot," said the jarl.

They followed the path for the rest of the afternoon, one on each side of the horse, occasionally catching sight of a lake on their left side. The trail got narrower and, in places, they had to squeeze through between the year's new growth on the young fir trees and scratchy juniper bushes on both sides of the path.

"Ssh! Did you hear that?" asked the jarl. "It was the sound of an axe. Listen, there it is again."

They moved slowly forward towards the regular sound of thumping and the occasional crash as a sapling fell. It was now quite late in the evening and the light was fading, making it difficult to see any distance through the trees.

"Can you smell the smoke?" asked Ivar quietly.

"Yes, there must be a house nearby."

Rognvald unsheathed his sword and they cautiously moved out of the trees into a clearing. In the far corner of the open

---

[26]   Byrnie – chain mail armour

space was a building made out of vertical logs, with a turf roof. The sound of the axe stopped; they had been detected. But it was not they that had been heard by the wielder of the axe: he had been alerted by the sound of his geese being unwelcoming to strangers.

Rognvald halted the horse and whispered to his young companion, "You do the talking. Tell them you are Danish and that we have come from the field of battle seeking care for our friend. No word about who he is!"

Ivar understood the reason for the jarl's request. The Danish King, Cnut, had claimed the Norwegian throne and he had been generous with bribes to curry favour with the people of Norway. Most Norwegians preferred a Danish king to King Olof. The owner of the house might be fooled into thinking that the two men with a wounded warrior on the horse had been fighting for Danish interests.

An old man limped across the clearing in front of them. He was holding a long-handled axe as if he was preparing to use it for another purpose than chopping trees.

"Who are you?" asked the man, his voice trembling with fear.

"We are Danish warriors. We have come from the field of battle. We need help for our friend; he is badly wounded. You do not need to fear us."

"Why have you come here?"

"We got lost when the great darkness descended in the afternoon."

Rognvald put away his sword to appear less threatening. Still holding his axe at the ready, the old man approached the horse and looked at the rider who by now was leaning forward, resting on the horse's withers. "He is near dead. Wait here."

The old man limped off towards the wooden house. Ivar noticed for the first time that a woman was standing in the doorway listening to the exchanges between the men. The man and the woman had a short conversation and then she hurried across the grass, scattering the geese which had thought that she had come out to feed them. She came up to the horse and peered at the hardly conscious Harald.

"He is but a boy! Bring him to the house quickly," she ordered.

The geese scurried after her as she made her way back to the door, and then hissed and nipped at the newcomers as they walked the horse up to the house. The building was surrounded by a fence of hurdles. In the space between the hurdles and the house there were chickens. The old man shooed the chickens away from the gate in the fence which was in front of the house door, and opened it to let the visitors go through while making sure that none of the chickens escaped.

Ivar held the horse while Rognvald lifted the wounded boy down and carried him through the open gate and then through the door, ducking his head down to get under the low door frame. Ivar tied the horse up to the hurdle fence.

Rognvald struggled to keep hold of the near unconscious boy as the jarl's eyes adjusted to the poor light inside the house.

"Here, put him here," said the woman, indicating a cot, the only bed in the room. "Help me to get this off," she added, tugging at the warrior's chain mail. It was clear that the old woman was mistress in her own home and had no qualms about the status of the man she was addressing.

There was no room for Ivar to help Rognvald so he stood in the doorway looking around the inside of the house which was illuminated by the fire burning in the hearth at the centre of the room. Over the hearth was a metal stand with three legs. The legs came together at the top and, from the apex, a pot hung on a chain over the fire.

"You, boy, let the pot down so that the water gets hot," the woman ordered Ivar.

He did as he was bid and lengthened the chain so that the pot hung just above the flames.

Rognvald undressed Harald. Under the byrnie, he was wearing a long rough linen shirt and baggy trousers, the legs of which had previously been tucked into his boots. The jarl gently pulled off the shirt while the woman held Harald in a sitting position. The wounded warrior winced as the sleeve was pulled over his bloodied arm. Both Rognvald and Ivar noticed that, under the shirt and on his belt, the warrior had a large money pouch which was bulging. There was no doubt that the woman had seen it too before Rognvald had removed it and put it on his own belt for safekeeping.

Ivar went back to studying the room. The floor was covered in rushes, presumably from the lake they had seen. The cot on which Harald was being tended was obviously the couple's bed. It was no more than a low wooden platform, just high enough to prevent vermin joining the sleepers. It was covered in furs and there were more furs rolled up at the end of it. On the other side of the room, there was a rough wooden table and four stools. Next to them was a weaving loom with some balls of wool stacked nearby. Cooking and eating utensils were piled on a second table. The ceiling had a large hole to let the smoke out and a flap which could be pulled closed to block the hole. The inside of the roof was birch bark stretched on joists. Two beams ran across the room under the ceiling and from these hung all manner of things. Food was stored there hanging to prevent vermin from reaching it. There was some kind of bread as well as smoked meat and fish. There were also clothes, tools, a bow, a leather quiver of arrows, and herbs which had been hung to dry.

"Bring me the water, boy," demanded the woman.

"My name is Ivar."

"Alright, alright, Ivar, huh, Ivar the red," she said, alluding to his ginger-coloured hair. "Hurry up. I am Frida and my husband is Ansurr."

Ivar suddenly remembered the husband. Where was he? The Dane gave the woman the water and went outside. Ansurr was standing by the horse examining Rognvald's byrnie which had been thrown over the animal to save carrying it. The emblems on the byrnie might well identify who Rognvald really was. The old man noticed Ivar and then pretended to be examining the horse.

"Take the horse over to the edge of the forest there and let her graze," said the old man, pointing to an area at the side of the clearing. He watched as Ivar led the horse over to a post near the trees where there was some long grass and tied the mare up.

"You and your master can sleep in the outhouse, but you will have noisy company. Come and see."

The man led Ivar around to the back of the house where there was a second building which was almost the same size as the dwelling house. He opened the large door and beckoned the boy to come in. Inside it was almost dark, but Ivar could just make out that there was a cot at the end of the building. There were also several stalls, two of which were occupied: one by an ox and the other by a cow.

"We will have to bring your horse in overnight. There are many wolves around here as well as bears and wolverines."

"Whose bed is this?" asked Ivar.

"That is my farm slave's cot. He went off to fight against the King. The law says that, when a king has used violence on his subjects or returns from forced exile, it is the duty of every citizen to try to kill him. The fine for not doing so is huge. I would have to pay three marks! I am too old to fight, so I sent my slave. I don't know if I will ever see him again, for the lord knows he was too clumsy to be a successful fighter."

"Did you want him to fight against the King?" asked Ivar cautiously.

"By the gods no, but he had no choice. I fear trouble though for, mark my words, the King will be back and he will be resisted again by the chieftains. Our local chieftain, Kolbjörn

Gunnarsson, has his longhouse only a day's walk from here. He has seventy warriors."

They walked back to the house. On the way, Ivar helped the farmer to draw a pail of water from the well which was by the hurdle gate.

Frida turned as they came into the house. "Boy, um... Ivar, go to the outhouse and run your hand around the ceiling beams, get as much cobweb as you can."

He did as he was bid and soon returned with his hands held apart with the sticky weave stretched between them.

"Wrap it round his arm," Frida said, holding up Harald's limp hand. She wound linen, torn from the young warrior's shirt, tightly over the cobweb. "Now, let's have a look at that leg."

When she had dressed all the wounds and bathed Harald's scalp, on which there was a large bump with a cut on it, she left the boy on the cot and busied about clearing up the bloodied rags, remnants of Harald's clothing, and put them on the fire.

"I have given him some willow potion to ease the pain and help him to sleep.[27] Now we will eat and you can tell us what brings a warrior and two boys to our farmstead."

She busied about preparing porridge and dried fish for their supper. Meanwhile, Ansurr had been outside leading the geese to the outhouse and putting the chicken away in a wooden coop. He called to Ivar to take the horse to a stall next to the cow, while he held the outhouse door open and stopped any of the geese escaping.

Later, when the peasant couple, the jarl and Ivar were sitting round the table eating, Frida became inquisitive. "You have come from a battle, I see."

"We have and, as you can see, it did not go well for us."

---

[27] Willow leaves and bark contain Salicylic acid, the main constituent of Asprin

The woman seemed to have no interest in who they had been fighting for or against.

"What's to become of the tall boy?" asked Ansurr.

Rognvald had seen that it would take some time for Harald's wounds to heal sufficiently for him to make the journey into exile.

"Can you keep the two boys here until he is able to travel?" asked Rognvald, pointing to Harald. "I have to leave tomorrow."

"We could, but it will cost you, and I see that you are not short of silver," replied Frida. "The boy will need to rest for some weeks and, by the time he is better, winter will be on us, and he will have to wait until springtime before he can go."

"I will pay you well. Here are five pieces of silver. You will get five more when they leave. I want no one to know that they are here."

"If our farm slave comes back, they will have to share the cot with him. And the healthy one will have to help me with my work," grumbled Ansurr.

"So be it," said Rognvald.

"Tonight, the boy can sleep in here, but tomorrow he must move out with the animals," added Frida.

Later, Rognvald took Ivar aside. "You were the King's servant. Now you are to be Harald's servant. How do I know that you won't just leave him here, or cut his throat and take the silver I must leave with him for the farmer and for his journey?"

"You have my word, sir," replied Ivar.

"Ha, the word of a slave. You are not a freeman; you can't give your word."

"I can swear on the bible."

"How do I know that such an oath would mean anything to you?"

"It would, sir. I am a Christian. I could write a promise."

Rognvald did not want to admit that he could not read. He scratched his beard and then said, "No, we have to do it another way. I will show you tomorrow."

"But when we leave here, where are we to travel to?"

"I will arrange for some of my men to wait for you after the melting of the snows on the other side of the lake from the fortress of Mjälleborgen[28] in Sweden. We passed it when we were marching to Norway. You must find a guide to take you over the mountains to the south-east."

"Where will we go then?"

"My men will take you to King Anund in Uppsala. I will be there making arrangements for me and my men to travel to Novgorod."

Next morning, before Rognvald prepared to leave, he carried Harald into the outhouse. Ivar watched as the jarl gently placed the wounded boy on the cot.

"Come here, Ivar."

Ivar moved and stood by the bed. Rognvald unwound the bloody cloth which was wrapped around Harald's arm. The injured boy winced as the wound opened.

"Ivar, give me your hand."

As the Dane stretched out his hand, Rognvald drew his seax with his right hand and grabbed the offered hand with his left. Ivar watched and grimaced from the pain as the seax was drawn across his palm. Blood immediately began to seep out of the cut.

"Hold Harald's wound, Ivar. Let your blood mix with his."

Ivar had already realised the purpose of this ritual and he knew the power of it. Influenced by the heady feeling of his new-found importance, he had already decided where, as a slave, his best interests lay. He seized the injured arm and held it tightly. Harald gasped and, for a moment, it appeared that he would faint from the pain. After some seconds, the Dane let go.

"You have pledged allegiance as a blood brother, Ivar the red. You will follow this man to the gates of Valhalla or

---

[28] Mjälleborgen – the fortress of Östersund

Heaven, whichever you believe in, and serve him faithfully."

"I will, sir," said the young man.

Rognvald replaced the dressing on Harald's arm and covered him over with a fur.

"I will leave after we have eaten. You will have more space in here tonight. I will be taking the horse."

At mid-morning, Rognvald climbed on the mare, gave her a kick, and reluctantly the horse slowly walked off along the path they had travelled the day before.

That night Ivar was woken by Harald screaming beside him. His fever lasted all that night and for two more days. Frida tried to force several different potions down his throat. On the second day, the fever reached a peak with Harald flailing his arms and sweating profusely. Then, suddenly, he slept, the crisis was over, but the boy was very weak and still in much pain from the suppurating wound.

As the autumn progressed and the days got shorter, the wounded Norwegian gained strength and gradually spent less time on the cot. Meanwhile, Ivar had replaced the farm slave and worked at Ansurr's bidding. Each day, he took the ox and the cow out into the clearing for them to graze, cleaned out their stalls and put the dung in the midden. Some days, he helped old Ansurr cutting timber around the clearing to maintain the open space; other days, he spent hours splitting logs for the winter firewood store. On several occasions, he accompanied Ansurr down to the lake to clear bushes around a meadow which provided the winter fodder for the animals. Ivar was anxious about these days working in the open field for, from where he worked, he sometimes saw people fishing from small boats, and he was anxious to avoid contact with anyone who might start asking questions about who he was and where he had come from.

By the time of the first snowfall, Harald was able to walk around the barn, and soon he could help Ivar with his lighter chores. Winter limited their activities but, once the ice was thick enough on the lake, Ansurr took the two young men to fish through holes they made in the ice. These were nervous expeditions and the two of them kept a worried watch around them to make sure that they did not get company.

Although the two young men lived and worked closely together, and a kind of friendship developed, Harald was often quick to remind Ivar of his place as a slave, an inferior being.

One night, at the beginning of spring, when the snows had almost disappeared, just as the two companions were about to go to bed, the door of the barn was noisily pushed open.

"What the devil's going on here!" shouted an uncouth voice which the two residents did not recognise.

Harald grabbed the seax which Ivar had left by the bed and the Dane reached for the war axe.

The owner of the voice came forward into the light of the tallow candle by which the barn was lit. A huge figure of a man in a coarse woollen cloak stood on the other side of the light. "Who in hell are you?" he demanded.

"We are travellers waiting for the snows to clear so that we can be on our way," said Harald. Unwisely, he added, "And who are you?"

The man boomed at the pair, "Who am I? I live here. This is my bed!"

"Ansurr thought that you were dead. Where have you been?"

"I got my head split in the battle, didn't I? By those bastard soldiers of Olof's. But we gave them a good beating. I was taken to Nidaros by boat to recover."

Ivar could sense Harald bridling with offence at the description of his brother's men. The servant grabbed the master by the shoulder to restrain him.

Harald's anger was diverted from the farm slave to the servant. "Get your hand off me, you impudent peasant."

Ivar let go, but his action seemed to have given pause enough for Harald to grasp that subterfuge was the best course.

"It would be best if you went to tell your master that you are back. He has been very worried for you."

"Worried that he might have lost his investment, you mean," said the man.

"What is your name?" asked Ivar.

"Alv. What are you called?"

"I am Ivar and this is my master, Harald."

Alv left them in the barn and followed Ivar's advice by going to the house to announce his return. Later, he came back into the barn and squeezed himself into the bed with the other two. He put his feet next to their heads and his head at the foot of the cot.

The next day, Alv woke first and announced loudly that he was going out for a pee.

"Thank the gods that it is time for us to go, Ivar. I was not born to be sharing a bed with two slaves."

"We have to find a guide to take us over the mountains," Ivar reminded Harald.

That evening, after all the chores had been done, Alv joined the old couple and the two young men for supper. He was dressed in a rough tunic and wore deerskin boots. His movements were slow and awkward, and his manner was resentful, almost aggressive. He was perhaps in his mid-thirties, but it was difficult to be sure. His face had a tortured expression and his hair was unkempt, both of which made him look somewhat savage.

"Ansurr, the snows must be melting in the mountains now. It is time for the two of us to go," said Harald.

"Um…might be a bit early yet. The spring comes earlier here," warned Ansurr.

"That's a chance we will take. But we need a guide to lead us over to Anund's country."

"You owe us five pieces of silver for your stay but, if you pay ten, you can have Alv as a guide," growled the old man.

"Does Alv know the way?"

"He came from near Mjälleborgen on the great lake, the place of the god Freyr."

Harald looked at Alv. "Is it true?"

"It is an accursed place. My mother sold me as a slave to pay her debts after my father was killed mining the iron." He spat out his words betraying his feelings for his current predicament.

"But do you know how to get there, Alv?"

"It is a hard climb, but you are young. Ansurr is right: we should wait another two weeks. The snow lingers late on the mountains and in some parts stays all summer. But we have to leave before the ice on the rivers melts. We must cross two great rivers and many streams."

They spoke no more of the matter and ate their porridge before returning to the outhouse.

Next morning, Harald took Ivar aside and said, "Can we trust this bumbling peasant to lead us?"

"He might just rob us in the mountains, and the price Ansurr asks is high."

"There are two of us; we can defend ourselves. I was not intended for the farming life. We have to find Rognvald. We will take this chance," stated Harald impatiently.

"We will need to carry enough food for two weeks' travel, and we will need warm cloaks for we will be sleeping in the open. We will have to pay Frida to make them for us."

"A few pieces of silver are of no consequence."

And so it was decided. Harald accepted Ansurr's offer and, two weeks later, the three of them set off on foot with heavy packs on their backs, carrying as much food as they could and such possessions as they had, except Harald's byrnie which was too heavy and was left behind. This was the start of their long journey to Novgorod, in the land of the Rus.

# Chapter 6

## Thayne Torkil's First Test

It was much later that Torkil remembered the map, but that was long after a servant had discovered that, on the morning that his grandfather had been found dead, the monk had gone, leaving his black robes on the floor of his room.

There were formalities attached to inheriting land: a fee had to be paid to the King and the transfer of succession had to be granted by him personally. But the King was well disposed to the new thayne of Selceeflet because of the royal visit to the island the year before, and since the King was currently residing in Wintoncaestre, just two days' journey away, they took the opportunity to seek an audience.

Torkil had travelled to Wintoncaestre with his mother and several armed retainers, to ensure their safety on the journey. While they were waiting for an audience with the King, they visited the Bishop to thank him for sending the monk to pray for the old man's soul.

"But, madam, I am perplexed. I sent Brother Ralf, an Anglo-Saxon Benedictine to attend to your father, but he was found drowned in the harbour at Hamwic. After that, I had no one available to send. So, I do not know of your Norman monk."

Torkil and his mother were greatly troubled by the conversation with the Bishop, but it was quickly put to the back of their minds by the distraction of a royal audience.

First, they had to visit the Royal Chancery to have the charter, describing the estate Torkil had inherited, written on a single sheet of parchment by a royal clerk. The document had to describe the land grant with precise boundaries. It was written in English rather than Latin, as the King preferred use of the vernacular. The text was prefaced with a cross and, in addition to the description, several curses were written foretelling what would happen to anyone questioning the authenticity of the charter. Two strips were cut partially across the bottom of the parchment. On one, the royal seal would be affixed when the King had approved the grant; the other was to be used to tie up the document.

They met the King in the great hall after waiting for some time in the queue of petitioners. King Edward, while having a statesmanlike quality about him, was not an impressive figure. He was clearly overweight, and his choice of dress and general demeanour seemed to confirm the rumour that he preferred to be concerned with spiritual matters and hunting rather than affairs of the realm. Unlike his courtiers, he had an unfashionable long grey beard. Many of those around him, to judge by the language of their conversation and by the fact that they were clean-shaven, were Norman and not Anglo-Saxon, and they were impressively attired.

The court seemed to be very busy with many people coming to and fro, and messengers arriving at frequent intervals. The King quickly conducted their business, but they noted that he seemed to be bad-tempered, perhaps because of the many interruptions. They returned to the Chancery and the impressive seal was placed on the charter. It was double-sided; both sides had an image of the King sitting on the throne. On one side, he was shown holding a cross and, on the other, a bird symbolising peace.

At the Chancery, they learned why the King had been so

preoccupied when they had met him. News had just been received that Earl Godwin was making preparations to leave Flanders and return to England from exile, by force, with two of his sons. Further, that two of his other sons, Harold and Leofwine, were planning to invade the west of England from Ireland.

The royal clerk told them that the King had ordered that a fleet of forty ships should be sent to intercept the Earl and had put his forces in the West Country on a war footing. Everything was to be done to prevent the troublesome, but powerful Earl re-establishing himself in England. The King also had fears about what retribution the Earl might seek for the fact that he, the King, had given the Earl's sixth and youngest son Wulfnoth and his grandson Hacun to Duke William of Normandy as hostages, to guarantee that, when Edward died, the Earl would not interfere with the process of the Duke becoming King of England.

These were troubled times and the family from Selceeflet were anxious to return to their estate while the country was still in a state of relative peace. Their business being completed, the visitors set off homewards, staying overnight at Hamwic before embarking on their boat.

Their sailing craft, a cog, had recently been built for the family. The ship was built of local oak. It was normally used for fishing, but it also served as a transport for goods and passengers. The creek which led to Selceeflet was tidal and, in order that the vessel could be used in most states of the tide, the wide-beamed hull had been designed so that boat could float in water which was only half the height of a man, even when loaded. It was flat-bottomed so that it could rest in the mud at low tide. The cog had a square sail, but also two oar ports on each side so that the crew could row when the wind was not fair or for manoeuvring the craft when it was being berthed. In the centre of the boat, there was a large hold with a wooden cover for keeping the cargo dry.

The fine summer weather afforded them a moderate north-easterly wind which, filling the large square sail, quickly carried them back to their island creek. What they were unaware of was that the same wind was carrying others in their direction.

It was mid-morning on the day after their return from Wintoncaestre. Edlin was introducing Torkil to the business of running the estate and they were discussing with the estate steward the sale of the remainder of their grain. This was the hungry month. His grandfather had bought up grain from several of his tenants to hoard until July when prices would be best. The two of them became aware of someone shouting outside the house. The voice got louder as the source of the noise got closer. Torkil got up and pushed a window shutter open to its maximum so that he could see down the approach road to the house. There was a shabbily dressed man running towards them.

Soon the young man in the window could hear what the man was shouting. "Master, mistress, we are being attacked!"

Torkil ran through the house to the front door just as the man reached it. He recognised the man as a fisherman but even if he had not known him, the smell of fish pervading the air would have easily identified him.

"Young master, we have just come ashore after fishing all night." The man was out of breath from his exertions and paused to inhale deeply several times.

"Yes, yes, but what news have you?"

"At dawn we saw a great fleet, perhaps twenty vessels sailing from the east. When they came opposite to Hamwic, they turned south and entered the river towards Werrar."

"Could you see whose ships they were?"

"No, master, but they were not like the English fleet of King Edward. And we could see smoke rising from the village. When we came into the creek, we saw three of the ships pass by. I think they may be going to Eremue."

By this time, Torkil's mother was standing behind him listening to the messenger.

"Has the alarm been raised in Creektown?" she asked.

"Yes, mistress. The men are raising the chain across the entrance to the creek."

The fisherman was referring to the village's main defence, that of raising a heavy chain across the narrow entrance to the lagoon in front of Creektown. This had saved the village and Selceeflet from unwelcome intruders several times in the past. It was quite difficult for an invading force to land and attack as there were dangerous shoals off the coast on either side of the creek entrance. To the east and south of the two villages, there was thick forest which acted as a protective barrier against intrusion. On the west side, there was a ditch and a laid hawthorn fence which marked the boundary of the Selceeflet estate. The defenceless village of Eremue which lay further west was a far easier target for raiders.

"Go back and tell the churl[29] in Creektown to mobilise all fit men with what weapons they have and to take up position on the coast in case men try to come ashore from the ships," said the woman.

Torkil felt angry that he had not thought of that. The master of Selceeflet should not be seen to be relying on his mother to make such decisions. This was just the start however. His mother called a servant to go round the village to call all men to arms and then turned to Torkil and said, "We must hide our silver."

She ran off into the house and Torkil had no option but to lamely follow.

During the rest of the morning, there was feverish activity with Edlin barking orders at staff. The woman supervised as their steward dug a hole in the garden which was large enough to hold their iron-banded chest. The servants were busy packing items of value into the chest before Edlin placed two heavy leather pouches which she had retrieved from a hiding place in the house, known only to her. For although they had been

---

[29]    Churl – the lowest rank of freemen in the Anglo-Saxon hierarchy

safely hidden, she knew that, should the house be burned down, all would be lost. The only secure place for their silver would be under the ground.

As ordered by his mother, Torkil helped the stable boy to take their horses to hide them in the forest. When the two of them were walking back towards the house, they saw a thick pall of smoke down the coast towards Eremue. Outside the house, there was a bustling crowd of men with pitchforks and reaphooks, the only armament that most of them had. The steward, an old soldier, was trying to organise them to form a defensive line to the west of the village in case the raiders should march from Eremue.

Torkil stood idly by as arrangements were made. He had no experience of warfare and really had no option but to stand and listen to the orders being given.

Unbeknown to Torkil and his family, and indeed to the King, Earl Godwin had made his move. His fleet had sailed from the Yser on 22 June. At first, though he had eluded the English fleet which had been sent to stop him, he had been beaten back by storms. When he heard that the English fleet had then been disbanded, he made a second attempt to break his exile.

*When Godwin, the Earl, learned of that, (that the English fleet had been disbanded), then he drew up all his sail, and his fleet, and then went west direct to the Isle of Wight, and there landed and ravaged so long there, until the people yielded them so much as they laid on them.*

The Anglo-Saxon Chronicle AD 1052

During the afternoon, Torkil was called to see his mother. She was in the hall, together with the steward. The steward, Simon, had long served the family. The old warrior had somehow come into the employ of thayne Alric, Torkil's grandfather, many years ago. Now that Edlin was widowed and the old man was dead, his advice and support were even more important to the family.

"Torkil, we must seek help from the King, for we fear that it is Earl Godwin who has attacked the island. We think it would be best if you sail on the afternoon tide for Hamwic and then make haste for Wintoncaestre to tell the King what is happening here so that he can send a force to thwart Godwin."

"But, Mother, why me? I am needed here to protect you and our estate."

"You would best serve the estate if you do this. You are familiar with the journey, and the King knows you."

Whether it was to protect her son from the ravages of the enemy or whether she genuinely believed that he would be the best person to inform the King, the steward did not know, but he nodded sagely, realising it was best to agree with his mistress.

Edlin, however, knew exactly why she wanted her son to make the journey: she did not want him exposed to the looming danger to their village. With a woman's guile, Edlin cleverly added, "And, son, it will be risky. You will have to evade the raider's ships."

This last statement gave Torkil some comfort that he was being asked to do an important task with attendant danger and, though with some resentment, he went off to prepare for the journey.

The steward chose two fishermen, Seward and Irwin, to take Torkil on the voyage. There should have been a crew of four, but men were needed to guard against attack and thus no more could be spared.

By the time Torkil got to the jetty, the crew were already preparing the boat. The incoming tide was just beginning to lift the hull from the mud and the moderate south-westerly wind was gently rocking the craft.

Torkil helped the two men to raise the square sail which immediately filled with the breeze. They were carried all the way down the channel to the lagoon with the favourable wind and, even though the incoming tide slowed them down, they did not need to row. As they approached the narrow opening through which they would have to pass to reach the sea, the men standing guard by the heavy chain recognised their ship and lowered the chain to let them sail through. The crew rightly anticipated that the current would be much stronger through the entrance, and the two men took an oar each to help to propel the boat while Torkil steered.

Soon, once clear of the land, the ship was carried quickly by wind and tide in the direction of Hamwic. The day was fine and the good visibility assured them that they were alone on the sea. They followed the coast of the island as close in as they dared, to avoid being seen on the open water until they made their crossing to the mainland. However, as time went by, the wind began to drop and their progress was slowed.

It was as they were approaching the northernmost point of the island that they caught sight of the fleet. There were around twenty ships all at anchor off the entrance to the river which led to Werrar.

"Looks like they are waiting for the tide to change, master," said Irwin.

"Yes, then they plan to voyage west perhaps," suggested Seward.

"No matter what they plan, we have only one option. We can't get back against wind and tide; we have to cross to the other side as quick as we can," said Irwin anxiously.

Torkil, who considered himself commander of the ship, realised that he really should follow the crew's advice. The two men looked at him waiting for the order to turn north.

"Are you sure that we can't turn back?" he asked.

"If we do, the journey will be extremely slow, and there is a risk that, when the tide turns, the fast ships from that fleet could catch up with us. We would be leading the raiders straight to our village! We must go north now!" urged Irwin.

"Look, two of them are moving!" shouted Seward.

There was now no doubt about the urgency of the situation. Two of the warships had raised their anchors and were being rowed westwards towards the lone craft.

Torkil changed course for the river estuary which led to Hamwic. Shortly afterwards, the two craft being rowed changed to a more northerly course in an attempt to intercept them. On this course, the large ships had less resistance from wind and tide, and it was becoming clear that the warships would soon block the trio's passage to the estuary. The ships were already close enough for Torkil and the others to see the rowers and the armed men standing behind them.

"Get the oars out. Let's row as well!"

"Master, it will make little difference. We have no choice but to surrender. We are trapped," said Irwin.

Seward agreed. "If we give them the ship, they may spare our lives. But they are going to be very disappointed that we have no cargo."

"Drop the sail," ordered Torkil reluctantly. "If they ask where we have come from then say Eremue."

Their ship drifted slowly towards the warships which had now stopped moving. As they got nearer to one of the craft, the three of them could see the sweating oarsmen, many of whom were slumped over their oars trying to catch their breath after the exertion of the chase. The armed men were preparing to take on any resistance from the smaller ship.

When they came within earshot, a figure on the afterdeck of the nearest boat called out, "Who is the master of your vessel?"

Torkil stood on the gunnels holding a shroud for support and answered, "I am!"

There was a roar of laughter from the nearest ship. Someone called, "Shouldn't you be home with your mother? You are too young to even grow a moustache."

The laughter increased. The armed men relaxed and some of them sheathed their swords.

The figure who had spoken first shouted, "Where are you bound, and what is your cargo?"

Torkil hesitated and then answered, "We are going to Hamwic to get a cargo of iron."

"Your journey is going to be longer than you had expected!"

There was more laughter from the other crew.

"We will come alongside and pass a line to tow you to our fleet."

The larger craft was guided alongside them and, as it pulled slowly ahead, a line was thrown over the stern for Irwin to tie onto their bow. Once made fast, the rowers started their work again, and soon the three from Selceeflet found themselves being dragged towards the anchorage where the rest of the fleet lay.

And so it was that the young Torkil, master of Selceeflet, and his two companions were enlisted to serve Earl Godwin. Torkil's grandfather had recommended that the young man should seek to serve the cause of the Anglo-Saxon Earl, but this was not the way that the boy had expected to do it. He realised that he could not identify himself as he did not know what the Earl's attitude would be towards the son of one of Swegen's henchmen, and he certainly did not want to risk the fleet raiding the creeks by saying where they had really come from.

When their ship had joined the rest of the fleet, a sailor from one of the other vessels was appointed to take over command, and two more crew were assigned to join the original three. There was general relief among the three of them that the newcomers treated them well, though Torkil was made to feel that he was very much the junior member of the crew.

When the tide slackened, the fleet made ready to leave their anchorage. The wind had changed to a light north-easterly and, before the sun had set, Torkil's ship was following a long line of square sails westwards.

Irwin asked the new commander, "Where are we going?" He was still fearful that the fleet might raid the creeks.

"Earl Godwin left the island in a hurry. A courier arrived this morning to tell him that his two sons Harold and Leofwine who had sought sanctuary in Ireland have arrived with their fleet at Portland and they are awaiting his arrival. It is just a day's sail away".

At daybreak, they could see in the distance, surrounded by a light mist, the high hump of Portland.

*With great joy the father and the brothers looked on each other again and marvelled at each other's labours and dangers, now at an end. The sea was covered with ships. The sky glittered with the press of weapons.*

Vita Edwardi Regis, 1052

After the merry-making which followed the Earl's reunion with his sons, the crews were told that they would be sailing east and that they would increase their force to such a size that they would be able to force King Edward to capitulate. And that is what they did. As the fleet sailed along the south coast, as peaceably as possible, they requisitioned more ships and crews. They stopped at Romney, Hythe, Folkestone, Dover and Sandwich. Such was the popularity of Earl Godwin and the dislike of the King's French friends that many volunteered to join the swelling army.

The whole journey was one of huge excitement for Torkil. There was the thrill of the voyage in their open boat but, most of all, as time went by he felt more and more like a veteran among the original crew as newcomers joined them. And the crew of the ship gradually began to treat him with more respect, a respect born out of working together and sharing the pleasures and the dangers of the voyage. Finally, there was the great day when, after their fleet had been stationed on the south bank of the Thames overnight, they moved to encircle the King's fleet of fifty ships on the north bank. Earl Godwin also had a land army marching against the King from the north. The sovereign was trapped and had to offer terms to the returned exile. The old warrior was reinstated to his earldom and the King was forced to outlaw his close French advisors. Once more, the country was under Anglo-Saxon influence.

At the end of September 1052, when it was announced that their fleet was no longer required and was to be disbanded, Torkil, like many others, realised that he could now sail home. The announcement also marked a change in attitude on their ship. Irwin and Seward had been treating Torkil as any other member of the crew, but now the hierarchy was restored. However, Torkil was no longer the spoilt, hesitant young master who had left Selceeflet. Two months at sea had toughened him, and the company of the warrior sailors on a long voyage had served to make him more robust and resilient. As time had gone by and Torkil had become sea-hardened, he had revelled in the danger and excitement of sailing the flat-bottomed craft in bumpy waters for which it was ill-designed. But, in particular, the boy had enjoyed the companionship and camaraderie of his shipmates. He had also developed a desire to emulate their skill at arms for, although they had not been called on to fight during the voyage, he admired their confidence and swagger when facing down the forces of King Edward.

"Master Torkil, 'tis a long journey we must undertake with just the three of us. We need more crew," said Seward.

Over the last few weeks, Torkil had learnt to respect the seaman skills of his original two companions, and he took Seward's view seriously. He considered how they could enlist help. He felt confident now about introducing himself as the thayne of Selceeflet to Earl Godwin, but he was a man of such lofty importance that it would be difficult to get an audience. He decided to try to approach Earl Harold, Earl Godwin's second eldest son. What none of them knew was that, on 29 September, Earl Godwin's eldest son, the disgraced Swegen, had been killed outside of Constantinople while on a pilgrimage to the Holy Land to seek forgiveness. Harold was now Earl Godwin's eldest son and heir.

"We must talk to Earl Harold," said Torkil.

"But will he want to talk to us?" asked Seward with doubt in his voice.

"His ship is moored on the north bank. We could move over to there and go alongside."

"But, master, it would be risky to row over. There are just the three of us and there is no wind to sail."

Torkil realised that he should heed the advice of his skilled companion but, with his new-found confidence, there was a growing stubborn streak about him which occasionally could not be denied. "Do you want more crew or not?" he demanded.

Seward and Irwin realised that there was no point in arguing. They glanced at each other in exasperation. They pulled sacks of straw out from under the afterdeck and hung them over both sides of the ship to protect the hull when they came alongside the other ship; then they raised the anchor. The tide was beginning to flood and the Earl's craft was upriver of theirs so they would have to row their heavy ship across facing into the tide and try to drift slowly down to the warship.

The two men pulled hard at the oars while Torkil steered up tide. The plan seemed to be working well until they got to the far side when they hit an eddy. The crew struggled to hold the boat steady, but it started drifting backwards more quickly than they had planned.

The crew on watch on the warship saw the danger as the cargo vessel drifted towards them and fruitlessly tried to hold the vessel off with poles as it approached. Despite the straw sacks, there was a loud bang as the smaller vessel thumped into the side of the larger one and started to float down alongside the hull. Irwin leapt up and passed a line quickly to one of the watch crew who made it fast to the warship. The cargo ship banged again against the hull as it came to a stop.

By this time, there was a row of men peering down at the deck of the smaller ship and most of them were cursing the stupidity of the three men on board. Then the crowd parted and a tall man of about thirty with the conventional Anglo-Saxon moustache and long fair hair looked over the side.

"Who the hell are you?" demanded Earl Harold Godwinson.

Torkil stood as tall as he could and looked up at the menacing figure above them. "Sir, I am Torkil, the thayne of Selceeflet on Vectis."

"What happened to old man Alric?"

"He died three months past. I am his grandson."

Harold turned to the company around him. "You hear that, men. Here we have a thayne of Norse and Anglo-Saxon blood, like the best of us, but more wet behind the ears!"

Torkil swelled with pride at the description of his lineage, but the comment about him being a child rankled.

"I may be young but I have served the Earl this last two months as well as any man among you," retorted Torkil impudently.

Harold glared down at Torkil. "Listen, the pup has a bark!"

"He also has a bite, and will gladly use it in the service of your lordship."

There was a roar of laughter from the crew of the warship who were listening intently to the exchange.

"Perhaps before you set about making my enemies tremble, you could tell me why you have disturbed me and my crew by your lack of seamanship."

"Sir, we are but three on this vessel and we have to make the long journey back to our home. We need some more crew and provisions for the journey."

Harold turned and started talking to some of his companions. Torkil could not hear what was said. Then the Earl swung quickly round, leant over the side of his ship and shouted, "Come aboard, Master Torkil, let us discuss the matter."

One of the warship crew threw a rope and Torkil took it to help clamber aboard the bigger ship.

# Chapter 7

## A Royal Mission

At the stern of Earl Harold's flagship, there were some benches under the cover of a sail which was stretched high over the deck. The Earl was sitting there with several other men.

"Sit, Master Torkil," he commanded, gesturing towards a space on one of the benches.

The young man did as he was bid. Judging by their demeanour, fiercesome appearance and the arms they carried, he was immediately aware that he was in the company of seasoned warriors, Harold's leading housecarls. These were his personal bodyguard, tough men with a reputation for their skill at arms, who had seen action with Harold and were his most trusted soldiers.

Harold looked at Torkil and addressed him. "My father's army has disarmed the Norman mercenaries who were serving the King. The Normans have fled north to seek refuge in Scotland. However, this humiliation of the Normans has displeased the Duke of Normandy, William, and our King Edward wishes to keep the peace with him."

Torkil listened intently. He was aware of the rumours that Edward had chosen Duke William to succeed him as sovereign of England when he died. It was said that, to give a guarantee of this intention, Earl Godwin's youngest son and grandson had been presented to the Duke by the King as hostages.

Harold continued, "We have a hoard of swords, shields and battleaxes which were taken from the Norman mercenaries. The King wishes to return them to Normandy as a goodwill gesture."

The master of Selceeflet knew only too well the cost of well-crafted weapons. This was the reason that they had had very few to defend their village. Such a hoard would be very valuable.

"We need a well-found cargo vessel to take them to Normandy. Your ship will be perfect to do this. However, we have had a demonstration of the quality of your seamanship and so I will be putting one of my sea captains, Egbert, in command of your vessel and three of my housecarls will sail with you."

"But how can I get back to my home, My Lord?"

"When you return from Normandy, you will take my men to Hamwic and leave them there to find their way to Wintoncaestre. Then you are free to sail home."

The exciting prospect of a journey to Normandy on a goodwill mission for the King compensated for the insult Torkil felt in having the command of his ship taken from him. But he did wonder why his ship had been chosen as it was not the best of vessels to make an open sea voyage: the hull was far too shallow.

"When should we leave?"

"Tomorrow we will tow your ship to the wharf and load the weapons. They are being greased now to protect them. Then, if the weather permits, you should leave immediately you are loaded. Soon will be the season of the autumn storms, and we want the weapons to arrive safely."

Torkil returned to his ship and informed his crew of the mission they were to be sent on. Neither of them had crossed the channel before and both were concerned about the length of the voyage and the danger of autumn storms. But their fate was sealed, and there was clearly no alternative but to do as the Earl commanded.

By mid-afternoon the following day, the ship's ballast, large stones and rocks, had been swapped for the cargo. It was securely stowed and they had taken provisions on board. The three warriors came aboard with Egbert. He looked around the vessel and then told Torkil and his two companions to go ashore with him. He took them to another ship which appeared to be stocked with all manner of equipment, and there they obtained some more cordage, two stone anchors and an extra barrel. Once these items had been stowed on the cargo vessel, he gave orders for the barrel to be filled with weak ale.

"Our water won't stay sweet if we are delayed by contrary winds. Go back to the supply ship and ask for a cartload of flagons of ale to fill our barrel," he ordered.

This seemed a sensible precaution to the crew as the ale would keep much longer than water without going off. But what puzzled Torkil and his two men were the anchors. They were large stone weights in a basket made of rope and, while they were normal in appearance, they were far too small to hold the cog if they had to anchor in bad weather and, in any case, the ship already had an anchor.

By evening, their ship was ready to sail on the next day's mid-morning tide. That evening, they received a visit from Earl Harold. He took his housecarls aside and talked to them out of Torkil's earshot, furtively glancing at the original crew to ensure that he was not overheard.

Then he addressed Torkil. "We have unexpected company for you on your voyage. The King has insisted that one of the two Norman warships berthed with his fleet should escort you to Normandy."

Torkil was not aware that there were Norman ships in the King's fleet, but it did not surprise him as Edward was allied with the Normans.

"So, the two of you will leave on the tide tomorrow." In a rare moment of gratitude, the Earl said, "I am beholden to you for the loan of your ship, Master Torkil. You serve me well and I remember such things. I am sure we will meet again. Your grandfather must have told you that, as a thayne in my earldom owning five hides of land, you have the duty to serve me for up to forty days each year or to provide a soldier with arms to do so."

"Even if I send soldiers, My Lord, I will come to serve you myself."

Harold clapped Torkil on the back and took his leave.

Next morning, preparations were made for their departure. The three housecarls and Egbert brought their foul weather clothing aboard and stowed it under the raised deck at the stern where the helmsman normally stood. There was no cover for the crew so, in bad weather, it was essential to have greased clothing available to wear for protection from the elements.

When the tide turned, they slipped their moorings and Seward, Irwin, Torkil and one of the housecarls rowed out into the mainstream where they turned downriver. As the tide gathered pace, they began to move more quickly.

It was not until mid-afternoon, by which time they were using the large square sail to propel the cog, that they noticed the ship following them. Egbert drew the crew's attention to the much larger craft which was sailing with its square sail only half-set, to keep the speed of the larger craft down to that of the cog, having caught up with it.

"Our Norman nursemaid has arrived," said Egbert.

Torkil studied the foreign vessel. It gradually drew level with them on their port side, and he could see the detail of the sleek craft. It was about twenty-five paces long and he counted sixteen oar ports, so it must have a crew of at least thirty-two. But there would also be officers and some warriors, so perhaps there might be around fifty on board. The craft was very similar to the classic

Viking design. But that was not so surprising: the Normans were descended from the Viking settlers who were given land by the French King, Charles the Bald, a hundred and fifty years earlier. The French King had granted land to the Danish Viking chieftain, Rolf, or Rollo as the French called him. It was the King's intention that, by allowing these Vikings to hold the land temporarily, they would stop other Vikings raiding his country. The plan did not work. Rollo kept the land and his successors expanded the area they controlled. Now there was a French kingdom and a separate Norman dukedom within it.

The two vessels continued their slow journey at the cog's pace for three days. The weather was kind to them and brought moderate winds which, for the most part, allowed them to use their sails. They travelled in sight of the coast, and their course took them along the route previously followed in the other direction by Earl Godwin's fleet. At night, both vessels kept a lantern lit so that they could locate each other. Egbert had told Torkil that, when they sighted the Isle of Wight, they would turn south for Normandy.

On the fourth day, in fair weather with a favourable wind, they were cruising well and making good speed. The Normans were travelling in their wake.

"What is the land on the starboard bow?" asked Torkil, pointing to a large finger of coast which stretched southwards.

"That is Seal Island, Selsey," said Egbert. He was steering the ship and seemed to be concentrating very hard on the island and the seas between them and the land.

Out of concern for his ship, Torkil hestitantly ventured, "Shouldn't we keep further out from the coast to be safe from the rocks?". He remembered that, when Earl Godwin's fleet passed the area, they stood well out to sea. There were stories that, in living memory, the old village of Mixon had been overwhelmed by the sea and that the rocky shallows formed by it was the site of many shipwrecks.

One of the housecarls looked at Egbert and said, "Perhaps you had better tell Master Torkil what the plan is."

Egbert drew a deep breath and turned towards Torkil. "As you see, our Norman friend is sailing directly behind us. Our course is going to take us right over the rocks you are worried about. I know these seas very well; we are in my home waters."

"Why take a risk when you could steer further out?" Torkil was very aware of the fact that he had a responsibility to get the ship home safely.

"Because, my young friend, your cog will sail over the rocks. We might just touch some, but we will not suffer much damage. The big ship behind us needs sea three times deeper than we do to float. We don't expect that their captain will know the danger under his keel. Sooner or later, they will hit a rock very hard."

"You would wreck their ship?"

The housecarl who had spoken before growled at Torkil, "The Earl has use for our cargo. Did you really think that we would hand it over to the Normans?"

The other two warriors and Egbert started laughing as they crowded towards the stern to watch the Norman ship. It was about twenty minutes later, just after they had passed over some water turbulence, that they saw the Norman ship suddenly jerk up and lean over on its side. Although the grounding had been violent, the noise of the sea prevented the Anglo-Saxons from hearing the bang which had reverberated through the warship.

"She has gone on too far to get off!" shouted Egbert.

They watched transfixed as the large craft toppled over on its side. Although the distance between them and the wrecked craft was increasing all the time, they could see men jumping into the sea and items of cargo falling off the sloping deck.

"What is the King going to say and, even worse, how will Duke William react?" asked Torkil naively.

The talkative housecarl turned round to face Torkil and

said threateningly, "What you have seen you will forget and not mention to a living soul. Shipwrecks happen all the time. Neither the King nor the Duke will know what happened to the ship. If any of the Norman crew makes it to the shore, they will be killed. The island people have no love for the Normans."

Torkil had more questions which he dared not ask, and he saw that Seward and Irwin too were intimidated by their companions.

They passed the headland and, after a while, Egbert began to steer towards the coast. They came closer and closer to a sandy shore and, after a time, they saw a break in the coastline which was the entrance to a waterway beyond.

Eventually, Torkil got up the courage to ask, "Where are we headed?"

"We sail for Boseham, to Earl Godwin's manor," Egbert said, "But we will have to wait for the tide to turn. With the ebb tide, the current will be too strong for us to get through the harbour entrance. We will anchor in the shallows to the east of the entrance."

After three hours at anchor, the wind having dropped, the crew manned the oars and guided the craft quickly through the harbour entrance as the flood tide swept them in. Egbert steered first to follow a waterway to starboard and then took the second channel on the port side. Torkil noticed small wooden shacks here and there near the high-water mark, with fish traps in the river frontage. Otherwise the shoreline was lined with bushes and low trees. As they came round a bend, they could see the town ahead of them, with the fine church behind the quay.

After they had berthed, Egbert said, "We have enough light to unload this evening."

The warriors, Torkil's crew and some hands on the dockside unloaded the ship before dark and placed the weapons on carts which came and went as they took the cargo for storage somewhere in the town. When they had finished, the crew had a meal of bread and meat which was spread out on a bench on the quay. Egbert drew Torkil aside and beckoned for him to follow him around the side of one of the quayside buildings.

They stopped out of earshot of the crew. "You are lucky. Earl Harold liked you and we have been told to see that you get home safely. But this mission is very sensitive, and we can't risk word getting back to the King or the Duke about what happened. People talk. We can't let your crew go back with you, and the cog will have to be destroyed in case it gets recognised by Norman spies."

"You mean you will kill Irwin and Seward and sink my ship?" Torkil was aghast.

Egbert was a big man and clearly not used to having his statements questioned. He grabbed Torkil by the throat and slammed him against a warehouse wall. "Listen, you brat, I've been told to give you safe passage, but that doesn't mean that you might not have an accident. Do you understand what I mean?"

Torkil nodded and gasped, "Yes."

Egbert let go of Torkil and marched back towards the others. Torkil stood, rubbing his sore neck, and tried to grasp the enormity of what he had just been told. After a while, he wandered back to join the others. Now, by the light of two lanterns, he could see that they all had wooden tankards in their hands and the atmosphere was jovial. Egbert thrust a tankard at Torkil. "Come, drink to celebrate our successful voyage."

Their junketing was eventually halted by rain. At first, soft fine drizzle, but soon after the raindrops got bigger. The housecarls and Egbert went on board the cog and recovered their rain cloaks.

"Torkil, you can sleep on board if you want to. We are going to find bed space in the warehouse over there."

Seward and Irwin agreed that there would not be much comfort to be had on board, but Torkil addressed them both sternly and said, "This is my ship. You are my crew. You will sleep on board."

The two men looked surprised to be given such a stern and seemingly unreasonable order but, though they were both the worse for drink, they obeyed, albeit with some grumbling. The other men laughed at them and bade them goodnight.

Once on board, Torkil grabbed each of the men by the arm and pulled them towards him. "I fear that, unless we sail on the ebb tonight, the housecarls will cut our throats now that the job is done." He had decided not to tell his crew the whole truth.

"But, master, we can't navigate away from here in the dark. You saw how treacherous the channels were, and, besides, we have no ballast," said Irwin.

"I tell you that, if we don't leave tonight, we may never do so," whispered Torkil. "We must be very quiet. If we let go of the shore lines, the current will carry us down the channel," he added.

The two fishermen saw that it was useless to argue with the thayne. They quietly prepared the vessel for departure. When they were ready, Irwin went ashore and untied the bow line. The tide immediately started to turn the cog to face the direction they wanted to travel. Irwin gave a tug on the stern line to get some slack, released it and jumped aboard. The cog started to gather speed, and Torkil tried to steer the craft. But, without propulsion and the steadying weight of ballast, the hull started to twist round and round as it was carried downstream. The two crewmen tried to row to get the ship to head bows first downstream, but it was impossible to control their progress.

It was pitch-dark and the increasing south-west wind lashed the rain across the boat, soaking the hapless crew. They were hoping that the current would carry them down to the wider channel where they might have a better chance of controlling the ship. All at once, there was a thump and the cog lurched over on one side.

"Master, we have hit a mudbank!" Seward stated the obvious.

They peered over the side to identify the obstruction, but they could not see beyond the swirling water gurgling around the hull.

"We're finished. We are going to be stuck here until flood tide, and then we will be carried back up to Boseham."

As the tide dragged the water away from the channel, the boat leaned more and more on to its side. At first light, when the tide had turned, the crew could see their plight more clearly.

"Master, we should put out the anchor and then, as the tide lifts her, we can wait here until slack water and then try to row to the main channel."

The mood on board changed as they realised that all was not lost. The anchor was dropped into the mud at the bow, and the craft gradually righted itself with the influx of new water. The rain had stopped, and the crew became more optimistic about their situation – that is, until they heard the steady, regular splash of oars coming from upstream.

A small galley appeared around the bend from the direction of Boseham. As it drew closer, they recognised three of the six rowers as the housecarls who had accompanied them from London. Two other men sat in the centre of the boat and, at the stern, Egbert was steering with the side rudder.

The galley came alongside the cog and Egbert jumped aboard. "Master Torkil, you are troublesome and I will deal with you later. Raise your anchor and man your oars. Steer to follow us."

He turned to the two men sitting in the centre of the galley. "Come on board and take the other pair of oars."

With two pairs of rowers, the cog followed the galley against the run of the tide, toward the main channel. This they followed until they were in a wide area of open water inside the sea entrance which they had come through the previous day.

"Master Torkil, drop your anchor!" bellowed Egbert from the galley.

Torkil scrambled forward and did the captain's bidding. The cog steadied in the current.

The galley was brought alongside and its crew made fast to the cog. Three of them clambered aboard the bigger boat. Together with the others who had transferred from the galley earlier, they grabbed Seward and Irwin and tied their hands. The two fishermen swore and struggled but to no avail. Two of the housecarls pulled out the stone anchors which Egbert had had brought onboard in London. The ropes which Egbert had brought were used first to tie one of the stones to Seward's legs and then one to Irwin's.

"What are you doing? How dare you! They are my men!" shouted Torkil.

Egbert turned and cuffed Torkil across the face with the back of his hand. The young thayne was dazed and fell backwards onto a thwart with blood streaming from his nose. He looked up just in time to see two of the housecarls lifting Seward onto the gunnels. A third threw the anchor over the side and Seward was jerked violently into the sea, screaming as he fell.

Irwin, having seen what had happened, struggled fiercely to get free. As he was thrown over the side, he grabbed the gunnels and hung in the water with the weight pulling him down, desperately gripping the side of the boat. Egbert seized an oar and beat the fingers on the gunnels until they released their grasp and, within a short time, Irwin had met the same fate as Seward.

The job done, most of the men returned to the galley. One of them came back on board carrying a pouch. He took out a flint, a striking iron and some flax and started to strike the iron against the flint. In a short time, the sparks from the flint lit the flax. He took some wood shavings from the pouch and gently placed them on to the burning flax. As the fire flared, two of the others dragged the sail open and placed one corner onto the fire. The sail was made of waxed linen and immediately began to flare up. They placed oars onto the sail and parts of the wooden cover from the hold.

"Let's go," said Egbert.

The men climbed over the gunnels and into the galley.

"Come on, Master Torkil, or do you want to perish with your ship?"

There were ribald comments from the crew and some laughter.

"Quickly now, we shall have to push off before the fire spreads to the galley."

Torkil aroused himself from the misery and pain he felt and lamely climbed onto the galley. Then rowers immediately pulled away from the cog which was by now well on fire. After a short while, they paused and all looked back at the blazing boat.

"Right, no Norman ship, no cog and no crew to tell tales. Let's get back to Boseham," said Egbert.

Torkil sat amidships and watched as the flames and smoke became more and more distant. How would he explain this to his mother? But then he reminded himself that he had not seen her since that July day when he set out for Hamwic. By now, she would definitely believe that he was dead. Things had taken a huge turn for the worse for him. Two days ago, he was brimming with confidence and thrilled at the prospect of sailing the cog up the creek to Selceeflet and surprising his mother by his safe return. She would have been delighted to see him, and proud, for her boy had become a man and not just that: he could boast that he had served on a mission for the King and Earl Godwin. Now he felt so helpless and shocked. He had just witnessed the terrible murder of two friends, his crew, sailors whom he had journeyed with for two months. His shock gradually developed into rage and a determination to avenge the brutal murder of his men, but he had to hold his feelings in check. At the moment, he was powerless to do anything.

As they travelled up the last channel towards Boseham, Egbert gave the steering oar to another man and came forward to speak to Torkil. "As I said earlier, you have caused me a lot of trouble. I am going to give you a better chance than your crew had."

That said, he nodded to two of his henchmen and they grabbed Torkil, pulled him up and stood him before Egbert. The captain seized the silver ornament dangling from Torkil's neck and lifted the chain over his head.

"I'll have this," he said, putting it around his own neck. He nodded to the two men holding Torkil and they gave him a violent push which sent the thayne over the side of the galley and into the swirling waters.

Torkil was aware of the laughter of the crew before the shock of the cold water hit him.

# Chapter 8

## Back from the Dead

Although it was only late September, the summer warmth had left the sea, and immersion in the chilly water jerked Torkil out of the malaise he had been in after the shock of seeing his companions murdered, his ship destroyed, and the effect of the blow from Egbert. The weight of his body falling from the boat had caused him to sink quite deeply into the water, but then his natural buoyancy brought him up to surface. The galley was already some distance away, but he could see that those aboard it were all looking to see if he came back to the surface. Torkil spat out seawater from his mouth and, though spluttering and coughing from the effect of having swallowed some of it, shouted as loudly as his voice would allow, "Egbert, I curse you. I will have my bear's claw back after I kill you."

Some must have heard what he said because there was a chorus of laughter.

Torkil had never learned to swim, but he had fallen into the sea before. It was a standard children's summer game in the shallow creek at home to jump into the water by the quay. But there the water was shallow enough to be able to stand on the muddy bottom. He remembered that sometimes he had floated on his back just to pretend that he could swim.

Now he tried to find the bottom with his feet, but the water was too deep. He tried to raise his feet and float. He found that, when he did this, he was carried head first upstream by the tide. But he was getting very cold and his joints were getting stiff. He had to get out of the water. He twisted round to see what was ahead of him, but immediately he sank under the water once more. He turned to try to float on his back again and, at the same time, used his arms to push himself through the water.

Suddenly, he felt a slight bang on his shoulder. He turned to see what it was as the object slid past him. It was a pole which must be supporting a fish trap! He grabbed at it but it was already too far away, but then he sensed a second obstruction: it was another pole. This time, he quickly grabbed the slimy piece of wood and held on. He could support himself and hold his head well clear of the water. This gave him a chance to look around and get his bearings. There were four poles in a square which must have been supporting some kind of net under the water. He desperately tried to find the submerged line supporting the net. His strength was ebbing fast, and he was terrified of losing his grip on the slippery support. He kicked around with his feet and became entangled with a rope under the surface of the water. He pulled up his right leg and saw that, around it, there was a rope leading in the direction of the shore. It was covered in green weed and slime but he grabbed it with one hand, let go of the pole and pulled himself with all his strength towards the shore. Many times he went under the water, but he kept his grip on the rope. Eventually, he was aware of soft mud under his feet and he was able to stagger, still holding the rope, towards the shore. Now out of the water, he plodded slowly through the yielding mud until he reached the tide line which was marked by weed and small outcrops of grass.

Torkil sat on the grass shivering from shock and cold. It was still only early afternoon, but the day was overcast and chilly. Nevertheless, he gradually recovered some strength and started to investigate his surroundings. There were low bushes along the waterside and beyond them higher trees, but what caught his interest was the upturned rowing boat a little way from the fish trap. He got up and walked towards it. As he did so, he became aware of two small children peering at him through the bushes, and beyond them a rough wooden shack. The children ran away, shouting out loudly as he approached them.

Immediately, a man came running from the other side of the shack with a pitchfork in his hand. He was wearing a tattered cloak and was barefoot. His hair was tousled. His dirty hands and feet betrayed the fact that he had been doing some kind of garden or farming chore. "Who are you?" he shouted.

"I am Torkil, thayne of Selceeflet."

"What are you doing here?"

"I have fallen from a boat and just come ashore."

The man, staring at Torkil, held the pitchfork in front of him. His wet clothes made it obvious that the young man had not long ago been in the river. Footprints in the mud showed the route recently taken by someone from the water line, and the filth on Torkil's boots confirmed that the footprints were indeed his.

"I need to dry my clothes. I can pay you." Torkil suddenly realised what a stupid thing he had just said. Now the poverty stricken, pathetic figure in front of him would know that he was carrying money and might rob him.

"I'll take care of your seax first," said the man.

Torkil had forgotten that he was still carrying his knife in the sheath on his belt. He took it out and put it on the ground. The peasant beckoned him to move back so that he could pick up the dangerous-looking long blade.

"Come with me," he said and led Torkil towards the shack.

Outside the hovel there was a rack with fish drying and, behind it, the two little boys were trying to hide while watching the stranger approaching their home.

The man called out and a woman appeared at the door. She was dressed in a long woollen overdress with two wooden brooches at the shoulders. The dress was worn and grubby. Her hair was tied in a plait.

"Stoke the fire. We have a wet visitor." He turned to Torkil and bade him sit on a bench in front of the shack. "You mentioned payment."

Torkil had gone too far to pretend that he did not have money. He opened his pouch and touched the wet contents. He tried to find a small piece of silver with his fingers without allowing the man to inspect the contents.

He glanced down at the silver coin which he had taken out. It was the smallest he had. It really was too valuable a reward for the man's services. But he had no choice. "This is for you to dry my clothes and feed me before I leave."

The man snatched the coin in case the thayne changed his mind. "Take your boots off and pour the water out."

By evening, Torkil's heavy jacket and his trousers were still damp, despite the time they had been hung in front of the fire.

"You had better stay here for the night. I'll get some more straw," said the peasant. The whole floor of the shack was covered in straw and dried grass. The family had very few possessions apart from wooden plates and beakers and the clothes they were wearing.

In the early evening, the man disappeared for a while and, when he returned, he had several flat fish which he must have taken from his fish trap. The woman gutted them and prepared them for supper.

Torkil spent the night with the peasant fisher folk and left early next morning to start his journey westwards. He carefully skirted round the village of Boseham and soon found the trail leading westwards. The peasant had returned his seax, and this gave the young man more confidence as he tramped the cart track to Hamwic. Though he walked most of the way, occasionally he spent more of his silver to persuade carters to allow him to ride with them and to share their suppers. At night, he slept anywhere he could find which was dry; usually under a carter's wagon.

Once in Hamwic, Torkil used the last of his money to charter passage on a small fishing boat to the creeks. He was hardly recognised when he landed at the small quay. He had been given up for dead long ago, and no one was expecting to see him. When he had left, he was in his finest clothes to meet the King at Wintoncaestre; he had been the commander of his own ship. Now, on his return, he was dirty and dishevelled, but it was not just his appearance which had changed: the mollycoddled boy who had left three months ago was now stronger physically and mentally and had learnt a great deal about the world in a short time.

He was richer in experience, poorer in appearance, but with a new determination: he was going to get the steward to train him at arms. Next time in the service of the Earl, when he met the Godwin housecarls, they would treat him with respect and he would take revenge on Egbert.

As the fishing boat was rowed up to the Selceeflet quay, he caught sight of several children emptying eel traps. The appearance of any unknown craft always caught the attention of the villagers, and it was not long before a small crowd of children, having abandoned their tasks with the traps, had gathered. They pushed and shoved each other to be the first to grab the lines of the stranger's boat. Torkil was standing in the bow ready to jump ashore, and despite his unexpected appearance, he was quickly recognised. Two of the children scampered off up the track past the watermill towards the big house. They wanted to be the first to take the good news to the matriarch of the village.

As Torkil made his way up the road, he was greeted with astonishment by the villagers who happened to be working on his route. They all had questions about where he had been and where Seward and Irwin were. But he was in a hurry and only gave peremptory explanations telling no one of the misfortune which had befallen his crew. Nevertheless, he was delayed sufficiently for the news of his homecoming to have reached his mother and for her to meet him long before he reached the house. And when they did meet, nothing, not his age, his appearance or his effort to avoid her doing so, would stop Edlin throwing her arms around him. She was astounded to see him. She had given him up for dead for she had had no word of him since that day when he sailed off with Seward and Irwin. She had suffered huge remorse for having persuaded him to make the journey, especially as the raid on the island had never reached Selceeflet. Now, there was a joyous homecoming and general celebration in the village, apart from in the households of the two missing fishermen.

Edlin soon realised that the one whom she had sent away as a boy had come back a tougher, more self-reliant person. For, despite his ordeal, Torkil seemed to have a new sense of purpose and direction compared with the relatively idle and self-centred way in which he had lived earlier. He began to take a keen interest in the estate affairs, and involved himself in the running of the farm. He also helped greatly to relieve the poverty of the families of the two murdered seamen. And, as he had planned, soon after his return he had taken Simon the steward aside and requested that he should share the skills he had used in an earlier life.

# Chapter 9

## The Road to Novgorod

*Through endless woods I crawl*
*On my way now, with little honour*
*Who knows but that my name may*
*Yet be far and wide renowned*

From the Orkneyinga saga, words attributed to Harald Sigurdsson,
about the journey from Norway to Sweden

The journey through the Kjölen Mountains was cold and long. At first, through the foothills, Harald and Ivar tried to march quickly, but they were held back by the ponderous Alv who constantly berated them with the warning that they should save their energy for when the climb got steep. And that was good advice for, with their limited food supply, they had to ration how much of their bread and dried fish or smoked meat they could eat each day. Consequently, their energy levels declined.

After two days, they came to a great river heading down a deep valley towards Norway. The water was still frozen and they were able to cross it several times as they followed the route up the valley with the path, sometimes on one side of the iced waterway and sometimes on the other.

To their relief, they did not meet any fighting men, though they did overtake several traders travelling more slowly with pack animals. There was no sign whatever of any habitations on their route through the mountains.

Eventually, they came to a series of deep gorges where the sun had never touched the snow. The going became very hard as they plodded through the deep drifts. In these ravines, they found it very difficult to find places to camp overnight and to keep their fire alight through the dark hours to frighten off wolves.

After several days of walking, the gorges opened out into open country, and they trudged over a large, frozen lake. Further on, there was a huge plain. The only sight apart from the faraway, great snow-covered mountains was the sparse, stunted dwarf birches with black branches sticking out of the deep snow. It was on the plain that they discovered a deserted tent. Judging by the lack of snow depth around the tent, it had been abandoned not many days before. Further on, they found human bones, the remains of at least two people, and shreds of clothing.

"Wolves – they must be very hungry to dare attack a group of people," grunted Alv. "We must be careful to build our fire as big as possible tonight."

Despite the doubts about their Swedish guide, he did seem to know the precarious trail, but it was the perilous nature of the route which would prove his undoing and illustrate to Ivar the ruthless nature of his younger companion.

After three days traversing the plain, they started the descent on the other side, now following another frozen river. As they got further and further down the mountain, the ice on the river got thinner, and they could hear the water gurgling underneath them. Eventually, after crossing a frozen lake, they reached an altitude where ice no longer covered right across the waterway.

"We have to get across," said Alv. "The path continues on the other side. The river widens and gets shallower further down, and we can wade across on the rocks."

They found the place: the river swept round a huge, rocky

outcrop and then widened considerably and ran over the rocks which were just covered by the water. Alv told Ivar to use his axe to cut some birch branches and trim them. When he was satisfied with Ivar's work, he said, "Now we all cross at the same time, one behind the other. You, the tall one will lead the way. Hold on to one end of this branch. Danish, you hold the other end with one hand. With your other hand, hold my branch. Then, if one of us slips, the other can pull him out of the water."

Harald stepped into the icy water, followed by Ivar, and finally Alv. The rocks were slippery, but many had flat surfaces which made it possible to walk on them. Harald was almost across when he heard a shout. Alv had slipped into the water and was being dragged by the current. He was far too heavy for Ivar to hold though he tried and fell into the water himself. Harald held on to Ivar's pole.

"Let go of Alv or we will all be drowned," shouted Harald.

Ivar had no choice. The slippery pole fell from his grasp and they watched as Alv was carried downstream before being thrown on the rocky shore on the side of the river they were trying to reach.

The two young men completed their crossing and then ran down the bank to find their guide. He was about a hundred paces downstream. Ivar and Harald clambered down the rocks to help him. With great difficulty, they managed to pull him out. As he lay at the side of the river, he was whimpering with pain. It was clear from the angle of his right leg that it was broken badly. The man was shivering with the cold and shock.

"You can't leave me here. Stay, stay, I implore you. The wolves will make short work of me."

Harald looked at Ivar. "We can't carry him."

"If we leave him here, he will freeze to death or, as he says, the wolves will find him."

"He has served his purpose for us. I think that we can find our own way following this trail," Harald retorted.

"What, leave him here to die? Can't we wait until the traders catch us up? They could help."

"It will be several days before they get here and we don't have much food left."

Alv could not hear their conversation, but seemed to realise that they were planning to leave him. "If you are going to leave me, it is better you kill me first. Better for it to be quick than by being gnawed to death."

After a moment's hesitation, Harald picked up Ivar's battleaxe, walked over to the injured man, raised the weapon high in the air and swung the blunt side against Alv's head, crushing his skull.

"Help me get his backpack off. We can use his food."

Ivar helped to lift the lifeless form while Harald untied the pack.

"Get his feet," ordered Harald.

Together, they dragged the wet body back to the river and pushed Alv into the surging waters. They watched as the current dragged the farm slave down the hill and returned him to the country of his birth.

It was, as Harald had said, not difficult for them to follow the mountain trail down through the foothills, but before them lay a seemingly endless tract of forest and lakes. However, luck was on their side and, two days after Alv's accident, with their food store exhausted, they came across an isolated farm. Harald's silver once more paved the way for them to get help. After two nights' rest in the farmhouse, with their backpack food store replenished, it was agreed that the farmer's son would lead them through the forest paths to Mjälleborgen.

Four days later, they arrived at a small settlement on the shore opposite the island fortress. Rognvald had taken the precaution of sending some of his men who had been among the seven hundred warriors which Harald had taken to Stiklestad, and whom Harald would recognise and trust. Several of them were waiting in the village, and there was some celebration when they were reunited with the leader whom some of them had last seen carried off the battlefield near dead.

From then on, the journey was to be easier, for the meeting party had travelled on horseback and two extra mounts were requisitioned for Harald and his servant. This was just as well as before them lay by far the longest part of their journey: two weeks' travel south-east on forest tracks to the capital of King Anund's kingdom.

Spring was well advanced as the travellers made their way along the forest paths. The countless trees were surrounded by carpets of coltsfoot and white forest anemone, and the weather was mild. They travelled first south-east and then, when they came to the great river, they followed the valley to the lowlands on the coast. Several times on the journey south, they had to pay fishermen to ferry them across the other mighty rivers which, by now, were all ice-free.

At last, they reached the large village of Uppsala. News of their approach had gone before them and Jarl Rognvald was outside the largest building to meet them. "You are looking better than the last time I saw you!" he said.

"Thank God for that," replied Harald.

"Come, we will eat together and you can tell me of your journey. Ivar, take care of the horses. You can eat with the servants."

Ivar was shocked to be suddenly reminded of his status as a servant rather than a companion and friend of Harald's.

The Dane was shown to a table outside the back of the building where kitchen slaves scurried to and fro with food and drink for Ivar and the warriors who had accompanied them from the north. The ale flowed and the air was one of celebration for a task achieved successfully.

Towards dusk, Ivar heard his name being called and he left

the party to go to the front of the building where he found Harald looking for him.

"Come, Ivar, let's look around the village." Though this was more of an instruction from Harald than an invitation, Ivar was pleased to have the opportunity to talk to his master as he was anxious to know what was to happen next. He asked, "What is Rognvald planning to do?"

"I can tell you while we walk. He is coming to show us around."

This, the capital of King Anund, was a large collection of wooden huts and cottages around a main square and streets which branched off in several directions. It was not particularly imposing apart from two dominant buildings. One of them, the building where they had eaten, was Anund's house. It was by far the biggest building in the square and the ornate woodwork indicated it was the home of a rich and powerful man.

Rognvald came out of the house and joined the two young men.

"Is the King here?" asked Ivar.

"No, while he calls this his capital, this is the religious centre of his kingdom only. His centre of power is in Sigtuna."

Ivar remembered his visit to the impressive town of Sigtuna when King Olof had returned from Novgorod. They had landed there before their march to Norway.

"Will we see him?" enquired Harald.

"No, he has taken his bodyguard to collect tribute from the villages in his kingdom."

Rognvald explained that this was an annual journey when the monarch collected taxes and gifts from his richest and most powerful subjects; in particular those where force might be required to extract payment. The work of collecting tribute from all the minor villages and farms was left to his tax collectors.

"This is the Ting's house," said Rognvald, pointing to a

large hall. "The Ting[30] meets every year at the end of February. They confirm the King's decisions and decide on the Leidang.[31] At the same time, they have the Disting, the annual market and the Disablot."[32]

"The Disablot?" queried Harald.

"You must remember Anund is a believer in the old gods. This whole province is pagan.[33] You will see later."

They walked through the huddle of cottages, behind which were three large mounds.

"The legend is that each of the mounds is the grave of one of the gods Freja, Thor and Odin."

Behind the mounds, they now saw a magnificent temple. Made of vertical timbers with a wooden tiled roof, the front was covered with carvings of mythical beasts. Chains of bright metal, which could only have been gold, hung from the roof over the façade between the carved animals. Two guards stood at the door.

As they came closer, they became aware of a strong smell: the stink of putrefaction.

"At Disablot each year, sacrifices are made to the three gods. The male of eight different animal species, and one human, are sacrificed nine times. The corpses are hung in the grove over there," said Rognvald, pointing to a wooded area.

The sacrifices which had been hanging there for three months could be seen hoisted on the branches of the trees.

"Are there no Christians here?" asked Harald.

"Yes, some, but they have to pay to be allowed not to attend the festival."

---

[30]   Ting – General assembly

[31]   Leidang – the contribution to the king's forces, in terms of ships and men, to be made by landowners

[32]   Disablot – an annual pagan festival involving sacrifices

[33]   The province of Uppland resisted Christianity until the second half of the eleventh century

*The sacrifice is as follows: of every kind of male creature, nine victims are offered. By the blood of these creatures it is the custom to appease the gods. Their bodies, moreover, are hanged in a grove which is adjacent to the temple. This grove is so sacred to the people that the separate trees in it are believed to be holy because of the death or putrefaction of the sacrificial victims. There even dogs and horses hang beside human beings.*

Adam of Bremen, 11th Century German Chronicler

The three men turned and started walking back to the square. Rognvald turned to Harald and said, "I have my ships at Östra Aros,[34] and over three hundred Norwegian warriors. Prince Jaroslav, the ruler of the Rus[35], has offered us sanctuary if we serve him. We will join the Varangians[36] in Novgorod."

Two days later, the voyage began, and Ivar found himself being transported back to Novgorod where he had once shared King Olof's exile. The eight ships were rowed down the Sala[37] River out into the great lake from whence they eventually emerged into the eastern sea. There, the captains set their courses in the direction of the rising sun and, sometimes sailing, sometimes rowing, they progressed until the sea ended and they entered a river, the Neva.

This was the entrance to the great trading route to the Orient. After rowing against the strong current of the Neva, the ships entered the Lake of Ladoga and then continued east until they found the entrance to a river leading south. Near the head of this river was a town: Staraja Ladoga. This was the first Norse settlement in the land of the Rus and was now a wealthy trading centre where furs, tar, walrus ivory and other Norse

---

[34]   Östra Aros – the port of Uppsala, five kilometres to the south of the village

[35]   Rus – the Slavic name for the Scandinavian settlers who had colonised parts of northern Russia

[36]   Varangian – originally a group of men bound together by an oath, but eventually meaning Scandinavian mercenary warriors

[37]   Sala River – now known as the Fyris River

produce were shipped south, and silver, wines and oriental goods were in the northbound cargoes.

Prince Jaroslav had married a Swedish princess, Ingigerd. She had been escorted on the journey from her home to Novgorod by a Swedish jarl. As a 'bride-price', her husband had given her ownership of Staraja Ladoga. She, in turn, had conferred the territory to the jarl who had brought her safely to Novgorod. His son, Eilif, was now lord of the town. It was Eilif who welcomed the Norwegians to the land of the Rus and showed them generous hospitality before accompanying them on the last leg of their journey to Novgorod.

Novgorod was as Ivar had remembered with fine buildings on both sides of the river. It was much more impressive than Uppsala with signs of wealth everywhere. The town's income was derived from trading and the tribute all users of the River Volkhov owed to Prince Jaroslav. It was a town rich in culture with a heritage of music and art. Its jewellers were renowned for their skills in making adornments of gold and silver for the wealthy. The artists' colony created paintings for the many churches in the town, and the recently introduced art of icon painting was the finest anywhere.

Jaroslav, who was called 'the wise' by many, had started an education system for the children of the most prominent citizens, and three hundred pupils attended his school. The town was administered from the Detinets, the Kremlin or town castle on the left side of the river. This was the citadel where the prince had his residence. The whole area was surrounded by a wooden fence and a rampart. Inside the citadel, as well as a military barracks, there was a church, many administrative buildings and the homes of the most prominent aristocrats who attended the Veche, the ancient parliament.

Yet the vast lands which the prince ruled on the west side of the Dneiper, all the way to Kiev, were constantly under threat and often suffered attacks from wild nomadic tribesmen.

And there were conflicts too with his neighbours to the west, in particular the Polish. The prince had a small private army, his *druzhina*. This was a personal bodyguard of some hundred highly trained warriors of high status who formed his retinue. They were responsible for his personal safety, but they were far too few to fight his enemies. For this, he relied on the Varangians, Norse fighters whom he hired because of their fearsome reputation and military effectiveness.

It was because of the prince's need for Varangians that the Norwegians received a warm welcome. Rognvald was treated with the utmost respect by the prince who had come to the harbour to meet the new arrivals.

"Welcome back, Jarl Rognvald. I hope that you will stay longer this time," said the prince, limping towards him. The Jarl knew that Jaroslav had been hit in the leg by an arrow in a campaign attempting unsuccessfully to seize Kiev from his brother, the grand prince.

"I will, sir. And I have three hundred men who wish to serve you."

"This is good. You will be well rewarded. I plan a campaign against the Læsir[38] in the summer. We lost many of our Varangians last year when we defeated the Chuds."[39]

Rognvald noticed the prince looking at the lanky youth standing behind him. "Sir, may I present to you Harald Sigurdsson, the half-brother of the late King Olof."

Harald pushed his way past others in front of him and confidently thrust his hand forward to the prince. "My sword is at your disposal, sir," he said.

The Prince looked at Rognvald and quipped, "Your companion hides his lack of experience behind the façade of youthful enthusiasm."

---

[38] Læsir – Norse for Poles
[39] Chuds – the inhabitants of what is now Estonia

Harald blurted out, "But, sir, I have experience. I led my men at Sticklestad."

Jaroslav, irritated at the interruption, said, "Led them to defeat, I believe."

Harald started to protest, but Rognvald intervened and sought to mollify both men by commenting, "It was a tragedy for all of us. Now, sir, we must talk of practical things."

"Yes, indeed. Come, we must talk terms for your employment and that of your men. Bring the young whelp with you. My steward will show your men where they have quarters."

The Orkneyman, Jarl Eilif, the young warrior and the Prince left the quay, accompanied by the prince's advisors, to discuss how the new force of Varangians would be paid and the practicalities of integrating them into the existing army of foreign mercenaries in Jaroslav's employ.

The next afternoon, the Varangians were called together on the large training yard in front of their barracks in the citadel.

Rognvald sat on a horse and addressed the men. "Prince Jaroslav has decided that you all should join a campaign against the Læsir. Jarl Eilif will be in total command. Your detachment will be commanded by Harald Sigurdsson."

There was a rumble of sound as the men reacted and commented to each other.

"Why aren't you commanding us?" called one of the men. Jarl Rognvald was famous as a brave fighter and good leader.

"The prince has invited me to join his *druzhina* as an officer. This is a great honour and I have accepted."

"But what is the pay?" shouted another of the men. There was a roar of approval of the question.

"Each man will receive three pieces of silver a week and a fair share of the plunder. Your contract is for twelve months."

There was much chattering among the men, but no dissent.

"Have fun tonight for we leave tomorrow. The transport

vessels are being provisioned already," bellowed Rognvald in an attempt to make himself heard.

The crowd of mercenaries broke up. Some formed small knots of men in discussion; some hurried off towards the town. The latter wanted to reach the ale houses and brothels before the crowd, for there were other detachments of Varangians walking towards the exercise yard to be briefed by their commanders, and doubtless there would be many of them who would later be heading in the same direction to indulge in the pleasures of the flesh and the ale barrels before possible death on a battlefield.

"Ivar, are you going to town?" asked Harald.

"I have no money," complained Ivar.

"I have. Come on, let's go," said Harald.

# Chapter 10

## Harald Sigurdsson the Commander

After their experience at Stiklestad, many of Harald's warriors were wary that their young commander might have the same hot-headed nature in battle as had his half-brother when he had broken out of the shield wall. They need not have worried. Perhaps it was just because of the lesson learnt from his half-brother's foolhardiness that Harald had a completely different approach to warfare. He was already becoming a cunning, careful planner and, above all, he was cautious to avoid casualties. However, Harald had another attribute. Right from the start of the first campaign in the employ of Prince Jaroslav, success seemed to crown all his ventures and he quickly earned the epithet 'lucky'.

The land over which Prince Jaroslav reigned was called the Kievian kingdom. This huge state was constantly at odds with its neighbours; in particular, the kingdom of the Læsir. In 1031, Prince Jaroslav decided that it was time to wreak retribution for attacks on his territory in the previous two years by the Læsir King, Miesko II. Prince Jaroslav had ordered Jarl Eilif to wrest a territory called Ruthenia from Miesko and destroy his defensive castles around the town of Belz.

The army's journey was very long. The convoy of ships crossed Lake Ilmen and then followed the Lovat River as it twisted its way south. The river ended in a large lake, and there the troops disembarked. A force was left to guard the boats, and the main army covered the rest of the journey to their first objective, a border fortress, on foot. The whole journey took a month.

As the Kievian army approached the castle, Eilif called his commanders together to discuss strategy. "The hill leading up to the castle is too narrow for us all to attack at once. Harald, I want your detachment to be in reserve and to stay out of the fighting at the beginning."

Harald was not entirely displeased with this order for he was not keen on pitching his men into an uphill battle when they had not fought together for almost a year and had not trained as a fighting unit since before Stikelstad. He had an alternative plan for them which might be less demanding as their first action of the campaign.

"But, My Lord, could my men not circle around to the back of the castle and cut off any retreat west by the garrison?" pleaded Harald.

Eilif scratched his beard. It was clear to him that the boy had a good idea, but he did not want the other commanders to think that his strategy was being dictated by a sixteen year-old.

"What do you others think of that idea?" asked Eilif.

"It makes some sense," said one.

"If the boy gets into trouble, he can't expect any reinforcements from us," said another.

The commander tugged at his whiskers for a moment and then said, "Harald, alright you can go, but you will have to move ahead of us so that you are in position before we charge. If you hear two long blasts on the trumpets then we need you back quickly to reinforce the main army."

"Yes, My Lord. We will leave immediately to circle around to the west."

"One more thing: Prince Jaroslav wants as many prisoners

as possible. He plans to settle the Læsir prisoners in the south of his kingdom to defend against the tribesmen. Don't kill more than you have to."

The Prince had ordered Jarl Eilif to round up as many prisoners as he could. They would be used to populate the troubled area in the south by the Ros River, where his territory was under constant threat from wild nomads, the Pechenegs.

Harald left the meeting and rode over to his men. He explained to Ivar what they were going to do and then the two of them rode round to groups of the warriors explaining the tactics. Shortly afterwards, Harald and his lieutenants moved off on horseback followed by the marching men. They made a wide circle through a wood and then started to move quietly towards the back of the castle. Very soon, they heard the sound of voices and the rumble of wagons. As they broke cover, they found themselves on a track leading to the castle and there, coming towards them, was a long line of old men, women, children and wagons drawn by oxen. The procession was being led by a small group of soldiers.

"Ivar, take as many men as you can and run to the end of the line to stop the Læsirs running back to the castle."

While Ivar ran off with a contingent of men, Harald led an attack on the soldiers leading the column.

The action was over quickly because of the superiority in numbers of the Varangians. Harald had to restrain his men from slaughtering the refugees, remembering what he had been ordered. But Eilif had said nothing about restraint regarding plundering the wagons. Most of these only contained the personal belongings of the people walking beside them. In some, there were sick people, but two of them were carrying silver and gold objects, chalices, plate and crosses, which must have come from the castle church. Clearly, the authorities were seeking to save the goods from the marauding foreign army.

All the Varangians were trying to crowd round the two

wagons to get a look at the plunder which they would get a share of and congratulating each other on their luck.

"A good start, master!" said Ivar.

"Yes, but only the start," the Norwegian replied.

Harald issued orders for the prisoners to be guarded and assigned a group of warriors to protect the two wagons from the attention of others of their army who might be consumed with envy.

The force continued up the hill and, as they did so, became more and more aware of the battle taking place for possession of the castle as the shouts of men and the clanging of metal on metal became louder. As they approached the rear entrance to the building, the gate opened and fleeing soldiers poured out of the opening. The fight which ensued was furious as Harald's Varangians tried to stop the castle defenders running down the hill in their effort to avoid the onslaught at the front of the castle. The defenders were desperate to escape and fought bravely while the Varangians tried to stem the exodus of the garrison troops. Eventually, the Norwegians prevailed, and the remaining Læsir laid down their arms. But it was not without loss for Harald: several of his men had been killed or wounded. Nevertheless, the stock of the Norwegian contingent of the Varangians rose considerably in the army, as did the wealth of the men when they got their share of the plunder after Jarl Eilif had taken his one fifth of the bounty and Harald, their commander, a similar share.

This was the first of several castles to be taken by Eilif's army before the town of Belz itself fell and the territory was returned to the possession of Prince Jaroslav. Such was the scale of King Miesko's defeat that he became hugely unpopular with his own people, and they forced him to flee into exile.

Harald's luck continued throughout the campaign. The plunder gained for his detachment of Norwegian Varangians made him a very popular commander, and any doubts about being led by such a young officer were dispelled. Increasingly, his shrewd advice at Jarl Eilif's war councils became respected by the older, more experienced commanders. However, Ivar had noticed that with his master's success came an unwelcome increase in arrogance and greed. The leader's share of the plunder had already made him a wealthy man, but he wanted more. And his arrogance was quick to assert itself on their triumphant return to Novgorod.

"Ivar, did you see Prince Jaroslav's daughter?" asked Harald when they had returned to their quarters after a celebration festival for the victorious Varangians.

"The little girl with the long plaits?"

"Yes, she will become a beauty, of that I am certain."

"Why do you ask?"

"I am going to marry her," replied Harald.

"But she is a child. She can only be eleven or twelve years old!"

"And I am sixteen. That's only five years' difference!" argued Harald.

Ivar knew better than to enter into a dispute with his master and commented no further.

"I have returned to Novgorod as a victorious commander, and her father respects me. I will ask him for her to be promised to me," stated Harald.

Harald got his chance the next day when the officers were called to the palace to be allocated their next assignments. He arrived early and asked to speak to the Prince before the meeting began.

Appreciative of his efforts on the campaign, the Prince acceded to his request. "Well, Harald, you wished to see me."

"Yes, Your Highness. As you are aware, I have been very successful in the campaign against the Læsir. As a reward, I want to ask for your daughter Elizavet to be my wife."

The prince was staggered by the impudence of the sixteen

year-old. His first reaction was annoyance, but it quickly turned to mirth.

"Tell me, young man, what wealth do you have?" asked the Prince teasingly.

"I have my share of the plunder from the campaign."

"And what lands do you own?"

"None, sir, but one day I will."

"You have little wealth, no position in your own country, and you presume to ask for the hand of a princess! No, no, a thousand times, no!"

Harald was not to be put off and asked, "What do you require of me to be a suitor for your daughter?"

"I require you to be a grown man with power, wealth and fame."

"Save your daughter for me. One day I will have these."

Other commanders coming into the room saved Harald from a venomous tirade from the Prince. Harald's employer just added, "I will see what action I can arrange for you this winter to further your fame."

When the meeting concluded, it was clear that the Prince had decided, perhaps vindictively, that Harald should be allocated the most unpopular and dangerous assignment: that of accompanying the *druzhina* on their winter tribute gathering.

Each winter, the prince sent some of his trusted bodyguard to collect taxes from his distant subjects. This was done in the winter so that the warriors could travel by horse and sled up the frozen rivers. The *druzhina* under the command of Jarl Rognvald needed a large band of Varangians to go with them so that they could enforce their will on the often reluctant local leaders and exact their tribute. The operation was uncomfortable: the soldiers often had to survive severe weather, sleeping in tents, and it was dangerous as the local landowners often paid mercenaries to fight off the tax collectors. However, there was a strong incentive for the force sent to do this work:

they were paid a commission on the total value of the tribute. Harald was instructed to choose a hundred of his Varangians to take with him.

"Ivar, we are going to spend the winter travelling in the far lands to the east of Nogorod," said Harald.

"What for?" enquired Ivar.

"We are to become tax collectors," replied Harald with some derision. "Now we have two weeks to prepare winter equipment, clothes and sledges so that we are ready when the snow comes."

Ivar felt that this was a good time for him to ask a favour of his master. "Sir, in the last campaign I fought with spear and axe, and served you well."

"I can't deny it," said Harald.

"I could serve you better if I had my own sword."

A warrior's sword was a mark of his status. The quality and balance of the weapon might not only mean the difference between life and death for him, but the mere display of a fine weapon could serve to speak of his potential and experience as a warrior. There was something contradictory about a slave owning a sword, and Ivar realised this. So the servant was surprised at Harald's answer.

"I have thought to have a new sword made to mark my success on the last campaign. I need a heavier sword now. You shall have my old one, but the hilt is too long for your hand is smaller than mine. We will get the swordsmith who makes my new sword to alter the hilt and the pommel on my old one to fit you."

It was true: Harald was still growing. He was already head and shoulders taller than any of the other Varangians and he had huge hands.

"Can we do this before the winter campaign, sir?"

"Yes, we must."

And so it was that Harald's sword of best quality Norwegian

metal came into the possession of the slave. The swordsmith altered the weapon, but Ivar had a special request. When he was a boy, his father had given him a bear's claw on a leather necklace. His father had, in his turn, been given the claw by his mother. Ivar asked the swordsmith to inlay the claw in the pommel of his sword. The legend in his family was that the claw would protect the bearer from death at the hands of a stranger. What better place to put it than on the sword which would accompany Ivar when he faced the dangers of battle.

As the days got shorter and the cold became more intense, Harald and his men waited for the rivers to freeze. As soon as they did, the small army set off.

It was when they were approaching the third village which they had to visit that the Varangians first had to actively support the *druzhina*. As their sledges progressed over the frozen ground, they noticed that the otherwise pristine snow was marked with hoof and footprints. There had been recent light snow which had dulled the sharpness of the imprints, but it was clear that a large band of travellers, perhaps thirty or so, had passed this way in the last few days, and the indications were that they were going in the same direction as the tax collectors.

Soon, the forest on the banks of the river began to thin out and, after a while, through the gaps in the trees, they could see plumes of smoke curling skywards in the cold air which was still on this windless day. Suddenly, they heard a blast on a trumpet being blown close to where they were, and then they saw a rider making his way as fast as he could through the deep snow towards the village.

The commander of the *druzhina* shouted back to Harald, "He was a lookout. The trumpet call has warned the village that we are coming."

The tribute collectors proceeded more slowly, now with their arms at the ready. As they neared the village, they could see that it was surrounded by vertical poles in the form of a palisade. But the fence was not a strong fortification; it was to protect the village from bears and wolves, not armed men. Nevertheless, around the perimeter there were watchtowers, and it could soon be seen that these lookouts were manned by armed men.

"The tracks we have seen must be those of a band of mercenaries in the pay of the village," said Rognvald to Harald.

"We need to get them outside of the village to fight them," advised Harald.

"The only way to do that would be to use fire arrows to set the village alight. We can't collect the taxes if we destroy the village."

This was the first of several occasions on the winter journey that Harald had the opportunity of learning military tactics from the wily Orkneyman.

"After nightfall, we leave some men at our encampment in front of the village. They should keep the fires burning and make plenty of noise to give the impression that we are all here. The rest of us circle round to the back of the village in the dark and make a night attack from the direction from which we are not expected," ordered the jarl.

And thus it was that, early next morning at first light, the Varangians smashed their way through the palisade with their axes and stormed the village. Those mercenary warriors who were not caught in the onslaught escaped through the gates at the front of the village only to run into the guard which had been left at the encampment. The village headman was forced to pay his tribute in silver and furs before being executed as a lesson to the villagers that Prince Jaroslav's authority was to be respected.

In early spring, before the thaw had broken the river ice, the *druzhina* and Varangians made a triumphant return to Novgorod. Most sledges were piled high with furs but one contained sacks of silver. Harald was greeted by the news that he was to be tested further. An even more hazardous expedition had been planned for him and his men for the summer. Jaroslav had decided that the time had come to exert his authority on his most distant subjects: the tribes in the far north-eastern province under the Ural mountains. The warriors of these tribes were considered to be so terrifying that, in Rus tradition, it was said that these were people who should be locked behind the iron gates until the Day of Judgement.

Harald's warriors joined other Varangian units whose task was to break the power of the tribes and to subjugate them under the Prince's rule. The campaign was very different from that of the previous summer against the Læsir. This time the Varangians had to learn to fight as cavalry. The enemies were accomplished horsemen and the Rus army had to adopt mounted tactics. The long summer campaign was conducted successfully, and Harald's reputation was further enhanced. In the autumn after the expiry of their contract with the Prince in Novgorod, the seventeen year-old commander, in his quest for further glory and wealth, offered his men to Jaroslav to serve in the south of his kingdom. There, on the important trade route from Kiev to the Orient, the fearsome Pecheneg tribesmen constantly intimidated the travelling traders and settlers. These warriors lived on the steppe north of the Black Sea, but roamed over great distances raiding and pillaging. They were very skilful riders and, though they used a range of weapons, they were most feared as mounted archers. They used a small bow, much shorter than that of the Norse, but nevertheless the weapon was extremely powerful as it was made of composite material. The wood of the bow was strengthened with horn and shaped into a double curve.

To counter the threat of the Pecheneg, the Prince's father had built walls from far out along the River Ros, all the way to the great marshalling docks on the waterway where ships assembled before going north or south on the trade route. The walls were constructed so that they were too high for raiders to jump over on their horses and thus prevented surprise attacks. The monumental structure was so long that it took over two weeks to march the length of it. It was known as the Snake Ramparts. At various points along the walls, settlements had been established, and they had been populated by prisoners of war who had been forced to settle in the villages. The strategy was that, as the villages grew and became stronger, the Pecheneg would be less likely to attack them. But the tribesmen had to be fought offensively as well as defensively and, in addition, the most vulnerable parts of the trade route had to be protected by mobile forces. Thus it was that Harald's Varangian warriors were contracted for another year, this time to work in the lands south of Kiev.

The journey south was a long one, not only in terms of distance but also time, for although the Varangians travelled south in their nine ships, the River Lovat ended before they reached the tributaries of the Dneiper, the great south-going waterway. The ships had to be dragged out of the river and transported overland for many days by rolling them over logs. At the end of the Lovat, there was a settlement where travellers and traders could hire teams of oxen, ox drivers and towing lines.

Transporting the nine ships was a huge enterprise. Six oxen were allocated to each ship and, in addition to these animals, the Varangians had to hire horses. All the men's heavy weapons and equipment had to be carried by pack horses, and some warriors had to ride fully armed to be on guard against surprise attacks from the nomadic tribesmen. The work was continuous and hard for the men for, while the beasts did much of the pulling, the crews also had to work. Some men were allocated to collect the logs as the ships rolled over them and rush the timber forward to the bow of the ship to maintain the carpet of logs. Others had to continuously spread animal fat onto the logs to help the keel to slide more easily. At times, the landscape was hilly, and the crews had to help the oxen to drag the heavy boats uphill. On the downhill runs, they had to hold lines behind the ships to prevent the vessels sliding too fast.

Eventually, they saw clear water through the trees ahead of them and, at a settlement on the river, they saw ships waiting to use the same oxen for their journey north. These were Norse traders who were returning with goods from the markets in Miklagård[40] and Arabia. They carried ceramics, jewellery, spices, wine and other things which were in demand in the north countries.

Harald rested his men for a day at the settlement, for them to recover from the arduous portage. In the afternoon of their arrival, he took Ivar to look at the trading vessels being pulled out of the water to begin their land journey north.

They walked along the riverside and inspected the piles of bundled goods in the ships.

"Those ships are too heavy to make the portage," said Ivar.

"All the cargoes have to be unloaded and transported by horses until they reach River Lovat."

"Very heavy work for the crews," ventured Ivar.

"Yes, but what wealth there is in each ship! The hardship must be worthwhile for them."

"These merchants have to work hard for their share of the riches of Miklagård."

"I think that it must be easy to get wealthy there. We shall serve the Prince for one year here and then offer our services to the Emperor of Miklagård."

"Will you never return to Norway?"

"Yes, when I have fame and wealth enough."

"How long must I be your servant?"

"Why do you ask?"

---

[40]    Miklagård – Constantinople, (Istanbul)

"I long to return to my own country, to see if any of my family has survived. I had property there too, though it was torched by your father's men."

"You have served me well, yet you are still my slave," replied Harald.

The commander thought for a moment and then said, "I want you to serve me for ten years more and then you shall have your freedom."

Ivar was disappointed, but he knew that to have argued would have been deemed as insolent, and he did not want the offer to be withdrawn.

"Thank you, sir," he replied.

# Chapter 11

## In the Service of Earl Harold

It was to be nearly four years before Torkil was called upon to honour the pledge he had made to Earl Harold: to serve him when required. Meanwhile, in 1053, a year after returning from exile, the old Earl Godwin died. He had been attending a royal banquet in Wintoncaestre when he was taken ill with a mystery ailment and died two days later. Rumours flew that the old man had become too powerful and that King Edward had found a useful opportunity to dispose of a rival who had become richer and more powerful than himself. But nothing could be proven, and peace reigned. Edward soon found that the new Earl of Wessex, Harold Godwin, while also potentially a rival, was a formidable warrior and a valuable ally. For, like a thorn in the side or an unreachable itch, King Edward had an enemy who could not easily be dealt with: Gruffyd Ap Llewellyn, King of Wales.

For years, the Welsh King had sent raiding parties into border areas of England to plunder and murder. But such was the nature of the country that the Welsh King always avoided being brought to battle. In 1055, with his army strengthened by Irish warriors, Gruffyd launched an attack on Hereford. Waiting to meet him was the English King's army, commanded by Earl Ralph.

*Earl Ralph collected a great army against them at the town of Hereford, where they met; but ere there was a spear thrown the English people fled, because they were on horses. The enemy then made great slaughter, about four hundred or five hundred men and on their side no one was killed. They went to the town and burned it utterly; and the large church also.'*

The Anglo-Saxon Chronicle AD 1055

The campaign was a disaster for the English; this insult had to be answered. The time had come for the King to appoint a new leader for his army – Earl Harold Godwin.

Torkil had spent four years learning the business of running his estate during a period of peace on the island. While tempestuous events were happening elsewhere in the kingdom, the narrow strip of water between Vectis and the mainland insulated the islanders from them. It was a time of prosperity with good harvests. The young thayne had shown skill at organising workers and supervising improvements to the estate buildings but also, throughout this time, he had been receiving training in the use of arms. His mentor, the steward, had encouraged him to select three young men from his estate to train with him, partly so that, in the event of future attacks on their village, there would be a core of men able to defend it, but also so that, when the call came to serve Earl Harold Godwin, Torkil would have some capable men to join him.

The four young men had learnt to use their swords and shields for attack and defence. They had practised the technique of forming shield walls so that, when opened, like angry dogs released from the leash, they could spring out from the formation and attack. Launching out from the protection of the shields, they trained to slash an enemy with the double-handed axe. There was considerable competition among them to perfect the accuracy of their spear throwing, and neither were the skills of hand-to-hand combat neglected, which led to several injuries to combatants.

And so it was in the early autumn of 1055 that the summons came from Earl Harold for the thaynes and the fyrdsmen[41] to be mobilised to form a great army to face the Welsh. Torkil had been waiting for this moment, and he made no effort to disguise the excitement he felt at having the chance to take part in combat.

"Can you not send your three fyrdsmen to serve the Earl?" his mother pleaded. "You only have a responsibility to provide armed men. You do not need to go yourself."

"Mother, don't you see, this is my chance to win honour for myself and the family, and there might be plunder for us to win."

"You have safer ways of making money here. The estate is too big for Simon and me to run alone."

"Nonsense, you will manage. I am almost twenty years old and I can decide for myself. If I don't take this chance now, it may be many years before I have another opportunity."

"Yes, it is a chance, a chance to get yourself killed. Please be careful, Torkil."

"Don't worry, we are well trained. We will bring honour to the village!"

With that, after packing his weapons and byrnie, he joined his three companions and set off for the quay. From there, they sailed to Hamwic where Torkil bought four horses, and then they rode to Wintoncaestre to join up with Earl Harold's army. Their stay there was short for, after a day, the commander led the army out of the city; their destination was Gloucester.

The army rested in Gloucester hoping to bring the Welsh to battle but, once again, when it suited him, Gruffyd withdrew to the mountains. Harold decided to advance into Wales to the Black Mountains. His search for the Welsh King was

---

[41] Fyrdsmen – Militiaman of the Saxon period; often a land worker called to arms in support of the king or a local lord

unsuccessful, but the Welsh made their hidden presence felt. Gruffyd's troops made small but deadly night-time raids on the English. Each time this happened, for fear of falling into an ambush, the English had to wait until daybreak to search for the marauding Welsh. But, by daybreak, the enemy were long gone.

With supplies running low, Harold decided to turn back and go to see the devastated Hereford. The Welshmen followed the English down the valleys, and the rate of attrition caused by their raids began to sap the morale of Harold's men. The night-time attacks continued and intensified.

One of Torkil's men, Eldred, approached his master as they prepared their camp for the night. "Master, we can't go on like this, fearing to sleep lest we have our throats cut by the Welsh."

"What would you have me do, Eldred?"

"We know that the Welsh must be watching us as we march. They don't know where we are going so they have to follow. If a band of us rode ahead of the column and hid in the country around our next encampment before our army got there, we could try to ambush the Welsh as they followed our troops."

Torkil considered the idea. It was true that the Welsh must be following the army as it marched. They would not be directly behind but spread out on one or both sides to avoid being ambushed by the English rearguard.

"I will talk to the officer Godric," said Torkil.

The thayne found the officer coming out from Earl Harold's tent.

"Sir, if I might have a word?" he called to the figure who was hurrying away.

Godric turned. "Who are you?" he asked.

"I am Torkil, thayne of Selceeflet."

"What do you want?"

"Sir, I have a suggestion to hinder the raids on our troops by the Welsh."

Godric looked Torkil up and down. He saw a well built warrior not much younger than himself, of medium height with shoulder-length red hair and the conventional long moustache.

"Well, what is your idea? God knows we have to find some way to make the Welsh suffer for their barbarity."

Torkil outlined his plan. Godric listened intently.

"Wait here," he said. He went back into the tent which Torkil had seen him coming out of. The thayne could hear voices from inside the tent, but could not make out what was being said.

The tent flap was thrown open and the tall figure that he had last seen on a ship in London emerged with Godric.

"Your plan is interesting, Master Torkil." Harold stopped and looked at him closely. "Haven't we met before?" he asked.

"We have, My Lord. You used my ship to transport weapons to Boseham."

"Ah, yes. That was unfortunate for you. But I see that you survived."

"Yes, My Lord, but my men did not, and I have a blood feud with Egbert."

"Um, that is as may be. You shall have a chance to prove yourself a better warrior than you were a seaman. You are too inexperienced to command a force to do as you are suggesting. Godric will lead twenty housecarls together with you, your men and a force of mounted fyrdsmen. Tomorrow night, we propose to camp at Gafenny[42] where there is plenty of water for the horses and we can resupply. You will leave before first light so that you are not observed by Welsh spies."

Godric spoke. "Get your men and then come with me to the supply wagons. We must draw provisions for our journey."

Next morning, a cockerel crowing well before dawn woke Torkil and his men. It had been a quiet night with no

---

[42]  Gafenny – Abergavenny, the mouth of the River Gavenny

interruptions from the raiders. They prepared themselves for the journey and had some bread and porridge. There was a gentle wind blowing down the valley.

The sixty horsemen led by Godric set off west following the river bank in the early light of dawn. By mid-morning, they had reached a small hamlet by the river. By a bridge, a watermill was slowly turning, and smoke was rising from the smoke holes of the simple houses. As the soldiers were spotted, children were dragged indoors and adults scurried for the assumed safety of their houses.

Godric gave the order to dismount and led several soldiers to enter the largest of the houses. They smashed the door down and dragged a man out. He was dark-haired and had a black beard. His jacket was made of rough cloth and was covered in white powder.

"Master miller, we want you to guide us to the high ground overlooking Gafenny," said Godric.

The man cowered, shaking his head. He clearly did not understand English. The man pointed to a hut on the mountainside which the soldiers had not noticed.

"Torkil, go up and see what he is pointing at."

They mounted their horses and, together with his men, Torkil trotted up the grassy slope to the hut. As they came closer, they saw a crude wooden cross on the wall of the hut. They approached and the door opened. A monk came out.

Torkil looked down from his horse at the monk. "We need a guide to take us up through the hills. If the village people help, we will not harm them. If they don't, we will burn the houses."

The monk looked up at the riders and said in English, "Follow me."

The monk went with them down to the village and spoke to the miller in Welsh.

"Where do you want to go to?" asked the monk.

"The hills above Gafenny," explained Godric.

Soon the force was following the miller who, on foot, was leading them south, away from the river. They entered a forest and followed a path which gradually became steeper. As the trail rose, the forest began to thin out until eventually there were just low bushes.

Godric stopped the column of riders and turned his horse round to look at the vista behind them. The others did likewise. By now, the sun was high and they could see a long stretch of the valley to the north and, to the north-west, trails of smoke betrayed the site of the village of Gafenny.

"Look, there is the army," one of the riders shouted. " The vanguard is coming round the bend."

The horsemen sat and watched as the long column of marching men, mounted thaynes and housecarls, and wagons snaked around the curves of the southern bank of the River Usk. By mid-afternoon, when the rear guard came into view, the vanguard had almost reached Gafenny. The watchers on the hill continued to scan the valley below them.

"Look, master, on the north bank in amongst the trees, there are horsemen."

The lookouts strained to see what had been reported.

"Yes, look at the glint of sun on their weapons!" shouted another.

Soon, they all saw glimpses of the Welsh horsemen traversing the valley in the woods on the north side of the Usk. As this force came level with them, Torkil counted eighty horses.

Out of sight of the English army in the valley, the Welsh used the cover of the forest to come down on lower ground to hide on the north bank of the river. There was a sharp bend where the river turned south and later turned east again. On the first of these bends, after the English rearguard had passed, the Welsh dismounted and set up a temporary camp.

Seeing this from his vantage point, Godric called to one of the housecarls and gave him orders to ride down the hill to Gafenny and tell the Earl where the Welsh were.

"Tell Earl Harold that we will attack the Welsh after dark from the west side. He should take a force along the river from the east to trap them after we have attacked. Keep in cover so that the Welsh do not see you."

The slope of the hill to the east of them was less steep and the rider could clearly see the route to take to the village.

Godric gave orders that his force should retrace their steps to the miller's village down the steep slopes where they could cross on the bridge to the north side of the river. The return journey was precarious and slow. Even the sure-footed Saxon horses found the incline slippery, and the riders had to dismount frequently and lead their horses.

By the time the light had begun to fade, Godric's men were on the north bank of the river. Cautiously and quietly, they negotiated the forest path taken earlier by the Welshmen. After a while, they tied their horses to trees and proceeded on foot. The rising half moon helped them on their way, but also made it easier for them to be discovered. They were anxious to avoid any Welsh lookout that might have been posted to guard against attack from the west. But such was the confidence of their enemy that they had clearly not suspected danger from behind, and no sentries had been posted.

As the English stealthily approached the Welsh encampment, Godric stopped the men and issued orders. He detailed two housecarls to lead most of the fyrdsmen to attack from the north. Torkil was instructed to join them. One of the housecarls, Elgar, was put in command. Their task was to stop the Welsh escaping in that direction. The other part of their force, which, having most of the housecarls, was stronger, would attack from the west and drive the Welsh towards Harold's approaching troops.

Torkil's detachment turned off north, but it soon became

obvious that it would be very difficult to penetrate the forest on that side of the path without making a lot of noise. The brambles made an almost impenetrable barrier between the ash and beech trees which towered overhead. Suddenly, they all heard the whinnying of horses. Unbeknown to Torkil's group, the other force had walked straight into the horse lines where the Welshmen had left their animals on the west side of their camp ready to make a quick escape when necessary.

The noise of the horses alerted the Welsh to the fact that there were intruders and they came racing from their resting places to investigate. Very soon after the horses had betrayed the presence of the English, there was the ringing sound of metal on metal. The shouts and curses of fighting men rent the cloak of quiet which had prevailed in the forest.

Since they could not do as ordered by Godric, Elgar led his men back to the path and they hurried towards the battle.

Godric's men had had some advantage of surprise. They were also well armed and wearing chain mail which the Welsh had not had the time to put on. But the sheer weight of numbers gave the Welsh superiority over Godric's force. By the time Elgar's reinforcements had arrived, the Welsh were breaking through Godric's line and fleeing west, directly into the fresh detachment of fyrdsmen.

As soon as they made contact, the two housecarls who were leading the detachment and several fyrdsmen were cut down by the desperate Welshmen. But, in the half dark, unable to discern how big the reinforcing group was, the fleeing warriors turned and attempted to run north into the forest. They were trapped.

Torkil rallied the leaderless fyrdsmen and led a search for the Welsh along the bramble hedges. The English used their spears to awful effect, piercing the backs of the struggling warriors. Soon they were joined by the survivors of Godric's housecarls with their swords and axes, and the bloody rout was continued until no more Welshmen could be found.

When the troops of Harold's army linked up with Gordic's detachment, they searched the area and finished off the Welsh wounded, but they also recovered the injured English; among them Godric. He had been chasing the fleeing Welsh when one of the panicking horses had trampled on his foot. He had heard Torkil organising the chase after the fleeing soldiers.

The next morning, Harold called Godric and Torkil to attend him in his tent. The housecarl was hobbling with a spear for support but was otherwise uninjured. Torkil, however, had a bloody face which, though it looked dramatic, was not from an enemy sword but from the brambles he had sought to climb through in the chase.

The Earl looked at the two men. "Godric, you have done good work this night. I do not think that we will be bothered by the Celts again."

"My Lord, the idea was Torkil's, and he led the fyrdsmen to stop the enemy's retreat."

"And what have you to say, Master Torkil?"

"In fact, My Lord, the idea was not mine but that of one Eldred, a churl from Selceeflet."

"Let me warn you both, you will not find favour or glory in my army by being modest. Torkil, I owe you a favour. What would you have?"

"To become a housecarl, My Lord."

The Earl turned to one of his advisors. "There are precedents to thaynes becoming housecarls, I believe."

The counsellor nodded.

"Then so be it."

Godric slapped Torkil on the back and grabbed his hand. "Come, an ale before we march on, thayne Torkil."

The drink they shared that day was to be the first of many they drank together, sometimes in celebration, other times in commiseration for, unbeknown to them, they were destined to travel many miles and fight a score of battles as comrades-at-arms.

In the days that followed, the army marched to Hereford and did what they could to fortify the city against further attacks by King Gruffyd, including digging a defensive dyke. During this time, Torkil and his men were billeted in farm buildings outside Hereford. This was one of the few farmsteads which had been spared the Welsh torching of the area, but the farmer had been killed in the general slaughter of the English. Before that attack, the owner, a thayne called Beorn, had sent his young wife Odelia to find refuge in Lodelowe,[43] two days' journey north of the city. When she returned, she found that her husband had been murdered and she was now mistress of the farm and owner of what animals had survived the pillaging of the Welsh. However, by statute, as a widow with no children, she was only able to inherit one third of her husband's property and the morgengifu[44] he had paid when they had wed.

While Odelia was pleased to have the security of the soldiers living in her farm buildings, she and her two maidservants had to endure the frequent lewd remarks of the men and their unwelcome advances. These occurrences always happened behind the senior officer Torkil's back.

One evening, when his working party returned to the farmstead, Odelia was standing outside the storehouses which were the soldiers' quarters.

"Master Torkil, I would speak with you," she said.

The warriors cast surreptitious glances and grins at each other, but none dared to comment.

"Good evening, Mistress Odelia. Of course," replied Torkil.

Odelia strode off in the direction of her cottage and Torkil followed. She ushered him into the small dwelling

---

[43]   Lodelowe – Ludlow, from Old English 'hlud Hlaw' – the hill with a noisy river
[44]   Morgengifu – literally, the morning gift payable by a husband to a bride

house. Inside, the two servant girls were standing waiting.

"Tell the officer what you told me, you little fool," she said, addressing her remark to the shorter of the two girls.

The girl looked at the floor and mumbled, "I am to marry Eldred."

"Why, girl, why?" demanded Odelia.

"For he comes to my bed each night."

Torkil was stunned. Eldred had a wife in Selceeflet, but this was not the time to mention it.

"Well, Master Torkil, what is to be done?"

Torkil knew that the price to be paid by a man for bedding a maiden who was a commoner was six shillings.

"The compensation will be paid," he stuttered and then added, "May we speak alone?"

Odelia sent the shorter of the girls to draw water from the well and told the other to feed the chickens.

"Eldred has a wife at home," Torkil blurted.

The woman was half turned away from Torkil when, in a very matter-of-fact way, she said, "Then I shall give the six shillings to the girl and not keep it myself, as is my right as her mistress. But this has got to stop. Your men must be told to leave my girls alone," she hesitated, "and me too."

She turned towards Torkil and he saw that she was crying.

"Are you too troubled by the men, or what is it which upsets you?"

"What do you think? I am a widow; my husband not long dead. I have to deal with his affairs and, poor as they are, it is so complicated for me. The Welsh stole most of our animals and destroyed much of our property. I must sell the land to return two thirds of the value to the Earl, and I have to endure the violation of my servants and the lewd taunts of your men."

He began to understand the depth of her feelings. He looked at her. The candlelight accentuated the paleness of her face which was framed by the tresses of her blond hair, and picked out the course of the tears on her cheeks. He felt a strong urge to comfort her, but was not sure what nature of soothing would be welcomed. His instinct urged him to step forward towards her, but his shyness and inexperience held him back.

"You will not be troubled by my men again. You have my word."

Torkil made to leave and walked towards the door. He paused, turned round and said, "Tomorrow I will come and help you to deal with your late husband's affairs."

Back with the men, he gathered them together and threatened them, on pain of whipping or worse, that they should desist from contact with or comment to the farm household.

He took Eldred aside. "I hear that you make sport with the mistress's maidservants."

"Well, they are pretty, master."

"Your conscience is your own affair but, when you return home with a debt of six shillings to me, you must decide if you wish me to explain the transaction to your wife or whether you will do so."

With that, the affair with Eldred was closed but, for Torkil, it was just the beginning. The frequency of his visits to the cottage and the length of his stay each time increased as, with the onset of winter, the length of the days decreased.

With the completion of the dyke, three weeks before Yuletide, the army was disbanded, and Torkil and his men returned home. However, an agreement had been made. By statute, a widow was not permitted to remarry for a year after her husband's death. In the summer of 1056, Torkil would be travelling to Hereford to bring his bride back to Selceeflet.

# Chapter 12

## In the Court of the Duke

*Earl Harold's journey to Normandy (From the Bayeux Tapestry)*

It was six years before the housecarl thayne Torkil was to be called upon to fight for Earl Harold again. During this period, each year, the four warriors from Selceeflet had attended summer training with the army to maintain their military skills, but for the rest of the time they led their normal lives in Selceeflet. The thayne looked forward to the annual summer gathering of the local fyrd in the fields outside Wintoncaestre and the chance to practise combat in the manoeuvres. Most years, Godric attended the exercises, and the two of them spent many raucous evenings together in the housecarl's quarters.

In the meantime, Torkil's family had increased as Odelia had borne two sons: Finn was born in 1058 and Edward in

1060; and his wealth had grown. The proceeds of the sale of Odelia's estate in Hereford had financed further expansion of the thayne's landholding.

And so the family prospered. But Torkil's enthusiasm for the military life did not please Edlin who, at the age of forty-six was an old woman. She found it difficult to show an interest in all the tales he regaled Odelia and her with when he returned from the yearly training sessions. Her primary concern was that he should not be called to active service again. She feared for his safety, but also she was worried about how the affairs of the estate could be managed in his absence. For, by now, partly because of her age and partly because the estate had grown, dealing with the tenants and conducting the business of their own farm was too much for her. Thankfully, the annual military training was timed so that the fyrdsmen and the officers could return to their farms in time for the harvest.

As the family prospered so did the village, with the Hall at its centre. These were good times and, to an extent, the thayne shared his good fortune with the villagers. After certain important dates in the religious calendar, and after the harvest, it was traditional for the thayne to provide a feast for his churls. It was the custom for the thayne to hand out bread as the guests arrived, as a gesture of his care for them. On these occasions too, any son of a churl who had reached the age of sixteen attended his first feast and had to swear the oath of loyalty to the thayne. The feasts were almost the only time that villagers tasted meat, for the herd of cows and the flock of sheep belonged to Torkil, and they were kept for milk and wool.

The womenfolk of the most important churls were allowed to attend the feasts, but they sat at a separate table together with Odelia and Edlin; that is, when the old lady was not fussing in the kitchen directing the slaves who worked there.

They had never had to buy slaves at the Hamwic slave market. There was a ready supply of girls and sometimes boys in Selceeflet and the surrounding villages. Most frequently, the slaves taken on were children of parents who could not afford to keep them. Occasionally, Edlin took a child as a slave in payment of a debt to the estate which a family could not afford to pay. This was unusual as most villagers were prudent and relatively prosperous. The land was fertile and food stocks were readily supplemented at most times of the year by fishing. Flatfish, eels, oysters and mussels abounded in the creeks, and churls had the right to fish in them. And nature provided many other foods which balanced the churls' and the slaves' diets. In spring, the roots of cuckoo pint[45] were harvested, as well as silverweed[46] with its delicate leaves and golden flowers which were eaten raw or ground into flour. Ox-eye daisy[47] with its long stems and white petals with a yellow centre had many medicinal uses and the young plants were eaten as a salad; stalks of tall burdock[48] were gathered for eating too; and, in May, young shoots of bramble and goose grass[49] were boiled as a vegetable. In late summer, hazelnuts, blackberries and wild cherries were plentiful. The autumn provided rose hips and haws which were infused with water, and sloes from the blackthorn bushes and elderberries were used for wine-making.

Each village family also produced vegetables from their own narrow strips of land which they farmed for themselves when they had the time, for every churl had a primary duty to work on the thayne's land.

It was at the times of feast days that Godric came to visit Torkil. Godric had no family of his own. It was not an uncommon occurrence that both his wife and his child had

---

[45]   Cuckoo pint – Arum maculatum

[46]   Silverweed – potentilla anserine

[47]   Ox-eye daisy – Leucanthemum vulgare

[48]   Burdock – arctium lappa

[49]   Goose grass – Galium aperine

died during childbirth. On his visits, the two men spent most of their time hunting. Torkil's falcons were well trained by one of the slaves, and their day excursions along the creekside paths often resulted in a fine bag of ducks and geese for the table.

At other times, groups of churls would go hunting with the two men to seek bigger game – deer or boar. All the men of the village had an obligation to train with the bow, and Torkil selected the most able of them to accompany him on his hunting trips. If they were successful then the meat was roasted on an outdoor spit in the village and all the families shared it, though the best cuts were kept by Torkil's family.

Although there was frequent turmoil in the King's court, and both political and ecclesiastical disputes, these seldom reached the shores of the island, and the years passed peacefully through the periods of winter, seedtime and harvest. However, the years did not always pass in family harmony.

Edlin had had her husband chosen for her by her father. She did have the right to refuse his choice but, although she was doubtful about the man he had chosen, she recognised that the proposed union with the son of a well-connected thayne from the other side of the water could bring benefits to their family. Very soon after the marriage, it became clear that, though her husband's family were well-connected, they had no wealth. Indeed, Alric soon found that the material requirements of his son-in-law were endangering the financial well-being of his own family. Edlin had been thrust from girlhood to womanhood in a torrent of tribulations. There had been disputes, physical violation and, ultimately, physical cruelty to her, her children and her father. She had conceived twice and, to her joy, never again. The law gave a woman the right to leave a husband, but to have done so would have left her penniless and her husband as heir to Selceeflet.

The marriage had transformed the winsome country girl into a tough woman with a very strong character. When she received news of her husband's death in a drunken brawl, it was if she had cast off a heavy yoke. But her character was now moulded and, when her darling son Torkil, always a boy to her, brought his wife to live at Selceeflet, there were severe problems of adjustment. For Odelia was also a determined woman and, having once been the mistress of a landed household, she fully expected to assume that position in her new home.

It was to take many months, indeed several years, before the two women agreed on the roles they should take. In the early period of the marriage, Torkil frequently had to intervene in disputes between the two women. Things did not really settle until 1058 when Finn was born. Odelia found herself fully occupied as a mother and was content to leave the running of the household to Edlin. Paradoxically, as Edlin got older, somewhat infirmed and less able to manage her responsibilities, she was secretly pleased to hand over much of the running of the household to Odelia. This need was particularly acute in periods of Torkil's absence, when she had to run the estate with Simon.

The advent of grandchildren had also had a softening effect on Edlin. She spent as much time as she could playing games with the boys, games she had learnt herself as a child such as board games and 'knuckles' where the player had to pick up small stones in one hand as quickly as possible. And there were extravagances for the children too. At feasts, Edlin often arranged for jugglers, acrobats and musicians to entertain everyone, and in particular the children.

It was thus much resented by Edlin when this pastoral idyll was interrupted by events which gave her son opportunities to vent his enthusiasm for military ventures.

Torkil was twenty-six when he received a summons from Earl Harold to join him on another campaign against Gruffyd Ap Llewellyn. Edlin was aghast at the prospect of her son participating in action against the Welsh. Their reputation as merciless killers of the English had grown on account of the sacking of Hereford and, as time went by, the stories told about this event had been embellished and exaggerated. Odelia shared Edlin's horror, for she had already lost one husband to the Welsh.

It was a cold October afternoon when a messenger arrived with Torkil's orders. Edlin immediately made an effort to persuade her son that his responsibilities in Selceeflet should be cited to the Earl as a reason for being unavailable to join the campaign.

"Torkil, your duty is to the estate. There are many mouths which will only be fed if we prosper. Who will deal with all the difficulties of ensuring a good harvest? For, without grain in our barn, people will starve."

"Mother, you exaggerate. You and Simon can manage perfectly well."

"And what about your poor wife? She has already suffered because of the Welsh."

"That is exactly why we must put an end to the threat from across the border!" Torkil was now raising his voice. "Odelia understands that; she knows what the Welsh are capable of!"

"She says nothing to deter you because she does not dare. A wife must do her husband's bidding, but I can say what I like and I speak for her too."

"There is nothing more to discuss. I have no choice anyway. I have to obey the order from the Earl."

"And your children – don't you fear that they may become fatherless?"

"Enough! I have heard enough. Get the servant to prepare food for me for the journey. I leave on the morning tide."

Resentfully, Edlin stalked off in the direction of the kitchen. She was humiliated but not defeated. She had always regarded deviousness as an attribute in the hard world she inhabited. Now was the time to show her stubborn son that she was not to be underestimated. When she had made arrangements as requested by Torkil, and when she was certain that he was busy with the preparation of his weapons, she called the steward to attend her.

"I want you to catch the evening tide and take a message to Earl Harold in Wintoncaestre. Hire a horse in Hamwic and ride through the night so that the Earl has this letter by morning."

"But the master is going to need the ship tomorrow morning and, besides, would it not be better for him to take the letter?"

"No, I want you to take it. Send the crew back with the boat immediately you have landed. Tell no one of your journey. Return shortly and I will give you the letter."

Simon was perplexed, but rushed off to make arrangements for a crew to be ready as soon as possible. As dusk fell, with the letter in his pouch, the steward was transported down the creek to the accompaniment of the feathered waders' evening chorus.

As dusk fell a day later, Torkil was kicking his tired horse to try to hurry the animal so that he could join his army comrades before dark. He found the encampment by the river on the south side of the town. But he was surprised how few tents there were. It seemed that only a small force had gathered there. He found his way to the officers' tents and sought out Godric.

After greeting his friend, he asked, "What is going on? Why are there so few warriors here?"

"The Earl is coming here tomorrow morning to explain the strategy. He has persuaded the King that we need to try a different way to trap King Gruffyd."

The two joined other old comrades, and soon the sounds of ribaldry and laughter echoed around the encampment.

Next morning, Earl Harold arrived with his hench people and his brother Gyrth. He gathered his officers and explained his plan. He told them that, having failed repeatedly to defeat the Welsh King in battle, a different strategy was to be used. King Edward had agreed that an attempt should be made to assassinate his Welsh enemy. He had agreed to let Earl Harold put together a small band of exceptional warriors for a lightning raid into the heartland of Wales. The operation was planned to take place in the winter when Gruffyd would be least expecting an English action.

When he had finished explaining the plan, Harold looked across the crowd to where Torkil stood.

"Thayne Torkil, I have heard from your mother that you can ill afford to be away from your estate, even though it is wintertime. I remember good mistress Edlin from when we had a royal visit to Vectis. A formidable lady to whom I am beholden for her hospitality. You are free to return to your estate on this one occasion."

Torkil was dumbstruck, frozen to the spot. As the gathering broke up, there were guffaws and sneers from his comrades as they passed him. His shock quickly gave way to fury as he chased after the Earl.

"But, sir, this is not my wish. I have come to serve you!"

The Earl half turned and shouted, "Go home, Torkil. Look to your wife and mother." With that he hurried away.

All around him, housecarls were busy breaking camp and preparing for their journey. Torkil went across to where Godric was packing his weapons on the armaments cart.

Godric turned as he approached and said, "Never suppose that you have won an argument with a woman, Torkil."

"By God, I will kill her!" growled Torkil.

"I think that such an action would displease the Earl. He seems to have some affection for your mother," joked Godric.

"The devious witch deserves a thrashing."

"Pack your goods and go spend the day in an ale house in Wintoncaestre. Drink deep and consider your good fortune to have womenfolk who care about you for I have neither wife nor living mother."

Torkil considered his friend's words for a few moments then slapped the housecarl on the back and seized his hand. "Be careful, old friend. Come back safely." With that, Torkil set off to follow Godric's recommendation.

By the time the master of Selceeflet returned to his home, his temper was cooler but nevertheless, after heated arguments with his mother, he was determined that he should never suffer such humiliation again. And, for her part, Edlin was quietly content that her will had prevailed, for she realised with some concern and not a little pride that over the last few years her son had not only developed into a physically strong man but that his strength of character and will power were seriously rivalling hers.

A few months later, when the Earl once more required Torkil's services, Edlin did not have the opportunity to interfere. At the annual training camp, Godric related to Torkil how the attempt to assassinate King Gruffyd had failed. Harold had force-marched his troops to the north-eastern border of Wales and then crossed the country to Rhuddlan on the River Clwyd, where Gruffyd had his palace. The surprise was total for the Welsh but, remarkably, Gruffyd had managed to escape. Since his force was relatively small, Earl Harold did not have the resources to initiate a hunt for the fleeing monarch. By way of retribution, the English had burnt the palace and the Welsh fleet before retreating.

During the training period, it was announced that King Edward's patience with his Welsh enemy was now utterly exhausted. There had been further raids on the English border areas. The King had decided that Earl Harold should embark on the biggest campaign to date against the Welsh. The Earl of Northumberland, Tostig, Harold's younger brother, was to lead an army southwards through North Wales, while Earl Harold took the fleet to land an army in South Wales and marched with his force northwards. The ships then should take station to prevent King Gruffyd escaping by sea.

Once again, there was no pitched battle. Instead, after weeks of chasing small groups of Welshmen using traditional methods, Harold decided to use his troops in a different way. They abandoned their heavy armour and, in small bands, the warriors ranged the country as irregulars seeking out the enemy where they could find them. Savage fighting continued for three months until Gruffyd's supporters, worn down by the English oppression, turned against him and offered terms to Earl Harold. Since many of his men had been decapitated by the Welsh, the Earl demanded Gruffyd's head before he would agree to make peace. The Celtic King was pursued into Snowdonia by his own men who later returned and presented the Earl with the monarch's head and the golden prow of Grufydd's personal ship. The Earl duly presented both to King Edward.

Earl Harold had reached the apogee of his career. The invincible Welsh had been broken and brought to heel by his outstanding generalship and the calibre of his troops. He was recognised as the greatest Anglo-Saxon warrior of his age and the King agreed for him to have the title 'subregulus' – deputy king. Earl Harold imposed harsh regulations on the Welsh including a law which stipulated that any Welshman found armed on the English side of Offa's Dyke[50] would have his arm chopped off. However, in view of his terrible decimation of the Welsh male population and consequent imbalance of males and females in the country, he introduced a new law which permitted English men to marry Welsh women, something which previously had not been permitted. To set an example, he announced that he would marry Ealdgyth, the late King Gruffyd's wife.

It had become clear to those closest to him that Earl Harold, now aged forty, considered himself to be the rightful heir to the fifty-nine year-old English monarch. However, it was also apparent that the King was not inclined to make public who he considered should ascend to the throne on his demise. There were several who laid claim to the right to succeed, but no one who could show an absolute right. The least popular and most feared candidate was the Norman Duke William. Many had the suspicion that King Edward, under the influence of

---

[50]   Offa's Dyke – an earthwork boundary between England and Wales built by King Offa in the eighth century

his French advisors, had already secretly made a pact with the Norman Duke.

Earl Harold needed to declare himself as heir, but there was a massive obstruction. The Earl's brother Wulfnoth and his nephew Hacun were still held by the Normans as hostages. Should the Earl declare his intention to succeed the King, it was likely that the two hostages would be put to death. Something had to be done to recover the two hostages.

Early in 1064, Torkil received a letter from Earl Harold that he was required to go to see him at Boseham. Further, that he should bring his sister Emma. The message was most mysterious, for what possible business could Earl Harold have with his sister who, now aged twenty-seven, was a nun at Wilton Priory? The Earl's request was not to be questioned, and Torkil travelled to Wilton to negotiate with the Abbetissa[51] for his sister to have leave of absence from the nunnery.

Torkil's crew sailed him to Hamwic where he disembarked and bought two saddled horses: one to ride himself and one for his sister. From Hamwic, he took the trail north to Sarum where he stayed the night. The next day, he rode the short distance to Wilton and, arriving at the nunnery, beat the blunt end of his axe on the large wooden door to attract attention. Eventually, a small flap in the door was slid open and a female voice demanded to know his business.

"I am Torkil, thayne of Selceeflet on Vectis. I am here on a mission for the Earl of Wessex. I must speak with the Abbetissa."

"Can you verify who you are?" asked the nun. Her hesitation was understandable as, within living memory, the nunnery had been destroyed by interlopers and, on more recent occasions, nuns had been kidnapped to fulfil the lewd wagers made in taverns by men short of female company.

---

[51]  Abbetissa – (Late Latin) the female superior in a house with more than 15 nuns

Torkil pulled out of his jacket the letter written to him by the Earl's scribe, rolled it up and thrust it through the open flap.

"Wait here," said the nun.

Invoking the name of the Earl was the key to getting immediate attention, for he was a significant benefactor to the nunnery. Nevertheless, it was a while before the sound of bolts sliding across the inside of the door indicated that his message had been read.

Two nuns of indeterminate age appeared in the opening. One said, "Sister Annis will take your horses. Come with me."

Torkil dismounted, gave the reins of his horse to the sister and, after untying the leading rein of the other horse, passed that to her too. He then followed the nun through a cloister. The place seemed completely deserted, but he realised that all of the nuns had probably been sent to their cells to avoid them seeing and being seen. A door in front of them was opened by an elderly nun who beckoned Torkil to enter the room. She followed him inside.

After exchanging greetings, Torkil said, "Abbetissa, I have a request from Earl Harold for my sister to accompany me on a visit to him in Boseham. He has—"

The nun interrupted Torkil. "Yes, yes, I have read the letter. This is a most extraordinary demand," she said as she handed the letter back to her visitor. "Sister Emma has been here for many years. She is very unworldly. I cannot think why the Earl would want her company."

Fearing that the nun might refuse the request, Torkil stuttered, "But I will be responsible for her. You need not be troubled for her safety."

"How do you propose to travel?"

"I have brought a horse."

"A horse! She has not been on a horse in her life. You cannot expect her to make a long journey in such discomfort."

Torkil had not considered this. However, he did know that

what the nun had said was not quite true: Emma used to ride at Selceeflet. He realised that it would not be politic to argue this point and said, "Then can I borrow a cart?"

"It could be arranged, but you will have to pay."

Such arrangements were made; the thayne was not in a position to argue. Torkil left the Abbetissa who went to inform Emma about the journey she was to make, and waited outside the nunnery with the door closed once more. Eventually, he heard a rumbling sound as a cart, driven by a nun, came round from what must have been the nunnery farm at the back of the building. His two horses were tied to the back of the primitive vehicle. The cart stopped and the nun driving it climbed down.

Torkil looked at the vehicle and wondered how long it would take to get to Boseham using this as transport. There was a flat platform for a passenger and a driver to sit on with their legs dangling over the front. The flat part had a low fence of split hazel hurdles around three sides to stop goods from falling off. The shafts of the cart which were tied to the horse with leather thongs were roughly shaped tree branches. The wheels were planks edge to edge, cut into a circle, with a metal hoop holding them in place.

Then the sound of the door bolts being drawn again announced that someone was coming. The old nun appeared together with another who was carrying a bundle. The second nun had her head down so it was not possible for Torkil to judge her age.

"This is Sister Emma," said the Mother Superior. "I charge you with responsibility for her well-being and for her safe return to her home here."

"A responsibility I am honoured to accept," answered Torkil.

The young nun looked up and, for the first time in thirteen years, Torkil's eyes met his sister's. Emma placed her bundle in the cart and climbed onto the seat.

Torkil addressed the old nun and said, "I am beholden to you, Abbetissa, I am sure that the Earl will show his appreciation."

With that, anxious to be off, he climbed up beside Emma. He shook the reins so that they slapped on the horse's hindquarters and the cart creaked into motion, jerking the two other horses tied behind and forcing them to follow.

There was a long silence before brother spoke to sister. At first, conversation was very slow and awkward but, by the time they were approaching Sarum where they would stay for the night, Emma was bombarding her brother with questions about the family she had left behind all those years ago, and how the estate was faring. These were questions which were easily answered, but her trepidation about the journey before them and the reason for it could not be soothed, for Torkil knew no more than her. At Sarum, anxious that their journey using the slow cart would take much longer than anticipated, Torkil persuaded her to ride the horse he had provided for her. He made arrangements for the cart to be taken back to Wilton, accepting that, on his return, he would have to face the wrath of the Abbetissa.

Two days later, in the evening, they arrived outside the manor hall at Boseham where Earl Harold was resident.

"Welcome, Torkil, and to you, madam," said Earl Harold in greeting them. He referred to the nun as 'madam' as, by virtue of her vows, she was considered to be married to God. She remained silent, but Torkil returned the greeting. "Good evening to you, My Lord. I trust that we have not kept you waiting too long."

"No, we have had a pleasurable time hunting and you shall sample some of our kill."[52]

The housecarl thayne was confused. The Earl had never before been so friendly and familiar with him, a socially inferior person.

---

[52]  According to the first picture in the Bayeux tapestry

"The womenfolk will show Sister Emma to her lodgings and make her comfortable."

The nun left the men and Torkil was ushered into the manor hall. From the noise, it was obvious that the mud-spattered revelling hunters in the hall had been imbibing freely to celebrate their successful day.

"Come, Torkil, join us," called Godric.

Torkil picked up a wooden tankard from the table and held it under the barrel of ale. After some preliminary pleasantries, he asked, "Godric, what is this gathering for?"

"The Earl is to go to Normandy. He has asked that you and I accompany him."

"And the purpose of the visit?"

"That you will have to ask the Earl."

Torkil's question was soon to be answered. After a short while, the Earl beckoned to Torkil and Godric to follow him to another room. In the room were several of the Earl's advisors sitting around a table. The two housecarls were offered empty chairs and the Earl sat at the head of the table.

"As you are all aware, the King is getting old and infirm. Yet he refuses to say who his heir should be, though it is obvious that I am entitled to the throne by virtue of being subregulus."

The Earl's advisors all nodded.

"But I cannot openly declare my intent to succeed."

"Why not, My Lord?" asked Torkil naively.

"You are not privy to matters of state, Torkil, but the answer is simple. My brother and my nephew are held by William, Duke of Normandy. This man lays false claim to the throne of England. He is cruel and ruthless. I have no doubt what would happen to them should I offend the Duke."

One of the advisors, to judge by the crucifix on a chain around his neck, a churchman, interjected. "So, our intention is to promote friendship between the Earl and the Duke with a goodwill visit. Earl Harold has received an invitation from the Duke to see him in Rouen. We will try to ascertain if it is possible to pay a ransom for the hostages or even, if the friendship is warm enough, the Duke may offer to return the Earl's relatives to England."

"But why have you asked me to bring my sister to Boseham?"

"We all have to make some sacrifice to solve the difficulty which I have described to you. As a gesture of friendship, I have offered to marry the Duke's daughter, Adelaide, to have as a second wife. The Duke is very protective of his daughter; he also a very religious man. He has asked me to provide a chaste, religious Anglo-Saxon female companion to be with Adelaide during our stay and on the journey back to England. He is worried that my ardour may be too strong to wait until the nuptials."

There was sycophantic laughter round the table before the Earl continued. "Sister Emma is the perfect companion for Adelaide. They will both speak Latin. Do you?"

"I do, My Lord. I was tutored by our priest."

"I have let the Duke know of my intention, and he was pleased because he remembered you and your sister from the visit he made to your home. He would like to repay your grandfather's hospitality. We must do everything possible to forge friendship while we are there. I am taking some of my hunting hawks as a gift as well as two dogs."

"But, My Lord, my sister is a nun at Wilton. She has lived in the nunnery for thirteen years. She is very unused to company. I don't think that it is possible for her to go."

The Earl broke in. "You will make the necessary arrangements for her to accompany us."

Torkil bridled; the idea of taking someone as unworldly as Emma on a long journey abroad seemed quite unreasonable. Harold saw Torkil's reaction, but ignored it.

The advisor spoke again. "There is some danger, of course.

Should things go wrong, the Duke might incarcerate the whole party. He is well known as an assassin and should he judge that Earl Harold is a threat then—"

The Earl interrupted, "That is a chance we will have to take. Hopefully, in your case, God will protect you, Bishop."

"When should we leave, My Lord?" asked Godric.

"If the weather is good, we will leave Boseham tomorrow for Rouen. We are a small group. The passengers will be you two housecarls, my clerk, Bishop Wulfstan, Sister Emma and me."

Godric, concerned for the safety of the party, tentatively enquired, "Should we go armed?"

"Yes, take your swords, armour, helmets and shields, but spears and axes will not be necessary. Now, let us join the hunters." And so saying, the Earl stood up and left the room to return to the revellers.

Torkil dallied in the room as the others left and indicated to Godric to wait with him. When the others had gone, he said to Godric, "This is a risky enterprise, I am most discontent that my sister should have to take part in it."

"But, Torkil, I am certain that the Earl has thought it through carefully and, besides, you and I will be there to protect her. You cannot disobey the Earl's orders."

Torkil thought for a while and then said, "I hope that you are right, for I have a bad feeling about this venture."

The six passengers embarked the next morning on the largest craft of the Earl's fleet. The sailing ship had a crew of six men and a captain. Besides the square sail, there was a bank of three oars on each side of the ship. It was by means of the oars that the vessel made its way to the narrow opening from the inland waterway to the open sea. Their destination: the mouth of the River Seine, the waterway to Rouen. The wind in the channel was from the north-west, their intended course was south, and so they were able to use the sail once land was behind them. Although the weather was fine, the wind increased in strength as the craft got further from land, and it soon became clear to the captain that he might be carried too far to the east. In reality, they were being carried even further east than he had expected.

As dawn broke, they found themselves off the French coast, and there was optimism onboard when the captain guided the ship towards a wide inlet which, as they neared it, seemed to lead into the river they were seeking. But this was not the Seine. Unbeknown to them, the bay in front of them was the Bay of the Somme. Worse still, the tide was on the ebb and, as they tried to enter the distant harbour, their ship grounded on the uneven, sandy ground outside of the tortuous winding channel. As the water dropped, the ship lurched over on one side, so much so that, when the tide had receded and the sand was no longer covered by sea water, those on board could, without much difficulty, clamber over the lower side of the ship onto the sand.

It was not long before their predicament was noticed by local fishermen, several of whom walked across the sands to investigate who the visitors were. Meanwhile, the Earl, after venting his spleen on the hapless captain, decided to walk ashore with his party to the village they could see from the ship. The village was Saint Valery-sur-Somme. It was not in Normandy at all, but in land which was the territory of Count Guy de Ponthieu. The Earl's misfortune was compounded when he was recognised by a French fisherman who had seen him in England. News of the stranding of such an eminent person soon reached the Count and he quickly had the whole party imprisoned and, apart from Sister Emma, placed in fetters while he considered how he could sell the group for a ransom.

The party languished in the Count's prison for a week before the Earl was able to bribe a gaoler to travel to Rouen to tell Duke William of their plight. On hearing the news, the Duke sent an emissary to the Count demanding that he release the prisoners and hand them over to the Norman's men together with all their goods. Very much against his will, the Count had to agree, for he was a vassal of the Duke's and to have refused could have had serious consequences for him.

The party was handed over by the Count at the village of Eu, on the border between his land and Normandy. They were given horses and then set off on the three-day journey to Rouen. When the group arrived, they were warmly greeted by the Duke.

The language that the visitors had in common with the Normans was Latin, though the members of the Anglo-Saxon party knew this language to varying degrees of proficiency. In case of linguistic difficulties, the Bishop had been taken along with the party to help if required as a translator.

"Welcome to Rouen, Earl Harold," said William. "I have made arrangements for you all to rest for a while as you recover from the Count's lack of hospitality. Tonight, we will have a banquet."

Torkil and Godric were led to a room which was to be their bedroom. Servants brought their clothes, weapons and armour, and placed them in the room. Sister Emma was also taken to her room. It was clear from the style of the welcome which they had received that the Duke wished to impress them. His manner was affable and, to some extent, Torkil's anxiety, based on the Duke's reputation, was eased.

The evening's event was lavish. As well as an extravagant range of food and drink, there was entertainment with musicians and jugglers. Harold sat next to the Duke at the top table. They were similar in age, around forty, but William was slightly heavier in build. Their demeanour was so hearty and friendly that they seemed like two brothers. They both enjoyed their wine with many toasts drunk through the evening.

Torkil and Godric sat at a lower table, but not together. In between them and around them were fifteen or twenty Norman knights. The atmosphere at the table was jovial and, despite language difficulties, there was much laughter and, as the evening wore on, taking their lead from the top table, there was a degree of wildness. Among the knights there was one whom Torkil recognised: Robert d'Evreux. He had aged and his hair was grey at the temples. It was, after all, fourteen years ago that he had visited Selceeflet, but there was no doubt – this was him.

Late in the evening, he barged between two knights sitting opposite Torkil and, in Latin, shouted across, "Where is your lovely sister, Torkil? She is not with the women." The knight pointed at the lowest table where some women were dining.

"She is tired from our ordeal with the Count and the journey. Life in a nunnery is not good preparation for this kind of adventure. She will join us tomorrow."

The knight was clearly the worse for alcohol. "'Tis a waste that what God has shaped for the pleasure of men he should keep for himself and clothe her in black."

"A Christian knight should respect that, for such chosen ones, spiritual service to God places them on a far loftier plane than most of us can aspire to."

"I am happy on the plane I inhabit and I know what little filly I aspire to!"

The Norman knights around Sir Robert laughed and slapped his back.

Torkil looked down at his beer tankard and stared deep into the foam, trying to control his temper. A voice called from across the table. It was Godric. He spoke in Anglo-Saxon. "Easy now, Torkil, we are guests here."

The thayne reminded himself of their mission in Rouen. His master would not thank him for causing a fight on their first evening. He looked up and calmly said to the knight, "Tell me, Sir Robert, I hear that you breed the finest warhorses in Evreux. Is it true?"

"Not true," shouted another knight. "The best ones come from the monastery in my city Caen."

The conversational diversion was successful, and a lively argument commenced around the table about the selective breeding of horses for which Normandy was famous. Whereas the Anglo-Saxon horses were generally never taller than eleven hands, the Normans had successfully bred horses for the use of their cavalry which were over thirteen hands. Huge sums of money had been invested in developing animals which were capable of carrying a knight in full armour at high speeds into battle. It was generally acknowledged that the most successful breeding programmes had been in monasteries. The religious establishments sold their animals for profit.

The conversation came back to Torkil, and one of the knights said, "I suspect that you will have a chance to try our horses. Can Anglo-Saxons ride?"

"I had a donkey when I was a boy," said Torkil. He was determined not to get worked up again.

"God protect us from the Anglo-Saxon donkey cavalry!" shouted one of the knights, to the great amusement of the crowd.

Godric got up from his seat and came round to Torkil. "I think it best we go to bed before this gets out of hand."

Torkil needed no second bidding. "Gentlemen, I bid you goodnight. I look forward to seeing your horses tomorrow."

Earl Harold noticed his thaynes leaving the table and took the opportunity of making his apologies too. He left the table and hurried after the two men. "The Duke is too genial. We must be careful not to be lulled into a false sense of security here, for we are very vulnerable. I have not had the opportunity to discuss a ransom for my brother and nephew. Tomorrow we will be shown around the palace and I will meet my bride. Be wary and keep an eye out to see what we can learn from our hosts. I bid you goodnight." With that, without looking back, the Earl opened the door of his room and went inside.

# Chapter 13

## Allies of the Normans

*He turns his horse and urges him forward*
*He aims a great blow with all his might*
*He breaks the shield and tears through the hauberk*
*He pierces the chest and shatters the breastbone*
*Pushed right through he pushes him off his saddle*
*And flings him dead a spear's length from his warhorse.*

Chanson de Roland (by a Norman poet ca 1090)

Next morning the Duke conducted the visitors around his palace. He was keen to show off the wealth he had accumulated through his campaigns against the French and other recalcitrant neighbours. The tour eventually led to the royal stables where the Earl and the two housecarls were shown the Duke's warhorses.

"These are giants," said the Earl.

The Anglo-Saxons were standing either side of a magnificent beast which was so tall that those on one side of the horse could not see those on the other side. At first, it appeared that the animal was black but, as the rays of the sun shining through the opening in the wall caught the newly groomed body, the tone was definitely brown. It had powerful hindquarters and huge hooves, though these were covered by white hair which almost touched the ground. Its head had a splash of white which ran from the top of the head down to the muzzle. As the Earl felt the horse's foreleg muscles, the beast showed its irritation by flattening its ears.

"These are our *destrier*,[53] warhorses. We use only the stallions. They will carry an armoured knight all day if the battle requires it," said the Duke.

He continued. "Each knight has three of these animals. One to ride for transport, one spare horse which his squire rides, and one to carry his armour and weapons."

The long wooden stable building was split up into many stalls and, in each one, there was a similar animal. In many of the stalls, the grooms were busy at their work brushing the horses or cleaning their hooves.

"We are preparing the horses for the tournament this afternoon. You will see the knights training. But come, now I must introduce you to my daughter. Your men can have a look around the stables."

With that, the Duke led the Earl off back to the main building.

Godric and Torkil wandered along the row of horses. At the end of the row, there was a door into a second building. Godric pushed the door open. There was a substantial hall with rows and rows of weapons.

"This must be the armoury," said Torkil.

They stopped by a rack of shields.

"These are very different from ours," Torkil observed.

The Anglo-Saxons generally used round shields, usually made of planks edge to edge. In the centre of their shields was a boss which protected the warrior's hand behind the shield. The shields they were now looking at were semicircular at the

---

[53] Destrier – specially bred Norman warhorses capable of carrying a knight in armour

top, but pointed at the bottom. They were covered by painted leather with different designs. There seemed to be ten of each pattern. At the demonstration in the afternoon they would see that the Norman shields were designed not only to cover the warrior's body, but to protect the left leg and the hand of mounted warrior which held the reins.

The two housecarls inspected the rows of swords in racks. The swords had long tapering blades with a rounded hollow running down the blade to make the sword as light as possible. The pommels, which provided the counterweight to the sword blade to make it easier to wield, were domed and decorated, and the wooden handles had leather coverings. Beyond the swords, armour hung on the walls.

"Their swords are designed for stabbing as well as cutting. And look at their armour: it is much longer than ours; it must reach to below the knees. Not very practical for infantry. It would be difficult to charge wearing these suits."

What Torkil was referring to were chain mail suits, or hauberks, which were designed for cavalry. The suits had a slit at the front and back to make it possible to wear the suit on horseback.

They passed rows of bows and quivers of arrows, but then they saw weapons they had never seen before: crossbows. These had a thick stock and a small bow. They would later see that the crossbows were loaded by pulling a lever and fired by pulling a trigger. The arrows were shorter than conventional ones.

At the end of the room, there were racks with lances. These were spears which were long enough to project in front of a horse's head when carried under or over arm by the rider, yet light enough to be thrown if necessary.

The two men could not fail to be impressed by the symbols of Norman military power they saw that morning, but more was to come. In the large exercise yard where there was to be a tournament in the afternoon, knights were training.

On the ground, there were two rows of wooden stakes, or *pels*.[54] The knights were doing sword practice using the stakes to represent their adversaries. The weapons they used were made of wood and were twice the weight of a normal sword; this to help them develop upper body and arm strength. Godric and Torkil recognised these exercises. They had both spent hours doing them, but what they saw next was very different from what they were used to.

On a different part of the large exercise yard, there were groups of horsemen. Each group comprised ten horses and men. These were *conroys*. Each *conroy* had shields of different, distinctive design. In turn, they charged pels which, in rows of five, were hanging from an overhead support.

Godric and Torkil walked across the yard to better see the action. As they watched, they saw the impressive horsemen line up in their groups of ten. At the blast of a trumpet, five would break away and, at the gallop, charge the pels, attempting to strike them with their practice lances which had a soft leather bag at the end instead of the usual point. As soon as the first five were a sufficient distance in front, the second five pursued them, aiming at the same target. The two watchers realised that the purpose of the second wave of riders was to continue the attack should any of the first five succumb to enemy arrows or spears.

This was completely new kind of warfare to the Anglo-Saxons. Their custom was to use horses for transport to the place of battle and then to fight on foot. They did not fight in the saddle. The two men continued to watch for a while as the knights changed their weapons from lances to swords and then repeated the same exercise time after time.

Later that day, the two English warriors found themselves back in the exercise yard. The Duke had arranged a formal

---

[54] Pel – from the Latin 'palos' meaning stake. Hence the English word 'pale' with the same meaning

tournament for his visitors to watch. They all sat on a viewing platform at the side of the arena. The pels had been removed and the whole exercise area was now clear. As they watched, some soldiers came in and placed rings, each about the size of a man's head, on five sticks which they pushed into the ground two paces apart. A *conroy* appeared from the stables, all the riders wearing full armour. Behind them, a second *conroy* took position.

"The rules are simple: the two *conroys* compete to see which can lance the most rings in a charge at the gallop," explained the Duke.

There was a trumpet blast and the five riders of the leading *conroy* kicked the flanks of their *destrier*. The horses leapt forward and were almost immediately at the gallop as they charged towards the rings. The riders lowered their lances as each one took aim at the ring in front of them. After the first five had attempted to lance the rings, the second wave took aim at any remaining rings. In some cases, riders in the second wave had no ring to aim at and so just rode without attempting to use the lance. The rings were then replaced and the second *conroy* did the same thing.

Each time for the first three rides, all of the rings were lanced by the respective *conroys*. It was on the fourth ride that one was missed. The Duke was obviously delighted.

"It is the *conroy* of my friend William Fitz Osborn from Breteuil which has won. He is not so young, four years younger than me I think, but he competes well with the young bloods!"

There were several similar competitions before the finale where the knights were to compete against each other in swordsmanship. Again, they used the heavy wooden swords but, though the swords were not real, they still caused considerable pain to anyone struck by them.

The Duke introduced the combat. "The two knights fight each other and score points according to the way they strike an opponent. For example, if they hit the body, the shoulder or the face, they get three points. If they immobilise or disarm their opponent, they get three points. If they hit other parts of the body, they get one point. They continue fighting until one of them asks for quarter."

The spectators watched transfixed as pairs of knights violently fought with each other. There were many heavy blows and, twice, bouts had to be discontinued because of one of the combatants being injured.

"What do you think of our warriors, Earl Harold?"

"I wish that they were fighting for me!" answered the Earl.

"Well, soon they could be for I have a proposal to make."

"And what, pray, is that?"

"I have heard about the brilliant tactics you used to defeat King Gruffyd in Wales. I understand that his army was elusive and could not be brought to battle."

"Yes, that was so."

"I have a similar irritant. My troublesome neighbours the Bretons continually raid my borders. It is time for them to be brought to heel."

"How will you do it?"

"You and I will lead a campaign against Duke Conan of Brittany."

The Earl was astonished, but tried to remain impassive.

Godric leant across to Torkil and said in Anglo-Saxon, "Did I understand that correctly? Are we to join the Normans in fighting the Bretons?"

"Yes, I think that is what he said."

The Earl looked across at the Duke and exclaimed, "But I have to return to England soon to deal with my affairs."

"Would you like it to be known that you were afraid of Duke Conan?"

The Earl, the Bishop and the two housecarls suddenly realised that, despite the generous hospitality they been shown by the Duke, in reality they were his prisoners. They would have to do his bidding if they were to have a chance of returning to England. For the moment, all thoughts of negotiating the release of the Earl's brother and nephew were abandoned.

"When do you intend to begin your campaign?" asked the Earl.

"We march in one week."

"We only have our swords with us. We will need horses and equipment."

"You will be supplied with all you need, and you and your men have a week to train with the knights to learn something of mounted warfare."

"Where exactly will we go?"

"My ally, Count Rivallon, is under siege by Duke Conan in a town called Dol in Brittany. We will go to lift the siege and take possession of Le Mont St Michel. I will show you these places on a chart after we have dined."

There was no more discussion. The Anglo-Saxons were to be co-opted into the Norman force to attack the Duke's Breton enemies. At the first opportunity, the Earl sought to be alone with Godric and Torkil to discuss their predicament.

"As you see, the Duke is very much in control. I fear that, if we do not accede to his wishes, none of us will see England again. The best thing is that we willingly do his bidding and continue to act cordially. We have seen no sign of my brother and nephew and I have not had a suitable opportunity to mention the matter yet."

The two warriors told the Earl of their tour of the Duke's armoury in the morning and of the quality and quantity of weapons there.

"It is clear that our host wishes to impress on us in every way how powerful he is. I assume that he deliberately left you two alone in the stables this morning so that you would find his weapons store and report back to me. The stables, the weapons and the tournament this afternoon were obviously part of his plan to strike fear into anyone considering opposing him and his claim to the throne of England."

"But he might be planning to take us, and you in particular, on the campaign so that we can be murdered and have it look as if the Bretons are responsible. That way the succession will be clear for him," suggested Godric.

"Yes, this might be so. Our best course is to acquit ourselves well on the campaign so that we gain respect and, hopefully, put the Duke in our debt. If we help him to achieve his military purpose quickly then we can test his will to let us go home."

"Are we taking the Bishop and my sister on the campaign with us?" Torkil asked.

"No," answered the Earl. "It will be too dangerous for them and certainly no place for a nun to be."

That evening, the Duke had a council of war with his senior knights. The Earl and two housecarls were invited to attend, but there were considerable language problems as several of the knights did not speak Latin and the council was held in Norman French. There were frequent breaks while translations were made into Latin for the benefit of the Anglo-Saxons.

By the time the meeting broke up, the three foreigners had grasped that the strategy was for the Duke to march south-west to Le Mont St Michel and to take undisputed possession of it by leaving a force there. There would be around three hundred knights as well as several hundred other cavalry and two thousand infantry; in total, about three thousand men.

Next morning, after his first training session with the knights, Torkil went to break the news to his sister that they would be leaving in a week's time and that she would be left at the palace with the Bishop.

"But, Torkil, you have brought me all this way and now you abandon me here in Rouen!"

"I am not abandoning you and you will have the Bishop for company."

"How long will you be away?"

"They say that it will take us seven days to march to Le Mont. Who knows how long it will take to do our business there? And then maybe two days to get to Dol where we suppose that we will do battle with Duke Conan. Then we have to get back. So I think that we will be away for about a month. Perhaps we will be back by the end of July."

"A month? What am I to do here for a month?"

"It would be good if you could spend as much time as possible with Adelaide and start to teach her our language."

"Can we return to England when you get back?"

"We hope so, but you must understand that we are detained here by the Duke. He will decide when we can leave. Don't you think that I miss Odelia and the boys? I want to leave as soon as possible too."

With that, the discussion was over. Torkil left his sister and walked down the corridor towards his own room. As he did so, he saw someone coming towards him. As the man approached and his face became clearer, Torkil began to get a strong feeling that he had seen the man before. The man, who was carrying a large key, passed on Torkil's left, grunting a greeting. The housecarl glanced at the man as he walked past. He had a scar through his hair on the left side of his head and part of his ear was missing.

Torkil racked his brain. Where had he seen the man before? And then it came to him! Thirteen years before, the mysterious monk who had disappeared after his grandfather had died. It must be him! But what was he doing here? Torkil glanced behind him. The man had stopped and was thrusting the key into the lock of a room, a room which was one of the few which the group of Anglo-Saxons had not been shown when they did their tour of the palace. Torkil turned and walked back down the corridor towards the room which the man had unlocked.. The double door, which was now closed was large and clearly was not one of the private guest rooms; these had smaller single doors. There was nothing to indicate what might be in the locked room.

For several days, Torkil kept a watch out for the mysterious man with the scar. He saw him on two occasions: once, going into the room with the double doors and, once, locking the doors as he left. Then, two days before the army was due to march, he saw the man come out of the room and lock the door but, to Torkil's astonishment, the man left the key in the lock.

This was too good an opportunity to miss and, though the housecarl should have considered the consequences if he offended their host by being over inquisitive, he waited until the man was out of sight, glanced round to see if he was being observed, and then unlocked the door. He paused and looked around again. All was quiet and there was no one in sight. He slipped into the room.

He found himself in some kind of large hall with a long table in the centre together with many chairs. On one wall, there were several windows which allowed the sun to illuminate the room. The opposite wall was covered in charts on vellum. On the biggest map, he recognised the outline of England. It was marked with several cities and ports. There were annotations in Norman French around each port. Then he noticed a series of charts of the south coast of England. These too were annotated. Further along the wall there were several maps of a place he knew very well – Vectis, the Isle of Wight. He looked closely at one of the charts: it showed his estates! The lands which he owned were shaded on the map and, at the bottom, in Latin, was written *Verified by Alric 1051*. The name Alric was in a different hand from the words *Verified by*; a very uncertain shaky hand: his grandfather's.

Torkil was astounded. How could the map his grandfather had shown him when he was on his deathbed have got here? It was quickly obvious to him: the monk had stolen it. But he was no monk; he must have been a Norman spy. That would account for the fact that the monk sent by the Bishop of Wintoncaestre, Brother Ralf, had been found drowned in Hamwic harbour. The spy must have murdered him and taken his place. But why did a Norman spy want to get information about Selceeflet? Then it dawned on him. The Normans were looking for suitable places to land an army as part of an invasion force. That was what his grandfather had once intimated when he questioned why Duke William chose to hunt on the island instead of the great southern forest.

Torkil looked more closely at the maps. Most of them were drawings of the central south coast around Hamwic and the island. This area must be the choice the Normans had made for a possible invasion. He suddenly became aware of voices in the corridor outside. The only hiding place he could see was under the table. He quickly crouched under it, but the noise of the voices began to recede. He walked over to the door, slowly opened it and caefully poked his head out to see if anyone was in sight. Confident that he could get out unnoticed, he slipped into the corridor and closed the door. He did not observe the smaller door opposite slowly close as he walked away. The man with the scar and the wounded ear smiled. The Anglo-Saxon fish had taken his bait.

Torkil hurried to find Godric and Earl Harold. They were getting changed for another training session.

"I have something important to tell you."

"I am afraid it will have to wait. We are late for the riding practice."

"But, My Lord, it is vital information."

"We can talk later," said the Earl, hurrying away towards the yard.

With that, the discussion was closed for the moment, which was just as well as, during the afternoon, in the breaks between exercises, Torkil had time to think. He realised what a long story it would be, for it started thirteen years ago. He tried to order his thoughts so that he could later tell the story cogently.

Torkil's opportunity came at the end of the afternoon. They had taken off their hauberks and given their weapons back to the pages to take to the armoury. The same pages had brought ale for them to drink after the heavy work in the warm weather. The three of them sat on a stone bench in the yard, watching others undergoing training.

"You had something to tell us, Torkil."

"Yes, My Lord. It is a long story which begins in 1051, thirteen years ago."

"Well, make it brief. I have matters to attend to."

Torkil began by reminding the Earl that the Duke had accompanied King Edward on a hunting trip to the Isle of Wight, and pointed out that it was a curious choice of venue. He proceeded to tell the whole tale up to the happenings that morning.

"Your story bears out my suspicions. I fear that, when I declare myself heir to the throne of England, he will do everything possible to stop me being crowned. But the fact that we know where they are planning to land in the event of an invasion is extremely valuable. Good work, Thayne Torkil, but you took a huge risk going into that room. If you had been caught, it could have gone badly for all of us."

"What do we do?" asked Godric.

"Nothing. We carry on with the campaign to Brittany. The most important thing for us is to eventually get back to England. When we are there, we can act on this information. Until then, we are allies of the Normans."

# Chapter 14

## Brittany

*The quicksands at Le Mont St Michel (From the Bayeux Tapestry)*

It was the last week of June 1064 when the troops assembled outside Rouen. The vast horde of foot soldiers had been camping there for several days as detachments joined them from different parts of the Duchy. Flags fluttered, identifying the position of the officers' quarters of the different detachments. The three Anglo-Saxons had been issued with the standard weapons for knights on the campaign: two lances, a sword, a shield, a mace and a conical helmet. Riding hauberks for the trio had been altered to fit them, by the Duke's armourers. Early in the morning, the knights had assembled in the exercise yard, all astride their *destrier*. Each squire rode next to their master on the knight's second horse.

The horsemen were dressed in normal clothes and carried only their swords and knives while riding in friendly country. All their other weapons and their hauberks were packed on their third horse which was led on a leash by the squires.

On the platform where they had previously watched the tournament, the assembly was inspected by Duke William and Earl Harold. Besides them were several officials who would be running the Duke's affairs while he was away, including Robert d'Evreux, the Bishop, the Duke's wife Matilda, Adelaide and Sister Emma. On one side of the platform, pages waited with the Duke's and the Earl's horses, and behind them were Torkil and Godric who were already in the saddle.

A knight carrying the Duke's standard rode up to the party and waited in front of the Duke's horse.

The horses in front of the viewing party were packed quite closely together and this clearly did not suit some of the stallions as they were restless, and occasionally one would try to bite another. Some riders struggled to control their mounts. There was a chorus of whinnying as one sparked off responses from many others and the noise echoed around the yard.

"Time to be away, Earl Harold. The horses need to work," said the Duke as he pushed past the onlookers in the direction of his horse. Harold followed and they both mounted their horses from blocks which had been placed on the ground. The Duke waved his hand to a trumpeter who gave a long blast on his instrument to indicate to the huge gathering, many of whom could not see the Duke, that departure for the campaign was imminent. The Duke spurred his horse and the Anglo-Saxons took up position behind him as he headed for the gates. As they moved forward, the knights fell in five abreast behind. At the back of each row of five, their squires and pack horses followed.

As the column made its way through the town, people came out of their houses to see the sight, but stood well back as several horses were very frisky and needed careful coaxing from their riders. Street traders pulled their barrows close up to the house walls to avoid having them turned over, and some children risked being trampled on as they ran along the side of the long column.

As they approached the encampment of foot soldiers, there was a long blast on a trumpet. The tents had already been struck and, as the trumpet sounded, men picked up their weapons and rushed to get into formation so that they were ready to follow the column when the last of the knights had passed. Finally, a long convoy of supply wagons fell in behind the marching men.

The Duke and his advisors had planned a series of overnight stops and had sent advance parties ahead to ensure that provisions and water were available when the army arrived. The plan was for the men to be on the road for ten hours each day. Since the weather was very warm, there were several stops for the men to get refreshment. Each evening, the wagons rumbled up to the camp to supplement provisions obtained locally. The latter were not plentiful as it was the hungry month season.

It was in the afternoon of the seventh day that the huge mound of Le Mont St Michel came into view. Since they were now near to enemy territory, the knights wore their hauberks and carried their weapons and shields. To approach the bastion, the army had to cross the Coueson River, the boundary between Normandy and Brittany. This river, which flowed all the way from north-western France to enter the sea at Le Mont, formed a wide estuary which could only be crossed at low tide. The army halted and waited until it was judged that the tide was low enough for the crossing to be made. If they got the timing wrong, one of the strongest inflows of tidal water in the world with a height greater than seven men would engulf their army.

"Send two knights ahead to check the level of the water," instructed the Duke.

There had been no opportunity for the knights to show their bravado on the long trek from Rouen. Now volunteers clamoured for the honour to bravely test the safety of the planned crossing.

The two knights selected for the task trotted down the estuary bank and across the dry sands at its edge. Rows of mounted men watched their progress as they began to traverse the wetter sand. Suddenly, before they reached the water flowing in the middle of the estuary, the leading knight slowed to a walk and gradually came to a halt. His companion came up beside him, and he too stopped. As the incredulous spectators focused on the pair, they saw the amazing sight of the horses getting shorter. They were sinking into the sand! The panicking stallions whinnied as they struggled to free themselves from the enveloping mire. Soon the bellies of the horses were at sand level. The knights tried to dismount but, as soon as they did, so they too began to sink into the quicksand.

Earl Harold turned to Godric and Torkil. "Bring your shields and follow me."

The Earl and the two housecarls dismounted and tore off their hauberks. They then ran on to the dry sand watched by the ranks of knights. All the while, the two in the quicksand were sinking deeper, and the horses barely had their heads above the yellow brown surface.

The Earl ran onto the wet sand, followed by the two housecarls. They were now no more than four or five paces from the struggling knights.

Harold threw his recently acquired Norman shield onto the sand with the front downwards and stood on it. "Pass me your shields," he said to the other two.

He took their shields and threw one of them onto the sand in front of him. He moved on to the next shield and then repeated the process. Standing on the last shield, he was able to grab the hand of one of the knights and prevent him sinking deeper.

The Duke had now realised what the Anglo-Saxons were about and ordered other knights to emulate what Harold and his men were doing, and to take ropes with them. Others ran to their aid, and shields were passed along the chain as a second group of men formed another corridor besides them to rescue the other knight.

By the time the two knights had been dragged to the shore, the horses had disappeared completely.

"A good day's work, Earl Harold!" said the Duke. But, despite his admiration for the rescue effected by his guests, he was resentful that it was not he that had taken the initiative. Nevertheless, the stock of the Anglo-Saxon warriors and their leader had risen considerably, and all could see that the Duke was clearly in their debt.

Eventually, a safe crossing was made and, without a fight, the Bretons in possession of Le Mont surrendered to the powerful force. After many of them were executed as an example to those who would dare to question the Duke's authority, a large garrison force was left at Le Mont, and the rest of the army proceeded towards Dol to lift the siege. However, by the time they arrived, Duke Conan had fled in the direction of Rennes. The army pursued him, and he was then forced to relinquish Rennes and found temporary sanctuary in Dinan. By this time, the end of July, the Duke had tired of campaigning. He sent his army to lay siege to Dinan while he, a number of his knights and the Anglo-Saxons travelled back to Rouen by way of Bayeux.

During the campaign, Earl Harold and his men saw much successful action and won such respect from the Duke that the Earl was honoured with an investiture of the Norman order of knighthood from the Duke. It was while the party were in Bayeux that the subject of the succession to the English throne was taken up by the Duke. He informed the Earl that he considered himself to be King Edward's rightful heir, and he required that the Earl should take an oath to swear loyalty to him as the future King of England. The Earl was in a very difficult position: he could refuse and probably be murdered along with his men or agree to take the oath and be bound by it. In the event, he decided to swear loyalty to Duke William's cause and to confirm his acceptance of the Duke's daughter in marriage, to unite the families of the two men.

Eventually, the party arrived back at their starting point, Rouen. As they rode through the gates, there were many there to greet them. Torkil looked for his sister in the crowd, but she was not to be seen. He handed his horse to a groom and went inside the palace. There was no sign of the nun. He went down the corridor to her room and knocked on the door. He noticed that the door appeared to be damaged: there was splintered wood around the lock. No one answered. He pushed open the door and there, sitting sobbing on the bed, was his sister. But she was not dressed in the nun's habit: she wore a shift and a skirt like the other women.

"What has happened?"

The woman looked at her brother imploringly. "Take me back to England please, please."

"But why are you dressed like this?"

"I can no longer wear the clothes of a nun."

"What has happened to you?"

"Robert d'Evreux has violated me. Please, please take me from here." The woman was shaking violently and sobbing.

The warrior blurted out foolishly, "But how, when?" He hesitated to comfort her physically. Their relationship had never been warm. The nun had been away from home for fourteen years, and he had never seen her during that time.

"He smashed the lock on my door, and I can't keep him out when he comes here drunk and violent."

"It won't happen again, I promise you," said Torkil lamely. He turned and quickly left the room. As he hurried down the corridor, he saw the Earl and Godric coming towards him.

"Why are you in a hurry, Torkil?" asked the Earl.

"That bastard Robert d'Evreux has raped my sister. I am going to kill him."

Torkil made to hurry on but Godric stuck out his foot and tripped the thayne who fell to the ground.

Torkil started to get up and Godric could see that he was about to swing a punch at him. The Earl grabbed his arm.

"Why the hell did you trip me?" demanded Torkil.

"Because it is better that you spend your anger on me than attempt to take on a Norman knight in a fury. Revenge is required, but you need to be calm and dispassionate when you take it."

The Earl intervened. "Listen, you want revenge for your sister's honour but, if you rush off to try to kill the Norman, you will probably get killed yourself. More seriously, everything we have done on this campaign, including my taking the oath, will be for nothing. We will never get away from here if you even tried to murder Robert d'Evreux."

Torkil's anger led him to impudently ask the Earl, "So what do you think I should do then? Just accept this insult?"

"Tonight we are going to have a celebration of our safe return. Wine will flow, many will drink too much, and d'Evreux will certainly be in that number. You should desist from drinking. Take the weak ale only. Act normally, show no anger, give d'Evreux a sense of relief, for surely he would have expected you to have done exactly what you had intended before we stopped you. Your enemy is a well trained and experienced fighter, more experienced than you are. But you have the advantage of youth: he is ten years older. And tomorrow he will be suffering from his libations this evening. I will speak to the Duke at table and issue your challenge to satisfy your sister's honour. I will suggest a joust between you two early tomorrow. No doubt the Duke will name the terms."

"But my blood is boiling. I could strike him dead now!"

"Do as I say for, if you cause us to miss our chance to leave this place, I will kill you myself. Godric, take him to your room and keep an eye on him."

The Earl strode off to his room, and Godric guided Torkil to their room.

At the evening's banquet, the Earl sat next to the Duke and, late in the evening, Earl Harold took up the subject of the retribution required by his housecarl.

"But, Earl Harold, is it such an important matter? If my memory serves me right, your own brother Swegen once did exactly the same thing to another nun, the Abbetissa of Leominster, I believe."

"Yes, but he had to flee the country for that and other crimes."

"So what do you want me to do?" the Duke asked reluctantly.

"Let justice be done. Permit my man to challenge Robert d'Evreux."

The Duke thought for a while and then said, "I do not want to risk losing my old friend, foolish as he can be, and you do not want to lose a good warrior. I will permit a duel, but only with practice swords, and both men must wear hauberks. We will use the same rules as in the training sessions you have seen."

"So be it. My man is seething with anger, and I would like this settled as soon as possible. What say at first light tomorrow?"

"Yes, let's get it done with quickly."

The Duke called both men to his table and then made an announcement to the revellers.

"Robert d'Evreux has offended the Anglo-Saxon Torkil. The housecarl has demanded that the honour of his sister should be satisfied by combat."

The Norman from Evreux was jubilant and, when he turned to face his friends, there was a loud cheer. He, having reached the stage of intoxication where good reason and common sense had deserted him, refilled his glass and drank deep.

When the Earl explained the rules of the contest to Torkil he was disgruntled and moaned to the Earl, "I would prefer to use real weapons. I want the man's blood."

"This is what I have agreed with the Duke and so that is what you will accept."

Torkil realised that further protest would be impudent and fruitless and so, begrudgingly, he acquiesced.

Next morning, Godric and Torkil made their way to the armoury at first light. There was no sign of the Norman. Torkil put on his hauberk and picked up a shield and one of the heavy wooden swords. The pair went out into the early sunshine and sat on a bench to wait for the adversary.

"Have you told Sister Emma what you are about?" asked Godric.

"No and, if she does hear about it, please make sure that she does not watch. Although she is deeply offended against, it is in the nature of her calling to forgive. I do not want to be hindered by her in seeking retribution."

After a while, the Duke and his friends arrived as did Earl Harold.

"Where is your man? Is he hiding?" Harold asked the Duke.

The Duke was irritated by the imputation that his friend was a coward and sent a messenger into the palace to seek the missing Norman. Eventually, he returned with Robert d'Evreux. The man looked dishevelled and somewhat sleepy. Clearly, it was not long since he had woken. The Norman went into the armoury and later emerged dressed and equipped for combat, his yellow shield bearing his coat of arms.

"Wait for the call," shouted the Duke as the two armed men walked out onto the exercise yard.

The men stood eyeing each other with hatred. Physically, they appeared to be reasonably matched, though the Norman was slightly taller than the stocky Anglo-Saxon. They held their shields and swords loosely by their sides awaiting the signal from the Duke to begin. They were two paces apart when they heard the command, "Commence!"

Both lifted their shields to the defensive position and slowly began to circle as they neared each other. Robert jabbed at Torkil's shield to keep him at a distance. The weight of the swords was such that it was impossible to make such swift movements as might have been the case with a real sword. When Torkil raised his sword to slash at Robert, the Norman had time to back away before the weapon whipped through the air in front of him. Counteracting the inertia of the heavy weapon as it missed its target left Torkil dangerously exposed to a counter-strike which, when it came, glanced off the top of his shield and grazed his head, dazing him for a moment. A moment was long enough for the Norman to sense blood, and he raised his sword as quickly as he could, high over his head to administer the coup de grace. There were loud shouts of encouragement from the spectators urging a quick end to the contest.

Torkil looked up and saw the weapon descending. He threw himself sideways, dodging the blow. Robert had put so much force into the attempted strike that he was temporarily off balance, dropping his shield arm and exposing his left shoulder. Before he could recover, Torkil swung his sword sideways and struck the Norman on the top of his left arm. There was a distinct grunt of pain from the Norman.

Both men recovered their composure and started to circle again. The crowd was shouting advice to the Norman, encouraging him to attack. This suited Torkil as he had already realised the best strategy was to let his opponent attempt a strike and then catch him with a counter-blow. At the back of his mind, he was also aware of the advice given to him by Godric. He had said, "Your best chance is to tire the man out. You are younger and, after a month's campaigning, probably fitter than Robert, and he was up late last night. The longer the fight goes on, the wearier he will be and the more mistakes he will make."

It was getting warmer now, and the heavy hauberk was beginning to be a burden. The prospect of trying to end this duel quickly was an attractive one, but Torkil decided to let the

Norman set the pace. Each time the taller man attempted to strike, Torkil dodged and looked for a counter-strike possibility. His shield was taking a terrible beating and, with each blow, the shock ran through his hand and up his left arm causing considerable pain. Soon he noticed that the Norman was breathing more heavily and beginning to move more slowly, but the force with which he smashed his sword onto Torkil's shield did not diminish. He was still very dangerous.

Then d'Evreux made his first serious mistake. Torkil raised his sword as if to hit the Norman on the head. Robert raised his shield to parry the blow but, deftly, the Anglo-Saxon dropped to a crouching position and swung the sword at his adversary's unprotected knees. The Norman did not react quickly enough and took a hard blow on the outside of his left knee. He instinctively dropped his shield lower to protect against a second blow, once more leaving his left shoulder exposed. Torkil leapt into the air and powered his sword down towards the Norman's head. Robert d'Evreux saw the strike coming and moved sideways taking the falling sword on his left shoulder. The force was such that d'Evreux dropped his shield.

Now, Torkil was faced with a man who was clearly in pain and who did not have the benefit of warding off blows with his shield. The Anglo-Saxon stepped back and allowed his adversary to pick up his shield. It was now obvious that his left arm was injured, for he had to pick up the shield with his right hand and push it onto his left.

The two men started to circle each other again though Robert was limping badly. Torkil knew what pain could be transmitted to the arm by taking blows on the shield, and so he now took the initiative and, at every opportunity, crashed his sword onto the yellow surface. Now the Norman was reacting too slowly to present the same danger with the counter-strikes, but nevertheless Torkil became too confident and took a heavy blow on his right shoulder before his relentless blows on the yellow shield eventually caused the Norman to drop it once more. This time, Torkil did not wait for it to be recovered, but swung with all his might at the injured arm. Even the chain mail could not prevent the resultant instant disfigurement of the wounded man's shoulder as it dislocated.

Torkil wanted his enemy to be reduced to total humiliation; he wanted him to fall to the ground. The Anglo-Saxon once more swung his sword at Robert's left knee, this time with devastating effect, causing the knight to howl and fall forward on his face.

There was a loud shout from one of the spectators. Torkil recognised the voice: it was Earl Harold. "Enough, Torkil, enough."

The Earl was concerned that his man might now beat the Norman to death with possible serious consequences for the party's chances to be allowed to leave Rouen.

Torkil stood over the knight, then turned and faced the silent spectators, threw his sword to the ground and walked off towards the armoury.

Later that day, the Duke met the Earl. "Your man has indeed wreaked revenge! But because you have served me so well, I bear no malice. It is time for you to travel back to England. I fear that Robert d'Evruex's vassals will not take kindly to the insult paid to him by your man. Your lives will be in danger here. A ship will be ready for you tomorrow. I have prepared gifts for you and the King. But, also in recognition of the service you gave me in Brittany, you may take your nephew Hacun with you."

"I am truly grateful to you. But what of my brother Wulfnoth?"

"He will return to England with me when I come to take over the throne."

The Earl realised that argument would be futile and so hastened to find the others to tell them the good news.

# Chapter 15

## Rebellion

*And then, after Michael's-mass, all the thaynes in Yorkshire went to York, and there slew all Earl Tostig's household servants whom they might hear of, and took his treasures: and Tostig was later at Britford with the King.*

The Anglo-Saxon Chronicle AD 1065

The year after their return from Normandy, at the beginning of October, the King was residing in Wintoncaestre when a messenger arrived with calamitous news. Three Yorkshire thaynes with two hundred men had rebelled against Earl Harold's brother Tostig, the Earl of Northumberland. The King immediately sent for Harold.

"Ten years ago you persuaded me to give the earldom to your brother. You said that he was generous, strong-willed and brave. But don't think I am fooled. By giving in to you, your family increased its immense power to cover almost every part of the country. You are as wealthy as I am!"

The Earl sensed that the King was in no mood to be argued with but, nevertheless, reminded him of the discussion ten years ago. "Your Majesty, Northumberland is the most lawless part of your realm. The people there are scarcely Anglo-Saxon: they have the blood and culture of the Norse. You wanted a strong man as overlord there."

"But we have seen that the appointment of an Anglo-Saxon from Wessex was resented by the northerners, and his attempt to introduce Saxon laws to replace their own was done savagely. He punishes wrongdoers with great cruelty."

"But, Sir, he is a righteous man who tries to be fair."

"Righteous he may be, but he has murdered all those who opposed him."

"They were traitors."

"They were local thaynes who tried to advise him to be merciful to gain popularity in the north."

"As maybe, but, Your Majesty, what has happened?"

"I have received messages from York that the rebels have slaughtered two hundred of Earl Tostig's warriors and that they are marching south. They have declared Tostig an outlaw and have elected the thayne Morcar as their earl. What can you do to stop them?"

The Earl was stunned by this news and quickly considered his options. "It will take time to raise the fyrd. I am on good terms with Morcar. As you know, my first wife Ealdgyth is his sister. I will take my housecarls north and parley with him."

The King agreed to the strategy, and Earl Harold hurried away to make arrangements.

The next day, a small sailing craft arrived in the creeks and sailed with the tide up to the jetty at Selceeflet. Godric disembarked and hurried up the hill to the manor house. The sound of the dogs barking at a stranger alerted Torkil who was in the hall with the steward. He pushed the shutters open and immediately recognised his army comrade coming along the track to the house. Torkil rushed outside to greet him. The noise had also attracted the attention of the rest of the family, and the children followed their father with Odelia and Edlin not far behind.

"Godric! What a surprise. Welcome back to Selceeflet."

"Torkil, it is good to see you!"

"And no less a pleasure for me, Godric! Come, join us for supper."

"I am afraid that we have no time for supper as we must catch the flooding tide. We can take food with us. The Earl needs his commanders. But look how these little ones have grown!"

"This is Finn. He is now eight and his brother Edward is six."

"You named them well, Torkil. A royal name for the youngest son with hair as red as his father's and grandmother's," Godric said, patting the boy on the head, "and a Norse one for the eldest whose fair hair is styled like a housecarl!"

Godric acknowledged Edlin and Odelia, but before he could speak to them, Torkil broke in excitedly. "But tell me, what is the reason for this summons?"

"The wild northerners have rebelled and are marching south. We are taking a force to meet them to see if Earl Harold can talk some sense into them."

"Where are we marching from?"

"Wintoncaestre. The King is there just now, and the Earl has summoned the housecarls to his standard."

Odelia had been listening intently and with consternation. She knew that her husband would have to heed the call from the Earl, but resented the fact that Torkil would have to leave home and face danger again. She did not want another confrontation between her mother-in-law and her husband and so tried to prevent it by asking Edlin to take the children off to play. Then she turned to address her husband. "Torkil, surely you can wait until tomorrow to leave. Godric, please stay for the night."

"I am sorry, Odelia, this is very serious. We must make haste." Godric was trying to be as diplomatic as possible.

"But, please, can't you just stay to sup with us?"

"I am afraid not. We must catch the tide."

Seeing that there was no point in pleading further, Odelia rushed off to the kitchen to make arrangements for the two men to take food with them for the journey. Torkil hurried away to collect his byrnie and his weapons.

Within a short time, the two housecarls were ready to depart. Torkil first took farewell of his children and then his wife and mother, aware that they were both distressed at his sudden departure. His own sadness at leaving was greatly mitigated by the thrill of another military mission. His discomfort at having to leave the responsibility of running the estate with Edlin and the steward again was soon forgotten.

Torkil was excited to be reunited with Godric, his old friend at arms. He looked forward to the camaraderie of the housecarls and the prospect of a new adventure in the service of the Earl.

They arrived in Wintoncaestre late in the evening having ridden from Hamwic on requisitioned horses. The very next day, Harold led a force of five hundred housecarls north. Their route took them through Abingdon-on-the-River and Oxford. The march was hard as the autumn rains lashed the mounted column, but they knew that the northerners would be suffering the same privations and Earl Harold's hope was that the rebels might lose their enthusiasm for the march south. On the fourth day of their northward journey, the Earl received a message saying that the northern force had reached Northampton and that the town and the surrounding area were being sacked.

The next day, the force from Wintoncaestre was nearing the occupied town. As the leaders of the column reached the top of the high hill to the south of Northampton, they got their first sight of a large army camped between them and the town. Fires were burning in the town and in the villages around.

"Godric, take a herald and four housecarls down to where the standards are flying and ask for safe passage for our force so that I can meet Morcar. Exchange hostages if you have to."

In situations where trust had to be engendered between potential enemies, it was customary to exchange hostages to guarantee non-aggression. In the event, Godric returned with four Northumbrian warriors. He had had to leave the herald and the four housecarls as hostages.

The column moved forward down the hill through the vast encampment of the insurgent army. The rebels looked on sullenly as the impressive housecarls' column with all the men in full armour rode past them. Earl Harold's standard, the 'fighting man', was hoisted in the van.

As they rode through the outskirts of the town, there was destruction everywhere, and smoke rising from burnt out buildings. Bodies littered the side of the roads together with broken barrows and carts which had belonged to those trying to flee the onslaught. Here and there were small groups of the surviving townsfolk huddled together for what protection they could afford each other. The rebels had clearly been slaughtering the refugees as they tried to escape. But their grisly work had stopped while they now stood watching the southerners as they entered the town. The housecarls could see that many of the opposing force were not impressive soldiers, and some carried only simple weapons such as billhooks and clubs.

"By God, what a rough-looking lot," said Godric to Torkil.

"But there are lots of them. I am uneasy that we are walking into a trap."

"The Earl knows what he is doing," said Godric.

"We will soon find out. There is Morcar's standard." Torkil pointed to a house which was less damaged than most, outside of which was Morcar's wild boar standard flapping in the breeze next to another standard which they did not recognise: a yellow 'x' cross on a blue background.

Outside the house, there was a large armed bodyguard surrounding two men with decorated helmets, the only parts that Godric and Torkil could see of them. One must be Morcar, but it was not yet clear who the other one was.

The column halted, and the Earl dismounted and walked up to the bodyguard. He pushed his way through and greeted

Morcar. As soon as he saw the other leader, he realised that his mission was going to be more difficult than he had expected. There with the pretender Earl of Northumberland was his brother, Earl Edwin of Mercia. The two had obviously joined forces. The rebellion was now even more formidable.

Word gradually filtered up the mounted column that the Mercians had joined the Northumbrians in their venture to oust Tostig. The Mercian housecarls had a fearsome reputation as warriors: they were better trained and more disciplined than the northmen.

Eventually, the mounted southerners were given orders to dismount. They watered their horses and waited for their supply train to catch up so that food could be prepared for them.

"I do not know my bible well," said Godric, "but I have the feeling that Daniel must have had in the den of the lion."

"The feeling is justified. I have just heard some of the rebels speaking a language which I recognise as Welsh. The Celts have made common cause with the two Earls. There is no love lost between the Welsh and Earl Harold."

"We cannot stay in the town tonight. We'll all get our throats cut."

In the twilight, when Torkil and Godric had finished their supper, Earl Harold emerged from the house with the other two Earls. He shook their hands and strode away from them, over to where his commanders were waiting. "Issue the order to march. We leave immediately."

There were mixed feelings among his men. A night march in October with too much cloud for the stars and new moon to provide illumination, on a road they were unfamiliar with, would be tiresome. Yet, the prospect of a sleepless night surrounded by the wild northerners, the Mercian housecarls and the Welsh, thirsty for vengeance, held no attraction.

The southern housecarls prepared their horses, put on their helmets and took their weapons to their mounts. They climbed onto their tired horses and set off in the direction they had come from.

At the encampment, the Northumbrian hostages were released as the housecarls and the herald rejoined the Earl's force.

As soon as they were through the encampment, Earl Harold called Godric and Torkil to ride to the front of the column and join him.

"We will ride through the night to get as far away from the rebels as possible. They have over three thousand men. Most of them would not think twice about gutting the men of Wessex. More men are joining them all the time."

"How were your discussions with Edwin and Morcar, My Lord?" asked Torkil.

"It is impossible to negotiate with them. They say they will continue south to take London unless the King outlaws Tostig and confirms Morcar as the Earl of the North. We must hasten to raise an army to meet them."

The long climb up the hill proved to be too much for some of the weary horses. Some went lame, others just plodded very slowly with their heads held low. Gaps were appearing between the faster and the slower horses. It was clear that the column was getting strung out.

Earl Harold gave orders for all the men to dismount to ensure that all the stragglers had caught up, for it would be dangerous for the force to be split up should the northerners have a change of heart and pursue them. Since the horses were so tired, the column now continued south along the old Roman road with the housecarls walking, leading their mounts.

Progress was slow in the darkness, and they were forced to stop several times to rest the animals. Eventually, they came to a small town which was called Tófe-ceaster,[55] and Earl Harold decided that they should spend what was left of the night there.

---

[55]   Tófe-ceaster – Towcester, the camp on the River Tove

Torkil and Godric sat around with some other officers at their wayside encampment near to the town by the side of the river. Earl Harold had taken over a house in the town.

"Can it be worth a civil war to keep Tostig as Earl of Northumberland?" asked one.

"He is a cruel bastard who deserves to be exiled," said another.

"But he is our leader's brother," said Godric. A gentle reminder that they owed allegiance to their commander.

"This is true, but can we risk the losses in a civil war when we need to build our army to face our real enemy to the south?" asked the first speaker.

There were sounds of agreement around the fire.

"Godric, you have Harold's ear. Can't you point out to him that we may soon need the Mercians and the Northumbrians fighting with us, not against us?"

"Um, I'll think about it," said Godric as he stood up to go and relieve himself.

Over the next three days, Godric and Torkil discussed the prospect of giving the Earl advice he did not want to hear. They both knew how intransigent he could be, yet he had to be reasoned with.

When they eventually had the opportunity to speak privately with Earl Harold, they found that he tended to be compliant with their view. He was not keen on raising an army and facing the rebellion. In his determination to succeed King Edward, he had realised that he would need the support of the Mercians and the Northumbrians. To alienate them further would damage his cause. His brother would have to be sacrificed.

Ultimately, it was the King who would make the decision about the earldom of Northumberland, but that decision was hastened when, a week later, news reached the King that the rebels had reached Oxford. Morcar and Edwin now felt so confident that they rode south to negotiate with the King. The monarch had been hunting in Wiltshire with Tostig but, on receiving the news that the rebel leaders were on their way to meet him, he and his entourage hastened to return to Wintoncaestre. On 28 October, when they came to the crossing point of the River Avon at Britford, south of Sarum,[56] the rebel leaders were waiting for them. A Grand Council took place on the river bank and the King acceded to the rebels' demands. Tostig was outlawed, and Morcar was confirmed as Earl of Northumberland.

An embittered Tostig fled to Flanders. He blamed Earl Harold entirely for his humiliation. He reasoned that the Earl could have raised an army against the rebels, but did not. The love between the two brothers had turned to a hate so strong that Tostig vowed to destroy his elder brother. On his arrival on the Continent, he immediately started to negotiate with the enemies of England to do so.

Later in the same year, with peace made in the north, King Edward decided to celebrate Christmas in London, at his palace at Westminster. The court was very busy as not only were Christmas celebrations to take place, but the new abbey church was to be consecrated. However, on 26 December, the King was unwell and retired to his bedchamber. His health continued to decline and he was unable to attend the consecration ceremony on 28 December.

The King died on 5 January. During his last days, he reported to his family that he had had a vision. He had seen a green tree. On it was a prophecy that, within a year and a day of his death, God would punish the kingdom for its sins by delivering it into the hands of its enemy, so that devils would go through the land with fire and sword and havoc of war.

The dying man's last words were addressed to Earl Harold. Referring to his wife, (Harold's sister), he said, "I commend this woman with all the kingdom to your protection."

---

[56]    Sarum – a fortress town three kilometres north of the present city of Salisbury

These words were taken by all who heard them as irrefutable proof that King Edward wished Earl Harold to succeed him as monarch.

The Royal Council, the witan, met and immediately voted for Harold to be king. On 6 January 1066, King Harold was crowned.

# Chapter 16

## Byzantium

Harald Sigurdsson and Ivar stood a while watching the ships northbound from Miklagård being prepared to make the portage from the Dnieper to the River Lovat. They moved on along the quayside towards where all the oxen and horses were being fed prior to them starting their long trek.

As they walked past one of the waiting ships, there was a shout. "Well, by the gods, Ivar Olavsson!"

Ivar turned in the direction the shout had come from and saw a face he recognised. But it was an older and much more weather-beaten face than when he had last seen it. However, there was no doubt – it was one of his friends from Roskilde: Aksel, son of the sea captain.

"I'd recognise that red hair anywhere! What are you doing here? Have you become a merchant?" asked Aksel.

Harald interrupted. "I'll leave you for a while to talk to your friend." And, with that, he made off back to their ship.

"No, I'm not a merchant. I'm a warrior, though I serve as a slave. That man is my master," he said, pointing in the direction of Harald's disappearing back.

"Ah, so it was true! Some said that you had been taken by the Norwegians, but most thought that you were dead. Come aboard and have a cup with the crew. We are all Danes. Mead is the best we can offer, I'm afraid." Pointing to the bow of the ship, he said, "We have barrels of wine, but they will stay shut until we get to Hedeby[57] market."

Ivar clambered aboard the ship and took the wooden cup offered to him.

"So, how did you come to be here, and with the Norwegians? Now we are all brothers with them of course, our King Cnut rules Norway as well as England and Denmark," said Aksel in a scoffing manner.

"I have been very lucky. My master is good to me. Sometimes he is like a friend, but most often he treats me like any other warrior in the force. I even get to share the plunder. We have all done well so far."

"Why don't you join us? We lost men when we were attacked by the Pechenegs south of here. I could pay you well."

"I have taken an oath to serve Harald Sigurdsson until he releases me from it."

"What kind of oath?"

"A blood oath."

"Why did you do that? What exactly happened after you were kidnapped?"

Ivar recounted his story but, before he could finish, he was interrupted by the appearance of Harald and a large group of the Varangians.

"We have come to take some tribute for you using the trader's trail of our master, Prince Jaroslav," shouted Harald.

"What do you mean? We pay the tax when we reach Novgorod!" replied Aksel. His crew nodded and called out in agreement.

"This is a little extra payment to my men for protecting you here."

---

[57] Hedeby – in Viking times a prominent Danish market town, now in Germany and called Haithabu

"We don't need protection here. Where were you when we faced the Pecheneg at the great rapids' portage? Then we needed help. We lost two crew."

"That's as may be. I want some share of your cargo."

From the threatening manner of the warriors behind their commander, it was clear that Aksel might have to accede to Harald's demands, but first he tried to get Ivar to intervene. "Ivar, can't you do anything to stop this? We have worked hard to get these goods."

Ivar avoided eye contact with his friend and looked very uncomfortable as he told him, "There is nothing I can do. I am a slave."

"But at least you could try!"

"Sorry, it would be best for you to do as they ask."

Ivar knew what the Varangians were capable of. They might easily ransack the ship and, if resisted, there could be deadly results. He quickly decided on the best course of action to avoid a confrontation. "Sir, they have wine in the hold."

Aksel growled at him, "You treacherous bastard! Your father would be ashamed of you."

Harald shouted again, "Unload three barrels and quickly, or we will come and do it ourselves."

Ivar sat watching the men untying the covers which protected the barrels from the weather. To have protested to Harald would have been suicidal for him; a slave's life was cheap. But through his action, he had made enemies of his landsmen. He knew that Aksel and his crew would make sure that word of what they saw as his betrayal of them became known in his home town. He had put himself in the position of a permanent exile.

While the Varangians were enjoying their wine, the Danish crew quickly unloaded their cargo. So, by the time the Varangians came back in a drunken state looking for more to drink, the goods had been dispatched north on the horse-drawn wagons which would carry them to where their ship could once more be launched. The following day, Harald set off south down the river which would eventually flow into the great Dnieper and transport them to Kiev.

As the ships glided towards the quay at Kiev, the crews caught sight of the amazing St Sophia Cathedral. The building had thirteen cupolas which glinted in the June sunshine. Around some of them, there were still large wooden structures of scaffolding where the builders were putting the finishing touches to the magnificent cathedral. But Harald's men would not have the opportunity to go through the Golden Gate and explore the impressive city, for at the quayside they were met by a delegation of military officials. Word had already reached Kiev that the Varangian reinforcements were nearing the city. Harald was given orders to disembark and leave his ships in Kiev. His force was to be supplied with horses and, the next day, they were to leave for the Snake Ramparts where another group of Varangians were defending the settlements against renewed attacks by the Pecheneg.

During the summer of 1033, Harald's warriors had a number of successful actions against the nomads. The technique employed by the Norwegian was to be assertive in the defence of the isolated settlements. Instead of passively defending them against attacks by the wild horsemen, Harald sought out their encampments and took the fight to them. His success gained him more followers as members of the existing Varangian force joined up with his small army. By early autumn, when he made his way back to Kiev, he had over five hundred men under his command. But it was not only his generalship which attracted his new followers: the word had gone round that he intended to move on to Miklagård the next year.

After a winter and spring spent repairing and maintaining his fleet, preparations were ready for the veterans of Stiklestad and their reinforcements to travel south. Harald had been advised by the captains of trading vessels overwintering in Kiev that the best time to leave would be early June. This would bring them to the great rapids at a time when the water level was at its most favourable. To transport his extra warriors, Harald had bought several monoxyla ships. These were craft made by Slavic people which they sold to traders for negotiating the Dnieper to the Black Sea. They were simple but very large dugout logs which could transport up to sixty men.

The journey south was safe and fast until the ships reached the great rapids. There the ships once more had to be dragged overland until, further south, the river once more ran calmly. But this portage was a very dangerous one because the Pecheneg, aware that travellers were at their most vulnerable when manhandling their ships over land, often ambushed the crews. With his very large force and his aggressive tactics, Harald successfully avoided the nomads and, ten weeks after leaving Kiev, his fleet sailed out of the Black Sea and along the Golden Horn, the waterway to Constantinople.

The coast on their southern, starboard side ran in the direction of the setting sun and, as they sailed along it, more and more buildings came into view on the hills further inland. The city was surrounded by a wall along the shoreline making it appear very inhospitable. Since none of Harald's crew had been to Constantinople before, they did not know where to find a harbour. Very soon, however, they heard trumpets blasting the warning that a foreign force was approaching, and six war galleys appeared from a bay, heading towards them.

The Varangians prepared their weapons in case their reception was to be a hostile one. Very soon, the first galley, which was leading the fleet, approached Harald's ship. It stopped just out of arrow shot and waited for the others.

"Put your weapons away," shouted Harald to his men. As he did so, he climbed up on to the prow and held up both of his hands to show that he was unarmed.

The Turkish rowers took up their oars and, once more, the galleys started moving towards the fleet. The Varangians could now see armed warriors standing ready for action behind the rowers. When the Byzantine galleys closed on the fleet, a man standing at the bow of the first galley started shouting to them in a language they could not understand.

Harald tried shouting back in Norse, but he was clearly not understood either. The warriors in the galleys were staring menacingly at his ship.

"Sir, let me try," said Ivar.

"How can you do any better than I can?" Harald's indignation was plain to hear.

"I can try Latin."

Harald was surprised. "Do you speak Latin? What makes you think that they will understand Latin?"

"The rowers are slaves. There is a good chance that some of them are prisoners from a country where the language is spoken."

"Well, try then."

Ivar clambered over the warriors sitting at their rowing benches and joined Harald at the bow. He called out in Latin, "We are friends. We come to serve the emperor."

The man at the bow of the galley clearly did not understand, but there were shouts from among the crew. Several called out to the spokesman, obviously translating Ivar's speech.

One of the rowers was dragged forward to stand by the spokesman at the bow. The slave was instructed to call out to the ship in Latin.

"Do you come from the northlands?" he called.

"We do," Ivar answered.

"What did he say?" asked Harald tetchily.

"He asked where we come from," said Ivar.

The man called out again, "Follow our ship."

Ivar translated and Harald gave the order to man the oars. The other ships in the fleet, seeing what the commander was doing, followed the flagship's example. And thus the Varangian fleet made landfall in Prosphorian Bay, the bay of the communion bread. Ivar the slave became an important man in the negotiations which followed with the commander of the harbour until the Varangians were able to link up with other Norsemen who had been in Miklagård long enough to learn the language and could act as interpreters.

From the interpreters, they learnt that the most powerful figure in the land was not an emperor, for Byzantine now had an empress, Zoe. However, the empress had a new husband, her second, who, although designated as Emperor Michael IV, was subservient to his wife. It was the emperor who, having heard that the leader of the newly arrived force of Varangians was a man of importance, sent for Harald to negotiate terms and to give him instructions about his first assignment.

"What do you know about the new husband?" Harald asked his interpreter.

"Ha, he is a gold-digger! His family are not of royal blood. They are silversmiths and he has a reputation for silver clipping!"

"What's that?" asked Harald.

"He cut bits off silver coins before circulating them and kept the silver clippings. The old woman is forty years older than him and fell for his beautiful teenage physique!"

"When did they marry?"

"Well, that's a story. They married on Good Friday this year. Her previous husband was still alive that day but, by the end of the day, he was dead; found cold on the floor of his bath house!"

"Where are we going to meet him?"

"You are summoned to the royal palace today. Be careful. Michael is very powerful. Empress Zoe has put him in command of all forces."

Later in the day, Harald led his Varangians through the city streets, guided by their interpreter. The men looked in wonderment at the buildings, the houses, the fountains and churches in this the greatest and wealthiest city in the world. They saw exotic, colourful flowers and trees with fruits of types they had never seen before. Street vendors sold foods which were unknown to them and, as they marched along the streets, children called out in a language which was totally bewildering. And the heat – they had never before experienced such overwhelming, oppressive, baking air. For though, while traversing the Black Sea it had been hot, there was always a sea breeze to cool their bodies, but here in the still air, where the wind was hindered by the tall buildings, they gasped for breath.

Their route took them past the Strategion, the prison, and the Church of Urbicus before they reached the Wall of Byzantium which protected the royal city. Here, the warriors were obliged to leave their weapons at the guard post before being permitted to pass through the gates. Constantinople was a city of intrigues, and a band of five hundred armed men entering the heart of the city was a threat not to be accepted by the authorities.

Once through the gate, the breathless Norsemen had even more reason to gasp. There in front of them was the huge structure of the church of Hagia Sophia and, behind it, the Royal Palace. The men were led to the Hippodrome in front of the palace to wait and get refreshment while Harald and the interpreter were led off by royal officials to meet their new employer.

When Harald later emerged from the palace, it was with the news that his force had been assigned to hunt Saracen corsair pirates in the Aegean Sea. They were to man fast sailing and rowing craft called *ousiai*. These were designed to be fast and manoeuvrable enough to catch the Arab pirate dhows which were wreaking terror and destruction in the Empress's territory in the Aegean. Each craft carried fifty rowers and fifty warriors. Harald's forces would man ten of these vessels as a flotilla, under the command of the head of the navy.

And so it was that, for the first two years of their stay in

Byzantine, the Varangians fought sea and land battles against the Saracen pirates. The enterprise was very popular with the men as it was extremely profitable. Each mercenary was paid a living wage, but most attractive was the plunder. Many of the dhows they captured were heavily laden with booty from nefarious activities. For each ship they captured, Harald had to pay one hundred marks to the Empress, a relatively modest sum. The remaining value of the ship and cargo was shared among the crew. Since the rowers were all slaves and received no share of the plunder, the Varangian warriors began to amass large sums of money, and their leader, taking the largest share, became spectacularly wealthy. From this time, using traders as couriers, Harald and some of his men started to send silver and gold back to Kiev for safekeeping by Jaroslav. For, by now, Jaroslav had moved his court, his power base, from Novgorod to Kiev.

But, as well as becoming rich, the Varangians in the flotilla gained a significant reputation because of their success in their mission. Such was the recognition of their part in clearing the Aegean of pirates that, at the end of the assignment, Michael appointed Harald and his force to be part of the Varangian Guard. This was an elite troop of Varangians with responsibility for the personal safety of the Empress and her entourage. To mark his achievements, Harald was promoted to the rank of officer in the Guard and presented with his own standard, The Land Ravager.

In the following year, 1037, Harald's Varangian Guard troop was appointed to travel to the Holy Land. In Jerusalem, the Church of the Holy Sepulchre had been badly damaged in wars for possession of the city. Empress Zoe had reached an agreement with the Caliph of Egypt to be allowed to repair this, the holiest place in Christendom. An army of craftsmen had been assembled in Constantinople, and they were to travel to Jerusalem to rebuild the church. In addition, this presented an opportunity for some high-ranking royal family members to make a pilgrimage. Empress Zoe's two sisters, both of whom were nuns, were to accompany the craftsmen to the Holy Land. But the journey was long and very dangerous as the travellers would have to cross hostile territories. Thus it was that Harald was put in command of an armed escort charged with protecting the group on their hazardous journey. At the end of the successful venture, Harald and his men were richly rewarded.

In the years which followed, the Land Ravager flag flew in several countries where the Varangian Guard troop was engaged in campaigns to exert Byzantine power. But, in the three-year campaign to recover Sicily from the Saracens, the authority of Harald the leader was challenged for the first time. The commander of the Byzantine army, Georgios Maniakes, or Gyrgir as he was known by the Varangians, a man who was said to have a physique even bigger than Harald's, fundamentally disagreed with Harald about tactics. When Harald refused to accept orders from him, saying that as a Varangian Guard officer he answered only to the Emperor, the general excluded the troop from his army and told them fight the Saracen independently. Further animosity arose when, disaffected by Gyrgir's method of apportioning plunder, a force of three hundred Norman cavalry mercenaries joined up with Harald's force.

Once more, Ivar's skill in speaking Latin became of importance. He acted as interpreter and liaison between the Normans and Varangians. The Norsemen quickly learned respect and admiration for the Normans' style of fighting, their heavy horses, and their skill with the lance. But the allying of the Normans with the Varangians was greeted with fury by the general who then refused to apportion any of their previous plunder to the Normans. This caused the cavalry to defect and travel to Italy to offer their services to the enemies of the Emperor.

The defection of the Normans later made life very uncomfortable for Harald's men when they had to face the same Norman cavalry when combating the Lombard revolt in southern Italy the next year. It took great courage for the foot soldiers of the Byzantine army to face and defeat the solid rows of Norman horsemen who charged with their lances levelled against them.

The last four years of Harald's time in the employ of the Byzantine Emperor were spent with Michael in a long and bloody but ultimately successful campaign to suppress a revolt by the Bulgars. At the end of this long war, the Varangians returned triumphantly to Constantinople marching behind the victorious Emperor. The ferocity of the young Varangian Guard officer in the hard battles had earned him the nickname of Harald Hardrada, Harald the hard ruler.

The Varangians were well known in Constantinople as hard-drinking men. The nickname for them was 'winebags' and, on their return from the long campaign, it was not long before the celebrations turned into a long, drunken orgy lasting several days. Ivar was caught up in the general mood, and he joined in the festivities. This included visits to the Varangian concubine 'harem' where slave girls were kept specifically for the pleasure of the Varangians; the hope of the authorities being that this provision would save the female citizens of the city from being bothered by the drunken warriors. Frequently, a girl was 'adopted' by a particular warrior, and they lived as man and wife. Thus it was that some of the Norsemen never left Miklagård when their contract expired. They stayed on and were assimilated into the population.

It was in the harem that Ivar met a Norman slave girl called Aveline. He recognised her at once. She had been among the slaves which the Varangians had found on one of the Saracen ships that they had captured when they were in the Aegean. She had been sold on for silver to a Byzantine trader as part of the crew's booty. From his visits to the harem, Ivar learned that she was the daughter of a Norman merchant. She had been kidnapped by Breton raiders when she was a girl from the village of Domfront on the border between Brittany and Normandy. The Bretons had sold her as a slave to Arab traders. She was well educated, and Ivar was able to converse with her in Latin.

At first, he was content to share her with other warriors but, after several days, he became more possessive and then, impetuously, claimed her by paying the harem keeper for ownership. But, for Ivar, there was no option for him to settle with Aveline. He was a slave and owed duty to his master. Where Harald Hardrada went, he must follow. Indeed, he should have asked his master's permission to buy the girl, and he feared the consequences if Harald discovered what he had done. The reality was that he had to keep his ownership of the slave girl secret. The only course open to him was to hide Aveline. Money was not a problem for the Dane, and so he rented a small house near to the Varangian barracks for her to live in until he decided what to do.

What Ivar could not have known was that the influence of Byzantine politics would very soon force him to make a decision.

The campaign against the Bulgars had taken its toll on Emperor Michael. He was taken seriously ill shortly after the army's return. This illness marked a change in the fortunes of Harald and his men. As the Emperor was dying, there was a power struggle to contrive to find his successor. Under duress from his relatives, the Emperor agreed to adopt his nephew Michael as his son and heir. The aging Empress then fell under the influence of a new emperor, Michael V, one who did not approve of the use of foreign mercenaries. She was persuaded by him to appoint as her advisor Harald's arch-enemy, Gyrgir.

Within days of the installation of the new Emperor, Harald received a summons to attend a meeting with Michael and Gyrgir.

"Ivar, we are summoned to the palace on the orders of the Emperor. I need my ceremonial robes," said Harald.

"And your sword, sir?"

"Yes, the gold-hilted one."

As an officer in the Guard, on special occasions, Harald had the right to wear a white and scarlet robe. His rank also entitled him to carry a sword presented to him by the Empress. The gold hilt denoted his rank.

"Tell Halldor Snorrason and Ulf Ospaksson that, as my highest officers, they should come with me to the palace."

"In their ceremonial uniforms?"

"Yes. I want to impress the new Emperor to get his attention. I have decided that the time has come to return home. I have received word that my nephew Magnus has become King of Norway and Denmark."

"And you should have received precedence?"

"Exactly."

Ivar accompanied the party to the palace dressed in his military byrnie, a mark that his rank was that of mere soldier. They were ushered into a large room where the huge figure of Gyrgir sat together with a smaller man in a white robe. At regular positions around the walls, there were armed Varangian guards, but not of Harald's troop.

"Your Royal Highness, this is Harald, the Varangian officer."

The Emperor looked Harald up and down disdainfully.

"Your Royal Highness, I have a request to make," said Harald.

Michael was clearly annoyed that Harald had taken the conversational initiative. "I called you to a meeting, not the other way round," he answered, and then added inquisitively, "What is your request?"

"I wish to be given permission to leave the Emperor's service and to return to my country."

"Damn you, I will decide how and when you are to be discharged." Looking at Gyrgir, the Emperor said, "You deal with the formalities."

The general rose to his feet and glowered at Harald. "You

have become very wealthy in the service of the Empress – too wealthy. You have deprived her of what is rightfully hers. You are accused of fraud."

"But my accounts show the division of plunder is as the law requires."

"Guards! Seize these three officers and take them to the Strategion," ordered Gygir.

Resistance was impossible. Harald and his two fellow officers were stripped of their weapons, and their hands were bound before they were marched off to prison. Ivar moved forward to pick up the ceremonial weapons to take them back to the barracks. As he did so, Gyrgir stepped forward and smashed the back of his hand across Ivar's face. "Leave them, get out!" he ordered.

What Ivar and the three officers were not to know was that the real purpose of the arrest was to eliminate some of the Empress's loyal support, for Michael planned to depose her. Later in the week, Michael had her exiled to a nunnery and assumed total power himself with the help of disloyal Varangians. But his coup was short-lived. There was a huge revolt among the people when news spread that the Empress had been deposed. In the street fighting, more than three thousand people perished in one day before Michael was forced to flee to a monastery for sanctuary, and the Empress was reinstated. Her vengeance was swift. Harald and his officers were released from prison and he was given the responsibility of capturing Michael and exacting the traditional Byzantine punishment for treason: blinding. Harald's men dragged the fugitive from the monastery and Harald personally gouged out his eyes. And then there was further bloody work to be done: the disloyal Varangians were rounded up by Harald's men and then hung or put to the sword.

The coup was over and Harald Hardrada was at the zenith of his power and influence in the Byzantine court.

# Chapter 17

## Tostig's Treachery

*As soon as Harold took over the government of the kingdom he began to abolish bad laws and establish good ones, to become the patron of churches and monasteries, to show himself kind, humble and affable to all men, but hateful to malefactors, for he ordered his servants to arrest all thieves, robbers and disturbers of the kingdom. And for defence of the fatherland he laboured on land and sea.*

John of Worcester, English monk and chronicler, died 1140

King Harold wasted no time in impressing his rule on the country. The object which defined the King's rule for the people, most of whom were illiterate, was coinage. This was one of the King's first priorities. Dies were sent out from London to forty-four mints in the country with a royal command for a new issue of the only coinage in circulation: the silver penny. On one side of the coin was the King's crowned head and prominent on the reverse was stamped PAX (peace). But there were other urgent issues, and foremost among them was to establish a good relationship with the northern Earls so that the King could be assured of their support in the anticipated invasion by the Duke of Normandy. And so it was that, in early April, Godric and Torkil were once more in a column of housecarls riding north. The King was at the front of the column, and he had with him his friend Bishop Wulfstan. It was hoped that the Bishop's diplomatic skills would help lead to an agreement with the suspicious northerners. The Earls met the King in York.

"We must be united in the face of the threatened invasion by the Normans for, if we are disunited, we are too weak to overcome the enemy," reasoned the King.

Earl Morcar was unconvinced. "If the Normans should usurp you, Your Majesty, then we would form a separate kingdom in Northumbria."

"I have heard Earl William speak. He would have the whole kingdom and you would be too weak to stand up to him."

The Northumbrian Earl turned and whispered to his advisors. After a while, he turned back and said, "What do you want of us?"

"We need the support of your army to prevent a Norman landing in England."

The King needed a decisive argument to give the Earl no choice but to strongly ally himself to the English cause. This was the moment the Bishop had been waiting for, and the King left the much respected churchman to give voice to what they both knew would be a fact which would disturb the Earl greatly.

"You must remember that Tostig still has designs to recover his earldom of Northumberland. He is now allied to the Normans. It is likely that, if they were to prevail and to take possession of this kingdom, Tostig would be rewarded for his treachery by being restored to the earldom of Northumberland."

There was a long pause, and Earl Morcar said, "I will consider this and give you my reply tomorrow."

Later that day, the King sent for Godric and Torkil. "When we return to London, I want you both to join my brothers Gyrth and Leofine in supervising the mobilisation of the fyrd. We will put together the biggest army ever seen on the south coast. Our spies tell us that work is going on a pace with the building of hundreds of transport ships in Normandy and the Duke's army is gathering in Dives."

"Do you think the Northumbrians will join us, Your Majesty?" asked Godric.

"Undoubtedly, given the night to think about it. By morning, Morcar will be enthusiastic to support us if it ensures that he will retain his power in the north. His brother, Earl Edwin, will be with us too. But we must not take all his troops to the south. He must keep a force in York to defend the east coast."

"And your ships?"

"I want the whole fleet to be based off Vectis."

Just as the King had predicted, the next morning, Earl Morcar pledged his allegiance to the King and promised to support him militarily. That day, the King, the Bishop and the housecarls left for London, arriving there on 16 April.

The next month was a very busy one for the King's officers as plans were drawn up to mobilise and supply many thousands of warriors and fyrdsmen. Torkil spent two weeks in London and then marched for Hamwic with a detachment of several hundred housecarls and two thousand fyrdsmen. There, he supervised the deployment of his men along the shore of the great forest. Other officers were doing the same thing all along the coast from Hamwic to Dover, but the main force was to be stationed opposite the island.

In the third week of May, lookouts sighted a large fleet of vessels entering the waters between the Isle of Wight and the mainland. At first, it seemed as if this must be the English fleet gathering at their station as planned by the King, but fisherfolk scurrying to the shore in their small craft had another story. An invasion had begun, but it was not the Normans. A treacherous Englishman had agreed with the Duke of Normandy to test the English defences.

*Soon came Tostig from beyond the sea into the Isle of Wight, with as large a fleet as he could get; and he was there supplied with money and provisions. Thence he proceeded, and committed outrages everywhere by the sea coast…*

The Anglo-Saxon Chronicle AD 1066

The invading fleet split up and attacked different parts of the island. Soon, the English soldiers along the forest shore could see smoke rising from island villages. Torkil was desperate. He had an army, but no way to transport it across the sea to defend the beleaguered isle. He was even more distressed when observers he had sent out in small craft returned to report that ten or so ships had disappeared through the opening into the creeks. Worse was to come for, about an hour later, even from the forest shore, it was possible to see smoke rising from the area due south. He was powerless to defend his own home and family! Neither could he desert his post as commander to take one of the small fisher craft to cross to the island, a course of action which would have been suicidal for him anyway. A lone King's housecarl would have provided great sport for the pirates. He just had to wait until the ships departed from the creeks.

In the late afternoon, a lookout reported to Torkil that ships had been seen leaving the creeks and turning east on the flood tide. The thayne had already requisitioned all the fishing boats his men could find and, as soon as it seemed that the departing ships had gone down tide far enough not to be able to easily get back to intercept them, his flotilla of small craft loaded with armed men set off for the island.

It was early evening when Torkil's boat slid alongside the Selceeflet jetty. He leapt out, leaving his armour behind, and, sword in hand, ran along the wooded track towards the Hall. The five warriors in the boat followed him. He passed the burnt remains of his watermill and continued up the cart track. When he came out of the trees on to the path to his home, he stopped. On the hill where the Hall should have been, there was nothing. He started to run again and, as he got closer, he could see the remains of his home charred and still smouldering, the smoke adding to the light evening mist which was descending and beginning to shroud the ugly scene. But the mist could not hide the bodies strewn at the top of the track. Bodies which had once been Torkil's vassals and churls, now hacked and speared most awfully. In the twilight, Torkil searched amongst the bodies hoping desperately that he would not find what he was looking for – members of his family.

He found the old steward lying on his back on the ground, a sword still in his hand, an arrow in his chest. Torkil felt his neck: he was cold, cold as the clammy mist. Half in and half out of the burnt building were the charred remains of a woman. An axe head was protruding from her back, the handle having burnt off. One of the warriors helped Torkil to lift the body out of the still hot ashes. The ash fell off to reveal a blackened silver bracelet on her arm which Torkil immediately recognised as his mother's. The bracelet in the shape of a writhing snake, which she always wore, had escaped the attention of the plunderers. Her hair, once the colour of fire, had been consumed by that same element, leaving a blackened skull.

The master of the torched Hall stood back to see in the gathering gloom if any buildings were still standing. The outbuildings had had the same treatment as the house, but the granary which was some way from the house was still standing. Torkil and his men made up some torches and went to search the building. It was completely empty. The raiders had taken what grain had been in the store. The men stood in silence, each of them furious that they had not been able to intercede in this invasion and save the village from devastation.

"What was that?" asked one of the men.

"What?" Torkil asked.

"I heard voices. Listen."

They stood very quietly and, after a while, they all heard

whispering. It seemed to come from under the floor. The men reacted fast and rushed out to surround the building, weapons in their hands. The granary was supported on massive rocks which had been shaped to try to prevent vermin from getting into the building. This left a void under the floor. They tried to light up this area under the building with their torches, but had to take care not to set fire to the wooden structure.

"Come out. We are friends," called Torkil.

The two girls hiding under the granary knew immediately that the voices were not those of the raiders, for they had spoken another language. First one and then the other crawled out. In the light of the torches, Torkil immediately recognised the girls as scullery slaves from the Hall. They were dishevelled and shaking with fear.

"Master, master, it was terrible, terrible, they were butchers, vile butchers..." Both girls were speaking at the same time saying more or less the same thing.

"Stop, stop, you can tell me about it later. Where is your mistress and the children?"

The older of the two girls spoke. "Mistress Odelia ran into the forest with the children when we first saw the smoke rising from Creektown. I don't know if the robbers caught them."

The smaller girl added, "I saw them going towards the south path."

"What happened to my mother?"

"We were watching from the kitchen window. Mistress Edlin stood in front of the Hall and refused to let the raiders come in. She ran to lock the door but one of the robbers threw a hand axe at her. I don't know what happened then."

"Where was the steward?"

"He went off into the fields with the chest to bury it. When he came back, he ran at the soldiers with his sword, but they fired arrows at him."

Torkil had a dilemma. His instinct told him to go and search for his family, but equally he knew that it would be impossible to find his way through the great forest in the dark, and thus there was little chance of finding them until morning.

"We can rest in the granary until first light and then we will search the forest," he told his men. The girls had nowhere to go so they also climbed up the steps to the building.

The late May night should have been short, but to Torkil it seemed very long. He was trying to imagine what route his wife might take in the forest. She did not know it well. His thoughts ranged over many things. His mother was old; most of her life had been good; she did not have much time left; but he grieved for her nevertheless. What if the raiders had taken his wife? What was happening to her? Where had the steward buried the chest? If he could not find the chest, how could he afford to rebuild the house? Who was responsible for this outrage against his village? Was this the Norman invasion? If so, why did they not occupy the island?

Some sleep came to the weary warrior before, at first light, the men started stirring.

"Sir, we have some food in the boat. Can I collect it?" asked one of the men.

"Yes, go straightaway. You men wait here."

Torkil was not going to wait for the breakfast. He set off along the forest edge until he came to a path leading south. The path was dry, and the ground told no story of people passing this way by letting them leave foot tracks. Brambles overhung the trail and, as he walked, Torkil had to push them aside. After a while, he came to a small clearing. The cropped grass told of frequent visits by hares. In the corner of the clearing was a pond, a well trodden path which showed that someone often went there to fish or to collect water. Torkil started to call out his wife's name. The sound of "Odelia" rang through the forest.

There were two other paths leading from the grassy space. The one going east had a tangle of undergrowth, indicating that it was not used often, but on the one striking south the grass was worn by regular use. Torkil turned and started walking along this path, calling out as he went. Then he heard it! First, a woman's voice and then children's voices. From around a bend in the track, Odelia and the two boys appeared. They stopped and then started to run towards him.

As they walked back along the track, Odelia described the happenings of the day before and how she had run into the forest, and that they had stayed the night in a hovel which belonged to a strange old crone. Despite the trauma, Torkil's mind flashed back to a time when he had heard that hovel described before.

"The hut was filthy and stank, but we were grateful enough to stay there. The woman was some kind of sorcerer. There were strange signs and collections of feathers and animal bones. But what of Edlin? Is she safe?"

"I'm sorry, Odelia, the news is bad. My mother was killed by the raiders. It seems that she tried to stop them entering the house."

Telling Odelia of his mother's death made the reality of her murder really hit him, and they walked in silence for a long while with the boys running ahead.

In full daylight, the sight of the burnt remains of their home distressed them both, but there was no time for further sentiment or to search for the buried chest. Torkil had to get back to his warriors after doing what was necessary here. There would be time enough to look for the steward's hiding place when he returned to rebuild the house after the threat of the Norman invasion was over.

They buried his mother and the steward at the edge of the forest with the help of some villagers who had escaped the slaughter. Torkil told the village men to take care of the other victims.

"Odelia, I must go back to the army, but you cannot stay

here so I will take you to Wintoncaestre. You can stay with Emma. She will be pleased to have company."

"But we must rebuild our home," pleaded Odelia.

"I'm sorry, that will have to wait until we live in more peaceable times."

"How will we live in Wintoncaestre? We have no money now."

"I have plenty of silver in my pouch. The King pays me well."

As the warriors rowed the small craft down the creek, Torkil and his family gazed at the place that had been home, not knowing if and when they would ever live there again. The shrill, rising tone call of the oyster catchers, as they expressed their excitement about the prospect of good hunting in the newly exposed mud, was the only sound apart from the splash of the oars as the ship made its way down the creek on the falling tide, and what had been a vast expanse of water was becoming eddying channels. Once clear of the creeks, the vessel set sail for Hamwic to transport Odelia and the two boys to live with Torkil's sister and her baby.

It had been in March the previous year that Emma gave birth to her son. When they had returned from Normandy, Torkil had taken her back to the nunnery and she had thrown herself at the mercy of the Abbetissa. But it was to no avail for, despite the circumstances of her pregnancy, in the eyes of the Mother Superior it was she who was responsible for breaking her vow of chastity. At first, Edlin had insisted that Emma should come to live at Selceeflet, despite Torkil protesting that he did not want the bastard of Robert d'Evreux to be born in his house. But the matter had been taken out of their hands when, on hearing the news that a baby was due, King Harold made arrangements for her to live in Wintoncaestre. No doubt feeling that his insistence in including the nun in the party which visited Normandy had led to her current state, he provided a small house, an allowance and a woman servant to care for her.

Emma herself could not remember the point in the pregnancy when she had ceased to hate the nascent child in her womb. It had been created through the act of a man she abhorred, and that abhorrence had at first tainted her view of the being inside of her. But gradually, like any mother, a feeling of joy and anticipation developed and increased as the months went by. It was probably in the fifth month that her maternal instinct took over, and she started to tie the wax tablet with a prayer in Latin inscribed on it to her right foot, as prescribed by the Church, to ensure a healthy child.

But the birth was difficult for, at twenty-eight, she was very old to have a first child, and it was probably only the draughts of crushed pennyroyal[58] which had brought on the birth that saved her and the boy. Now things were better, and mother and child were thriving when Torkil, Odelia, Finn and Edward unexpectedly stood at her door.

"Emma, I beg of you to take in Odelia and the boys for some weeks. Our home has been destroyed and Mother has been killed."

"Mother dead! But why? Who has done this?"

"I was away from the estate and some rebels raided the island. She was defending the house. They murdered her and burnt the house. Fortunately, Odelia and the boys escaped. I must go back to the army until peace is restored. Can they stay with you?"

"Oh, poor Mother. Though in truth I have not seen her for many years, I think of her often. I will pray for her soul. You should have been there to defend her," said Emma acidly.

"Believe me, I wanted to be, but it was impossible."

The situation was awkward because Emma held her brother responsible for forcing on her a radical change in her lifestyle. In

---

[58]  Pennyroyal – Lamiaceae, a wild plant which can be used as a uterine stimulant

addition, Odelia was a stranger to her. They had never met, and now she was being asked to house her sister-in-law and her two young children. And yet her new way of life was one which was much to her satisfaction with the blessing of financial stability and a fine young son. In many ways, she was still a nun at heart and her Christian charity dictated, when she saw the distraught Odelia and her sons in need of shelter, that she should welcome them into her home.

"It will be very cramped. We have one large room, as you see. This is where we spend our days and where the woman who helps me and I sleep. You are welcome to share it, but it is not the fine home that you are used to."

"We have no home now, so we are happy to have a roof over our heads," said Odelia.

The baby started crying and the two little boys went to the crib in the corner of the room to look at their little cousin.

"Odelia, I must leave straightaway to rejoin my men. Here is money for your upkeep." Torkil crossed the room and forced himself to look at the son of d'Evreux. He kissed the baby, his sons and his wife, but not his sister. She was still a nun to him. "I will return as soon as I can. I wish you good health, sister."

He turned to leave, but then looked over his shoulder at those who were dear to him and, despite his strong sense of duty to the King, wished for a moment that he could have stayed.

# Chapter 18

## The Way Home

In his position of favour with the Empress, Harald Hardrada now felt confident to ask again for permission to leave her service and to return north. But, in June, Zoe took a third husband, Constantine, and delegated her power to him. So it was to the new Emperor that the Varangian officer had to go to ask to be released from his contract. Again, the answer was no.

Ivar was serving wine, bread and goat's cheese at a meeting between Harald, Halldor and Ulf as they sat around a wine-stained table in their barracks by the Tower of St Eugenius.

"Though our loyalty is richly rewarded here, we know what happens to those who are disloyal – blinding, hanging or worse. But how can we enjoy our money when it is all in store in Kiev?" complained Ulf.

"I have more pressing reasons for wanting to get back to Norway," said Harald.

"Do you think you can wrest the crown from Magnus?" scoffed Halldor.

"No, at first I will share it with him, until—"

"Until he is found dead in his bed with a mouth full of poison," interrupted Ulf.

Harald ignored the remark but added, "And I have a mission in Kiev too. I have a bride to collect."

"Do you think that Jaroslav will give Elizaveta to you now?" asked Ulf.

"Of course he will. I have fame, wealth and the prospect of a crown."

"But you can't get your crown or your bride, and I can't touch my money unless we can get out of this blasted oven of a city," shouted Ulf.

It was now the height of summer, and the heat was stultifying. The drinkers' thirst was increased by the hot, dry air.

"Listen, I have a plan. It is risky, but I think that it is possible," said Harald, lowering his voice and looking around to see that no one apart from his loyal servant was within earshot.

"All your plans are risky!" answered Ulf.

"Clearly we can't try to leave the city in daylight, so we have to leave at night."

"And how do we do that?" queried Halldor. "Our ships are on the wrong side of the chain."

Halldor was referring to the huge chain which, each evening, was raised from the sea bed to the surface of the Bosphorous. It stretched from the south shore to the north shore to prevent vessels making a surprise night attack on Constantinople. The Varangian rowing galleys were to the east of the chain, in the Prosphorian harbour. Immediately to the west of the chain, in the Neorian harbour, was the Byzantine naval base from whence galleys had come out to meet the Varangians when they had first arrived eight years earlier.

"The chain is heavy and is never right on top of the surface. If we row fast towards it and the crew all move quickly to the stern so that their weight makes the bows lift, I think that we could ride over the chain. Then the crew move to the bow and their weight will tip the galley over the other side."

"Madness! You must have had too much wine!" declared Ulf.

"Well, it's up to you. I am going to chose sixty of our best men and take two galleys to escape over the chain."

There was silence in the room while they all thought about the import of what had been said.

"And so you will leave all the other men behind?" asked Halldor.

"This has to be kept secret, and the more who know about it the more likely we are to end up with no eyes. And, besides, to try to move quietly with five hundred men would be impossible. Some would want to stay too; they have wives here."

Halldor held up his cup. "Ivar, more wine. When are you going to do this, Harald?"

"We have to wait awhile. I have a feeling that we are being watched by the Emperor's spies after I asked for permission to leave, just to make sure that we don't try to do so. But we have to leave by mid-August if we are to get to Kiev by October before the snows come."

"And then we could continue to Novgorod on the frozen rivers on horseback," ventured Halldor.

"Precisely. We will be in Novgorod by the end of the year."

The thought of being reunited with his money was too strong for Ulf to resist. "I am with you," he said.

"Me too," said Halldor.

"Good, I will command the first galley; Halldor, you command the second. If you see that we don't get across the chain then help us to get back to the bay before morning and then no one will be any the wiser that we tried to escape."

And so it was decided. Harald selected his crews, and two galleys were surreptitiously prepared for a long journey. But it was a journey which Halldor was never to make.

The conversation between the three men had severely shaken Ivar and plunged him into near panic. By virtue of his oath to Harald, he was bound to remain totally loyal, and yet now he had another obligation: to maintain and care for Aveline. From what Harald Hardrada had said, the escape attempt would be in a few weeks, so he had a little time in which to solve this tortuous situation.

For some nights, sleep did not come easily to Ivar while he mulled over the possibilities, or indeed lack of possibilities, to solve his problem. He had not dared to mention to Aveline that he might have to abandon her in Constantinople. Indeed, to mention to her that his master intended to escape would be a breach of trust. He had quite a large sum of money which he could leave with her, though his main asset was the plunder saved for him in Kiev. If he left her with money, sooner or later it would run out, and besides he had grown close to her and he did not want to leave her to other men. He had to find a solution which did not involve telling her about the escape plans.

Each evening on his way back to the barracks from the house where Aveline was living, he passed the quay by the Prosphorian harbour where their ships were berthed. Other ships came and went: traders' vessels, war galleys and sometimes ships bearing pilgrims travelling to and from the Holy Land. These pilgrims came from all over Europe and, in Constantinople, those making their way to holy places disembarked to continue their journey on foot. Their places were taken on the ships by pilgrims returning from Jerusalem. But there were always fewer of the latter than the former as many died en route from the many dangers they encountered.

One evening, as Ivar walked around the harbour wall, despite the noise of the crowded wharf, he heard the sound of women chanting. Curious to know what the source of the noise was, he pushed through the bustling crowd of merchants, sailors, vendors and stevedores. There, by the side of a large vessel, was a group of nuns. The state of their clothes and the demeanour of several of them betrayed the fact that they had travelled some distance. They were chanting a psalm in Latin, and several were praying.

Ivar turned to one of the onlookers and enquired what

was going on. He was told that the French nuns had arrived in Constantinople penniless and hungry after being robbed on the journey from Jerusalem. They were desperate to find passage back to France on the ship moored behind them, but they could not pay for the passage.

Ivar pushed his way to the front of the crowd and, when the chanting stopped, he beckoned to one of the nuns, the one who appeared to be senior, to come and speak with him.

"Sister, is it true that you do not have funds to travel back to France?"

"Yes, sir. We have travelled far, but now cannot go further until the Lord provides for us to sail home."

"How much does the captain ask for your passage?"

"Thirty pieces of silver for each of us. We are hoping that the good people of Constantinople will give us alms to pay for the journey."

Ivar looked along the line of nuns to be sure that he had counted correctly. If he did what he planned, he would have very little silver left. He left the nun and clambered on board the ship.

"Halloo!" he called.

One of the crew who was resting under an awning stood up and sauntered over to Ivar. "What do you want?" he asked tetchily.

"Where are you sailing to?"

"Massilia."[59]

"How much will it cost for these nuns to travel with you?"

"You paying in silver?"

"Yes."

The man drew a breath, looked across at the nuns, and did the same calculation which Ivar had done. "Two hundred and ten silver pieces."

---

[59]   Massilia – Marseille

"I want one more to travel and I will pay you two hundred."

"No, it is not enough."

"Then I will find another ship," threatened Ivar.

"Alright, alright, two hundred. But hurry; we leave at first light."

Ivar jumped off the ship and sought out the nun he had spoken to before.

"Sister, I will pay for your journey, but on one condition."

The nun looked at him with disbelief. "You will pay for all of us?"

"Yes, I will, but you must agree to my terms."

The nun was choking back tears when she said, "Anything, anything we can do, we will."

"I want you to take my wife with you. You must look after her and, when you arrive in France, you must arrange for her to travel safely to her home in Normandy."

"We will, we will. Rest assured, dear sir. Bless you, bless you."

The challenge now was for Ivar to explain the plan to Aveline. He retraced his steps to the little house and banged on the door. She was surprised but pleased to see him as he entered the house.

"Listen, Aveline, I have arranged transport for you back to France and then to Normandy."

"What…when?"

"Tomorrow morning."

"Tomorrow! You are coming too?"

"No, I cannot. But I will, believe me I will."

"But how shall I travel?"

Ivar explained the situation with the nuns and the undertaking they had made to see that Aveline was returned safely to her home in Domfront. She was excited at the prospect, but concerned that she would never see Ivar again.

"When we arrive back in the northlands, after I have served my master for the tenth year, he will give me my freedom. Then I shall come to find you."

Ivar did not return to the barracks that night and hoped that his master did not seek him to do any tasks. The next morning, just after dawn, the pair were at the harbour, as were the nuns.

Ivar paid over the two hundred pieces of silver to the captain and gave the rest of his silver to Aveline. An hour later, the ship was already so far distant that he could not make out the figure in the stern waving to him.

The night chosen by Harald Hardrada for the escape attempt was in mid-August. It was a moonless night so that the chance of the two galleys being seen as they were quietly pulled out of the bay were minimised. But this precaution was to contribute to the disaster.

In the poor light, the lead crew had trouble finding the chain. They were forced to row in towards the shore again and to follow it from where it was linked to the land. Eventually, Harald decided to make his run at the barrier. First, a lantern was dropped on a float to mark the chain; then the galley circled back to give the rowers distance so that they could get up speed. The crew pulled at the oars with all their strength and, by the time they were approaching the lantern, the boat had reached top speed. At Harald's command, the crew pulled in their oars and rushed to the stern. Exactly as Harald had predicted, the bow rode over the chain. The weight then being transferred to the bow, the craft slowly but surely slid down the far side.

Now it was the turn of the second galley. Harald's ship hove to near to the chain to watch, such as they could in the dark night. They heard the splash of the oars as the galley rushed at the chain, the grinding sound as the hull slid up the chain, a rush of feet as the crew transferred to the bow, and then nothing. Suddenly, there was a loud crack followed by the sound of splintering timbers and the curses of men. The galley had wedged on top of the chain and then the back of the ship had broken.

Men were leaping into the sea. Some could swim; most could not. Harald's ship circled round near to the wreck trying to pick up survivors, but in the darkness it was almost impossible to find them. Seven men were pulled from the Bosphorus, including Ulf. The others would never enjoy their wealth, the product of eight years' campaigning.

Time was of the essence. Harald's galley had to be a considerable distance from Constantinople before their disappearance was discovered. With the wreck and the drowned Varangians behind them, the rowers pulled away as fast as they could.

It was on the long journey up the Dnieper that Harald told his crew the truth. He stood in the prow of the galley to address his men. He looked at them; each one of the battle-hardened men had fought alongside him for nearly eight years, he knew them all by name. But he was also aware that, of the five hundred warriors he had taken to Miklagård, less than forty were going home with him. Some of them were rich; others had spent all their fortunes on wine, women and gambling. But they had all served him faithfully, and he wanted them to know why he had to leave Constantinople in such great haste, before they discovered for themselves.

"When we were in Constantinople, a trader passed me a secret message from Grand Prince Jaroslav. The letter put me in a position where I had to leave the employ of the Byzantine Emperor as quickly as possible."

There was a general low-toned buzz of comment between the listeners.

"Well, tell us then," shouted Ulf.

"The Prince is gathering his forces to mount a full-scale attack on Constantinople next year. His army will of course include Varangians. In fact, you are free to offer your swords to his army if you wish."

Ulf, the only man with high enough rank to dare to challenge Harald, stood up and interjected, "But that would mean that we would be fighting against our comrades, those who we have left behind!"

"Yes, this is true. But worse would it have been if we had stayed: we would have had to fight for the Byzantine Emperor against the army of Prince Jaroslav, the man who guards our money and controls the route back to our homes in the north."

"And who is your future father-in-law!" called Ulf.

There were many guffaws around the crew. It was common knowledge that Harald had his sights on Princess Elizavet.

Harald's persistent officer spoke out again, "Why didn't you tell us this before?"

"The Prince had sworn me to secrecy. He was afraid that if word got out about the invasion he would lose the advantage of surprise. But there is another reason why he wanted me to make haste to Kiev. We have detailed knowledge of the deployment of all the Byzantine army and navy. This information is very valuable to the Prince."

"So what are your plans now? Will we go on to Novgorod this year?"

"No, I will spend some time advising the Rus army and dealing with financial affairs."

All of the crew knew what Harald meant by the latter statement. He had freighted enormous quantities of precious objects to Kiev, as had some of them. These objects had to be sold and their value exchanged for gold and silver which could be more easily transported back to their homes in the north.

*Laden with the richest cargo, you launched your swift ship, Harald carrying gold from Gardar[60] – Hard-won with honour – westward. Through storm and gale you steered, sturdy chieftain. Ships wallowed deep until at last, through thinning spindrift, you sighted Sigtuna.*

Harald's skald, Valgard of Voll[61]

---

[60] Gardar – the land of the Rus
[61] Skald – court poet. Valgard accompanied Harald to Miklagård

★

In the event, Harald spent three winters in Kiev, as did many of his remaining men. When he requested the hand of Prince Jarolslav's daughter, the ruler of the Rus found no reason not to bless the union. In the spring of 1045, Harald started the long journey with his wife Elizaveta and thirty warriors, back to the northlands. In the autumn, they arrived in Sigtuna, and there they were once again welcomed by King Anund.

Through the long winter, Harald spent many hours in discussion with another visitor: a Danish earl, Svein, who had fled into exile from Denmark. Together they plotted an invasion of Zealand in that country to restore Svein to power.

Ivar was conscious that an anniversary had been reached, one he had been looking forward to for ten years.

"Sir, more than ten years ago, you told me that you required me to give you that length of service before I could become a free man." Ivar looked nervously across the table at the warrior leader. Harald was just thirty years old. His long, shoulder-length, blond hair framed a young face made older by the long moustache.

"But, Ivar, we have fought a hundred battles together. You have never flinched with fear. Now we are going to start a new campaign to restore Svein to his kingdom."

"But, sir, that is not a battle I want to join you in. My home is in Zealand. I have no wish to fight against my friends and family."

Harald tugged at his moustache as he considered his reaction. "Did you make much money in Miklagård?"

"I did, sir, and I am thankful for it."

"What would you do if I give you your freedom?"

"Sir, I am but two years older than you and I am an experienced warrior. When we were in Sicily, I heard from the Normans that there is constant fighting between the French, the Bretons and the Normans, many of whom are Danish born and most of Norse descent. I will offer my sword to the Norman cause. There is good chance of employment there."

"How will you use your money?"

"I will buy land in Normandy and settle there."

Harald smiled and intoned in a quiet voice, "So be it then."

When the spring came, Ivar, with his new found freedom, his silver, his sword and byrnie, took passage on a trading ship bound for Rouen.

# Chapter 19

## A Turbulent Year

*Easter was on the sixteenth day before the calends of May. Then was over all England such a token seen as no man ever saw before. Some men said that it was the comet-star, which others called the long-haired star. It appeared first on the eighth before the calends of May; and so shone all the week.*

The Anglo-Saxon Chronicle AD 1066

The appearance of a comet[62] which had not been seen for seventy-five years was regarded by many, on both sides of the channel, to be a portent of a great event. Most agreed that it foretold doom or disaster. And, for England, the first disaster was when Tostig attacked and plundered the Isle of Wight in May.

After resupplying his fleet with the proceeds of his raid on the island, the sixty ships, manned mainly by Flemish mercenaries, then sailed eastwards raiding coastal towns and recruiting English seamen and soldiers. Many willingly joined Tostig with the promise of plunder and land. King Harold was forced to raise a huge army to meet the threat but, at Sandwich, Tostig escaped a confrontation and eventually reached the Humber. There he was defeated by the northern Earls, but again he managed to escape, though with only twelve of his ships. He

---

[62] Halley's Comet appeared in spring 1066

sailed on north to the River Tyne, and there he waited. He waited, for he had an assignation with the greatest warrior of the age: Harald Hardrada.

Torkil had been summoned by the King to take his housecarls east to join in the unsuccessful campaign to bring Tostig to battle at Sandwich. He was charged with a desire to take revenge on the man whose mercenaries had killed his mother and burned his home, but the opportunity to settle this score evaded him when it became clear that Tostig had escaped. Torkil and his men were then transferred back to central southern England to strengthen the defences there. It was well known that William was making preparations for the invasion and that, from the beginning of August, his forces and fleet were at Dives on the Normandy coast, almost due south of the Isle of Wight. This fact, their experience in Normandy and the raid by Tostig on the island strengthened the King's conviction that the Normans would make their landing in this area. The view was reinforced by the realisation that the provincial capital and site of his treasury, Wintoncaestre, was likely to be the Duke's primary target.

Lammas was the time when most peasants would be harvesting the first wheat to make the new bread from the year's early crop. A good harvest would guarantee food through the winter and, of all the crops, the most important was wheat. While Europeans preferred rye, the English made their bread with wheat flour, using barley as a second choice. But this August, most of the harvesters were women, children and old men, for the King had called up all of the fyrdsmen. At the beginning of August, there was an army of almost fifty thousand men stationed along the coast. The King's fleet of seven hundred ships was now based in the waters around the Isle of Wight ready to meet the invasion. When it was decided to bolster the defence of the island, Torkil was given orders to take five hundred housecarls and two thousand fyrdsmen across the water to protect the island ports.

And so this massive force waited throughout August for the anticipated invasion. It did not come, and on 8 September, King Harold decided to disband part of his army and allow the fyrdsmen to return to their homes to help with the wheat harvest.

The King also decided to stand down the fleet, and ordered his ships to sail to London. But the autumn storms began early that year and, on its way up the channel, a large proportion of the English fleet was wrecked. This was the same bad weather which had been keeping Duke William in harbour and caused him to delay the invasion. But he had no intention of invading the Isle of Wight and Hamwic, though he had fooled the Anglo-Saxons into believing so. The south-east coast was his target.

Duke William moved his forces, which now numbered fourteen thousand men, east to Saint-Valéry. On this journey, he too suffered losses of ships and men through the ravages of storms.

In September, Torkil received orders to travel to London to join the advisors helping the King with his disposition of forces. The loss of part of his fleet concerned the King greatly as he had had word from spies in Scandinavia that Harald Hardrada, now King of Norway, was also making a claim on the English throne.

It was in the third week of September that the whole council assembled to consider the military position.

"We have left a substantial force on the south coast to deter William. As time goes by and the autumn weather becomes less dependable, it will be impossible for him to make a safe passage across the channel, and we can withdraw some of our troops. As for the Norwegians, they are even more dependent on good weather to make a long passage from the north," said the King.

"But there is still another month before such voyages would be too foolhardy. We must continue to maintain vigilance," said Gyrth, the King's brother.

"And what say you, Torkil?" asked the King.

"Your Majesty, since it is my island which suffers invaders first and most, I think that we should maintain the standing army on the coast until late November."

Just then, there was loud banging on the door to the council chamber. Two guards opened the door and a messenger strode in.

"What news have you?" demanded Gyrth.

"My Lords, the Norwegians are upon us with a huge army. They have made common cause with Tostig and have invaded the lands of the Earl Northumberland. They have sacked and burnt Skarthi's Burg."[63]

There was silence in the room while everyone considered this staggering news. All of their deliberations and decisions had concerned the threat from the south.

"Surely the northern earls can defeat them," said Leofwine.

"If they are moving down the coast then it is likely that they intend to attack York. The Earls Morcar and Edwin have their forces there. They will be able to defend it," said Gyrth.

"I don't trust those two. They might even reach an understanding with Hardrada," said the King.

"But they hate Tostig. They would never make a deal which involves him," answered Leofwine.

"In any case, I cannot rely on Earl Morcar to defeat the Norwegians. We must do it."

There was silence in the room while they all considered the possibility of quickly assembling a large army, thus denuding the defences against William. Their force would have to march almost two hundred miles to meet the Norsemen. They were all considering the options and where they would find the necessary troops when the King stood up, clenched his right fist and punched it into his left palm.

"Godric, Torkil, organise the housecarls for a march as soon as possible. Gyrth, mobilise the thaynes and fyrdsmen. We will

---

[63]   Skarthi's Burg – Scarborough

pick up more men on our way north. If we do this speedily, we may surprise the Norwegians. We must leave in two days."

There was no dissent; no one dared counsel the King that this was an extremely risky venture. Men quickly left the room to deal with their allotted tasks.

On the morning of 19 September, the great column of men left London on a forced march northwards. The army started out from Bishopsgate and followed the Roman road, Erninga Straete.[64] By the time they had reached Toteham,[65] six miles north, and units had joined from east and west of London, the eleven thousand man procession was nearly seven miles long. The more privileged, the housecarls and the thaynes, were mounted on horseback. They rode in pairs. The journey would be a huge strain on the animals so the horsemen travelled lightly, leaving their weapons to be transported in the wagon train. The fyrdsmen, the majority of the army, were on foot. They carried their shields strapped on their backs and walked with their spears in their hands or, in the case of the archers, they had a quiver of arrows and their bows over their shoulders. Behind the column, the long wagon train carrying the tools of war and supplies trundled at the best speed possible trying to keep up with the men. These vehicles were covered by greased awnings stretched on frames of split hazel wood to protect the goods from the weather.

Officers rode up and down the column with messages and to give encouragement and occasionally threats to the marching men who, covering around thirty-five miles a day on foot, were being pushed to the extremes of endurance.

Messengers were also sent out ahead of the column to the proposed overnight stops, which included Cambridge and Lincylene,[66] to ensure that preparations were in hand to provide

---

[64]  Erninga Straete – Ermine Street, the main Roman road north

[65]  Toteham – Tottenham

[66]  Lincylene – Lincoln

food and water for the huge contingent which would soon be arriving.

At the head of the column, each time they came to a populated area, the King's standard bearers unfurled the royal banners: the Dragon of Wessex and the Fighting Man. As the King had predicted, more thaynes and fyrdsmen rallied around the standards and joined the force as the procession passed through towns and villages. The army had swelled to fifteen thousand by the time they reached Tadcaster late in the evening on 24 September. It took over two hours from when the vanguard entered the town to when the last wagons rolled in.

En route to the north, the King received reports that the Norwegians had three hundred ships. The fleet had found its way up the Humber and into the river Ouse.

"With three hundred ships, they could transport almost twenty thousand men. It will be a formidable force which we go to meet, Godric," said Torkil.

"Our best chance to prevail will be to surprise them," answered Godric, stating the obvious, but privately considering what chance their largely untried army would have against the experienced and well trained Norwegian force which might be far superior in numbers.

"It could be that they have already been defeated by Morcar," Torkil said wishfully.

His hope was quickly dashed when another messenger arrived. He brought news of a great battle outside York. Morcar and Edwin had been defeated and their men slaughtered or put to flight. The two Earls had escaped and taken refuge in York while terms were negotiated with King Harald Hardrada.

After a few hours' rest, early on the morning of 25 September, the royal army left Tadcaster for York. On their way, the King received news that York was to be surrendered by the English Earls that day, and the remnants of their forces would join Hardrada's army to march south. The Earls had agreed to give Hardrada one hundred and fifty children of well-to-do citizens of their earldoms as hostages to guarantee that the Earls would serve him loyally. In return, the Norwegian was to give the Earls the same number of soldiers as hostage to guarantee that they were allied.

As they approached York, the King called to Torkil to come to him.

"Take twenty housecarls with you and ride ahead to the city to find out where this exchange of hostages will take place."

"I will meet you later at the city gate, Your Majesty."

Torkil gathered his force and galloped off to see Earl Morcar to get the information the King required. On arrival at the city gate, Torkil was relieved to see that there did not appear to be any Norwegian troops in the town. The streets were deserted, but there were signs of looting with many broken doors and smashed gates. With some difficulty, the small force found where Earl Morcar was hiding. At first, he was not willing to give Torkil any information but, when it was pointed out that the King was approaching York with a substantial army and that the Earl's lack of cooperation amounted to treason, Torkil found out what he needed to know. Later, as the column approached the gate, Torkil and his men rode out to meet it.

"The exchange is to take place at a crossing of the River Derwent, Stamford Bridge, today."

"How far is it from here?"

"Six miles to the east on the Roman road, Your Highness. The Norwegians have their fleet moored on the River Ouse at Richale,[67] six miles to the south."

"Then we rest here for two hours and prepare for battle."

The men gratefully dragged off their byrnies. Their faces were caked in grime from a mixture of sweat and the dust which had been raised by the tramping of thousands of feet on

---

[67] Richale – Ricall

the dry, hot road. They sat or sprawled wherever they could find a space in the shade to rest after their exhausting march.

The mood at the Norwegians' encampment at Richale was jubilant as they sorted the plunder they had assimilated from the sacking of York. But Harald Hardrada was worried. They needed massive continuous supplies to feed their army which, even after the battle and the loss of many troops, still numbered around sixteen thousand. York had been emptied of grain and meat. In consequence of this, the victorious commander had ordered that cattle from all over the hinterland of York should be herded to the place where the exchange of hostages was to take place and that the grain supplies from the surrounding countryside should be brought there too.

The morning of 25 September dawned sunny and bright, promising a fine day to come. Hardrada conferred with his officers, and they decided that two thirds of the army would stay to guard the fleet and he would take just over five thousand of the force with him, including Tostig and his English and Flemish mercenaries, to collect the hostages and the supplies. Hardrada's senior officers, including Olof his son, would stay to command the remaining army. Since the weather was so unseasonably warm and they had eleven miles to travel, most of the men on foot, the Norwegian King allowed those of his troops who wanted to to leave their heavy chain mail armour and spears on the ships. Almost all of the warriors, including the King, only took their shields and an axe or a sword.

When the Norwegians reached Stamford, they found that the place was well chosen: it was at the crossroads of several Roman roads and there was plentiful water for the cattle. The hostages had not yet arrived, but some cattle were already there and the soldiers set about herding them on the right side of the bridge. They had posted no lookouts on the approach roads as, after their crushing defeat of the English force, they felt secure. Thus, their commander was concerned when one of his men pointed out to him a huge cloud of dust in the direction of York. Very soon, they could make out the shape of men tramping towards them, their weapons reflecting in the sun. At first, Hardrada thought that the approaching force was some of his men sent to join him by Olof. But when the banners came into sight, it soon became apparent that this was not the case.

Tostig advised that they should make a fighting retreat to their ships as they had neither the numbers nor the equipment to guarantee a victory. But Hardrada saw this as an opportunity to add to his long list of successful battles for surely, if this was indeed the English army, their King must be at the head of it. He gave orders for three of his best riders to gallop back to the fleet to summon reinforcements and for his army to deploy on the right bank of the river around his personal banner, the Land Ravager.

As they approached the bridge, the English King ordered his advanced guard to go forward to attack the Norwegians who had been furthest from the bridge collecting cattle on the left side. The cattle scattered and the Norsemen were quickly dispatched.

"Gyrth, stay with the army in case ill should befall me. Torkil and Godric, choose twenty housecarls to come to the bridge with me to parley. I will act as my own herald. Do not mention that I am the King."

The small group of Englishmen rode up to the left side of the bridge. Seeing this, Hardrada called Tostig and his bodyguard, and prepared to ride up to the bridge on the right side.

King Harold had noticed that when a very tall Norwegian warrior tried to mount his black horse he was immediately thrown and had to try again.

"That big man must be Hardrada, Your Majesty," said Torkil.

Hardrada rode slowly up to the bridge. The forty-four

year-old English King studied the fifty-one year-old King Harald Hardrada intently for a short while and then, wrongly assuming that the Norwegian spoke no English at all, turned and addressed Tostig.

"Tostig, if you change sides I will restore your earldom and you shall have one third of the kingdom," said the King.

"In such a case, what would happen to Harald Hardrada?" enquired Tostig.

Referring to the Norwegian's great height, the King replied, "We will give him seven feet of ground or as much more as he is taller than other men."

"I would not have it said of me that I brought the Norwegian King here to betray him." With that, Tostig turned his horse's head, and he and his companions returned towards the defensive shield wall which the Norwegians had prepared.

"Who was that herald who spoke so well?" enquired Hardrada of Tostig.

"That was King Harold, my brother."

"Had I known, I would have killed him on the spot."

"I know you would have, but I do not want his blood on my hands," said Tostig.

As Torkil rode back towards the English line, he was pensive for he had seen a face from the past. One of the horsemen in Tostig's bodyguard was Egbert of Boseham. There could be no doubt about it. He was grey-haired now, but Torkil would never forget the man who had murdered his crew all those years ago. He must have joined Tostig's mercenary force when they were raiding the south coast.

The battle commenced when the English force again attacked a few Norwegians who had returned from herding cattle only to find themselves on the wrong side of the bridge. But when the King's men tried to get over the narrow bridge, their way was blocked by a huge figure of a man, the Norwegian champion, a man who had taken his armour and weapons with him to Stamford. He was valiantly defending the passage across to his comrades. This single man wielded a battle axe so effectively that he stopped the English advance and killed several of the advancing soldiers.

The King saw some of his archers taking aim at the man. "Hold, this man has shown great valour. I will pardon him."

The offer was made to the man but he refused it and did not budge from his position.

*But there was one of the Norwegians who withstood the English Folk, so that they could not pass over the bridge, nor complete the Victory. An Englishman aimed at him with a javelin, but it availed Nothing. Then came another under the bridge, who pierced him terribly inwards under the coat of mail. And Harold King of the English, then came over the bridge.*

The Anglo-Saxon Chronicle AD 1066

Hardrada had formed his forces into a semicircular line with his axe men in reserve at the back defending his standard.

The English archers fired several volleys of arrows at the shield wall before a rain of spears was launched at the defenders, pitched over their shields by the fyrdsmen. Then the housecarl axe men advanced. They crashed their axes on the wall of shields, trying to break through. Where they did find a gap, the swordsmen joined them. This was a dangerous venture as sometimes the Norwegians opened the wall slightly to let attackers in to slaughter them before closing the wall again.

The Norwegians fought savagely against the overwhelming numbers of the English until, when their shield wall was eventually beginning to break, it was suddenly opened and Hardrada, screaming in the manner of the Viking *berserks*,[68] led his warriors to counter-attack. They were at a severe

---

[68]  Berserks were Norse warriors who whipped themselves into a trance-like wild frenzy of aggression

disadvantage now in hand-to-hand combat; most were lightly armed with only swords, and few had armour or helmets.

As the giant Norwegian King launched himself, sword in hand, at the attacking English, he received a fatal wound, an arrow through his throat. He crashed to the ground, dying. The great warrior, victor of a hundred battles, had been killed by an arrow which his thick neck armour would have protected him from.

The now leaderless Norsemen continued to attack violently, but were slowly driven back. As the slaughter continued, Tostig retreated to the standard to protect their late commander's Land Ravager flag. There was no question of a pardon from his brother, and it was in front of the Norwegian standard that Tostig and his mercenaries were killed.

The battle was over, but there was still noise and confusion on the field. Injured horses and lowing cattle joined the chorus of the screams of the wounded and the cheering of the victors. Torkil joined the English soldiers as they began to plunder the dead and dying foe. This was a right always afforded by a victorious commander to his men. But Torkil was not interested in general plunder: he was searching for a particular member of the enemy. He wandered between the pools of blood where even the grass was red, the piles of discarded weapons, and the corpses. A few of the Norwegians had survived, but they were shown no mercy by the troops who had spent six long days marching to meet them, not knowing if they would be the victors or the vanquished, constantly worrying whether they would see their homes again. Now, as masters of the field of battle, in many cases that concern had turned to vindictiveness.

When Torkil eventually found Egbert, he was sitting among the corpses. He had a severe slash to his shoulder, but was still alive.

The sitting man cringed slightly as the shadow of Torkil fell across him.

"I have come to keep my promise, Egbert. Do you remember the boy you threw from the galley near to Boseham? The one whose pendant you stole?"

The old soldier looked up at the standing figure above him and, with the one arm he could use, slowly pulled at something under his bloodied shirt. He handed the silver chain with the bear's claw to Torkil.

"This was my promise," said Torkil as he raised his sword and then, with all his force, swept it sideways to sever the mercenary's head from his shoulders.

Torkil's quest for Egbert had distracted him from his duties as an officer. Over the moaning of the wounded, the whinnying of the injured horses, and the victory whoops of the English soldiers, Torkil became aware of renewed clashes of metal on metal. The fighting had resumed!

He looked round and there, streaming towards them from the south, was a huge army of men in full armour. The messengers sent by Hardrada to his fleet had done their work, and now the remainder of his army had raced to the field of battle. Wearing their heavy armour, it had taken them three exhausting hours to reach the scene in the hot weather but, despite this, they were a formidable force and almost immediately succeeded in breaking the English line which had been hastily reassembled. The fighting was even more intense than in the earlier battle, for now both armies were evenly matched in weaponry and armour. The English had lost many men in the earlier conflict, and so the numbers now were roughly equal on each side. While the Norwegians were very tired from their effort to rush to Stamford, the English were suffering from the physical strain of a six-day forced march and the earlier battle. The carnage was awful as the two sides attacked and counter-attacked. King Harold's line held and fierce hand-to-hand fighting continued until nightfall by which time all the Norwegian officers, except Olof who had stayed with the ships, had been killed. Taking advantage of the dark, the remaining Norwegians fled back towards their fleet.

The English pursued the Norwegians to Richale and set fire to many of the ships before Olof surrendered. Seeing that the foe were no longer a threat to his country, the victorious King Harold offered Olof and the survivors safe passage back to Norway. Of the three hundred ships which had brought the Norsemen to England, only twenty-four vessels were needed to take the Norwegian army home. But the English had also sustained great losses with almost five thousand dead; losses which they could ill afford in view of the other threat to the country.

The King and his housecarls returned to York where they stayed for two days, but the monarch realised that now he must hurry south to counter the menace of Duke William. He decided to leave with his housecarls, and ordered those of his army who were to make the long journey on foot to follow as soon as possible.

# Chapter 20

## The Battle of Hastings

At around eleven in the morning on 25 September, the Normans started landing on Pevensey beach in Kent. News of the landing was given to the King while he was making the gruelling dash back to London from Yorkshire. Before entering the city, he stopped to pray at Waltham Abbey, to give thanks for his victory over Harald Hardrada. He then hastened to London to consult with his brothers Gyrth and Leofwine about the new threat to his realm.

"The King is returned from Waltham," said Godric.

"Then we must hasten to attend him and counsel him to be prudent about early action against the Normans," said Torkil.

Godric and Torkil found the King in the Great Hall, already in conference with his advisors. Gyrth was speaking. "We have lost too many men at Stamford. We must wait for two weeks to gather all available forces. If we do, we can mount an army at least three times the size of that of the Normans."

"But now we have the foe trapped on the peninsula.[69] If we strike now, we can drive them back into the sea. They are killing my people, plundering Sussex, and burning towns and villages.

---

[69]   At this time the area north of Hastings was a peninsula with only a narrow strip of land as access

I have a duty to defend my people. We must also consider that the longer we wait, the more likely it is that reinforcements will arrive from Normandy," answered the King.

Gyrth was adamant. "They are pillaging and burning in Sussex to provoke you into a hasty reaction, a too hasty one. They know of our battle in the north; they want us to react while we are weak. And we are weak. Much of our army including the corps of archers is still marching south from York. They will be here in a few days. If we move now, we will have no bowmen to fell the Norman knights."

They were all aware of the investment which the Normans had put into their mounted armoured cavalry on heavy horses. But they were also aware that these knights were vulnerable to well aimed arrows.

"So what do you propose?" asked Leofwine.

"We should build up our forces to give us superiority. We need just a week or two. Meanwhile, we will burn everything between London and Hastings. It is now October. There is little enough forage for an army. If we destroy the hinterland in Sussex, William's army may not starve but their horses will, and that will make them easy prey for us."

There was a long silence while everyone waited for the King's reaction.

At last he asked, "How many men do we have?"

Gyrth looked at Godric and waited for the senior housecarl to provide the answer.

Godric hesitated as he knew that his answer would decide the outcome of the discussion, and the news he had to give would not find favour with the King. "Your Majesty, we have lost nearly a thousand housecarls. There are now only two and a half thousand. There are about two thousand thanes and three thousand fyrdsmen. We have a few hundred mercenaries but no cavalry, and only a small number of the fyrdsmen can be relied on to be effective archers. Some of the fyrdsmen fought at Stamford, but many are novices, serving their lords for the first time. Our horses are tired from the long journey from York. They have been pushed to the limit covering almost two hundred miles in each direction. To meet the Normans, they would need to travel another sixty miles. We learnt much about the Norman methods of warfare when we were in France. The army needs time to train to counter these."

Gyrth interrupted Godric. "So more than a third of our army at the moment are fyrdsmen, the weakest troops?"

The King dismissed Gyrth's statement. "But each of them has at least a spear and a shield to serve their masters. Some of these so-called novices can be used for non-combat roles: they can tend the horses, bring up water for the warriors and defend the wagon train."

Just then, there was a commotion at the back of the hall, and a monk was escorted in between two housecarls.

"Who is this?" demanded the King.

One of the housecarls said, "An emissary from Duke William, Your Majesty."

The King's advisors parted to allow the emissary forward. The monk stood in front of Harold and addressed him directly in Anglo-Saxon. "I am Hugh Margot of Fécamp. Duke William has sent me to demand your immediate surrender and for you to give recognition that the Duke is the rightful sovereign of England."

There was silence in the room while everyone waited for a response from the King.

"I will give you safe passage back to your master to tell him that the only part of England he shall have will be the six-foot hole which will be his grave."

The monk's skill at diplomacy was not apparent when he answered. "I am sure he will have a six-foot hole, but that will not be needed for many years after you have filled one for, if you refuse to recognise his claim, he challenges you to single-armed combat."

The King leapt out of his chair and grabbed the monk by the throat, forcing him against the wall. Both Gyrth and Leofwine ran over to try to restrain the angry monarch.

"Don't kill him, we need him to take a message back!" shouted Gyrth.

Harold glared at the dishevelled monk whose hood had fallen back to reveal the grey hair round his tonsure.

"Tell your master that there is no escape for him over land or across the sea. Norman blood will pollute the soil of this fair country ere long. Now go!"

Torkil spoke loudly. "Your Majesty, this man is no more a monk than I am. He is a spy. I have seen him twice before. I recognise the scar across his head and the wound to his left ear. Blindfold him before you order him out so that he cannot collect any more intelligence for Duke William."

The monk was seized by the two housecarls, blindfolded, and hurried across the room and out of the door.

The King was still visibly angry when he asked Leofwine, "What date is it today?"

"The ninth of October."

"We march on the eleventh. Godric, arrange for the fleet to move to Sandwich to cut off the retreat of the Norman army when they try to return across the channel."

Gyrth intervened. "If we wait just a few more days, the levies of new troops will start to arrive."

Voices were being raised now, but Torkil plucked up courage to interject. "Your Majesty, we can use this emissary to our advantage. If we send him back to the Duke with a question, it will take him at least three days to reach his master, a day to consult, and then three days to get back here with the answer. Meanwhile, we would have a week more to strengthen our army."

"And what question would you have him ask?"

"Whether, if you recognise William's claim, the great

Anglo-Saxon earls, including yourself, could keep their lands and privileges."

"Such a question would denote that we are in a position of weakness. We are not. We march on the eleventh," repeated the King.

"Then let me lead the army. If we lose and I am killed then you will still be alive to lead a second army to defeat the Normans when they are weakened," reasoned Gyrth.

"You and Leofwine and all my senior men will accompany me to see our victory over the enemy. My commanders must now make preparations. Give orders that, when reinforcements arrive, they should make haste to join us."

With that, the conversation was ended and the King left the hall. Torkil and Godric went out to spread the news to the housecarls. When they were out of earshot of the others, Godric turned to Torkil and said, "Our impetuous master may get us all killed."

Torkil nodded.

There were many preparations to be made in a short time. Weapons had to be sharpened, supplies obtained and packed ready for transport, and armour and weapons stowed in wagons, while some warriors had to be recalled from their homes. The latter was impossible in many cases as they lived too far from London. Thus it was that on the morning of 11 October, the army of just over seven thousand men, which marched eastwards out of London, consisted of a motley mixture of thoroughly hardened and battle-tried veterans, and fyrdsmen, many of the latter never having seen action before.

The long procession of men, horses and wagons got longer and longer as the faster mounted troops made better time. Each evening, when the leaders stopped, it took several hours for the slowest travellers to arrive at the night's encampment. A fine drizzle soaked the foot soldiers and officers alike on the second day. The previous night, most had got what sleep was possible lying on open ground; the lucky ones had found a billet in a village; some slept under the wagons, but most had only their cloaks for cover. Thus, the second night was even more uncomfortable as they dozed in their wet clothes. By the evening of the thirteenth, the leaders had reached the eastern end of the downs and emerged from the wooded hills on to Caldbec Hill. On the hill, there was an old apple tree. This had been designated the rallying point for King Harold's army. By two in the morning, the whole army was in place, and the men got what rest they could before the inevitable battle on the morrow.

At first light, it was apparent that another hill, Battle Hill, would be the best strategic position for an army to occupy. Duke William had also realised this, and a race began to take possession of the hill. Harold sent his mounted infantry to lay claim to the position while foot soldiers struggled to reinforce the occupation. William sent his archers to attack the foot soldiers. For the first time, the Anglo-Saxons had a taste of the deadly effect of a new weapon: the crossbow. This shattered the morale of some of the fyrdsmen. But Harold's men prevailed, and the hill was taken and occupied by the Anglo-Saxon army.

All of the King's horsemen dismounted as fighting on foot was their custom, and the horses were taken to the rear. The King's standards, the Dragon of Wessex and the Fighting Man, were flying in the centre of the army's line which stretched out four hundred paces on each side. In the front row were the housecarls and mercenaries in their coats of mail, each wearing a helmet and carrying a shield. At the beginning of the battle, they were armed with javelins, their swords and double-handed axes placed behind them for later use in hand-to-hand fighting. The fyrdsmen were placed in the row immediately behind, together with the thaynes.

This formidable force looked down on the enemy. The Norman army, although equal in numbers, comprised more seasoned professional soldiers and a more varied force, with cavalry and archers which the Anglo-Saxons lacked. The Normans were well rested and better armed.

Both commanders addressed their men, riding up and down the ranks, exhorting them about the strengths of their armies and the weaknesses of the other's. But, in Harold's case, he was already concerned that some of the untried fyrdsmen had deserted after experiencing the crossbow fusillade. He urged the army not to break ranks but to hold their order.

William organised his army for the general advance. He was mounted on a fine warhorse, a gift from King Alonso of Spain. He was in the centre of the line of Norman soldiers and archers with his standard bearer. To his left were Breton soldiers and on his right, mercenaries and French troops. William too was worried about the morale of his troops, and decided to take a gamble to boost their confidence. He called for a volunteer to meet an Anglo-Saxon in single combat. His gamble paid off and the volunteer, Taillefer, killed his Anglo-Saxon opponent before he himself was killed when, alone, he charged up the hill to his enemy's line.

Then the Normans began their advance. Torkil was standing with the housecarls on the right of the line, two hundred paces from the King. They watched as the Breton soldiers laboured up the hill towards them. The fyrdsmen had a supply of missiles: hatchets, javelins and even rocks to bombard the advancing troops with. Unsettled by the rain of arrows flying towards them, some of the fyrdsmen started throwing the objects while the advancing troops were out of range.

"Wait, you fools; let them get closer," shouted Torkil.

The advancing bowmen were finding it difficult to shoot accurately while ascending the hill. Their arrows were either going over the heads of the defenders or hitting their shields, and thus they were having little effect.

"Now!" shouted Torkil. The housecarls threw their javelins

and then stooped behind their shields while the fyrdsmen in the rows behind dispatched their missiles.

The Normans took terrible casualties and made no impact on the Anglo-Saxon line. Some of them started to withdraw, and William saw that he must play his trump card. He ordered the cavalry to charge. But the demands made on even the Normans' strong horses to charge two hundred and fifty paces up a hill carrying a knight in full armour meant that, by the time the attackers reached the defenders, their pace was slow.

As the cavalry approached the Anglo-Saxon line, the housecarls broke ranks, dropped their shields and picked up their axes. They spread themselves out as much as they could so that they were able to swing their deadly blades. Horses, knights and soldiers were hacked and mercilessly slaughtered as the housecarls went about their work. There was general panic amongst the attackers and they started to stream down the hill in full retreat.

The effect on the fyrdsmen of seeing their enemy fleeing the field was immediate. Previously, the shield wall had been compact and continuous but now, since the housecarls had broken ranks to wield their axes, there were gaps. Many fyrdsmen streamed through the gaps in pursuit of the enemy.

"Stop, you idiots! Hold the ranks!" screamed Torkil. But to no avail. Many of the fyrdsmen were already too far down the hill to return when the Breton cavalry wheeled about and attacked the lightly armed Anglo-Saxons in open country.

Harold decided to exploit the Norman retreat by advancing the shield wall down the hill. In their confusion, the Normans were powerless to resist the advance. Chaos reigned in their ranks as William was thrown from his horse, and the false rumour spread that he had been killed. Nothing could stop the Anglo-Saxons now with their enemy fleeing before them in disarray.

A trumpet sounded to halt the advance. "Why are we stopping?" the nearest housecarls demanded of Torkil.

"I don't know. This is madness. We have victory in sight!"

He sent a messenger down the line to where the royal standards were fluttering to enquire why the advance had halted.

After a time, the messenger returned.

"Earl Leofwine has been killed, and the King is rearranging the command on the right."

William, mounted on a new horse, had regrouped his men and led a charge which forced the Anglo-Saxons back up the hill with serious losses. The shield wall reformed but, in furious hand-to-hand fighting, Earl Gyrth was killed. In the middle of this skirmish, William was dismounted again and had to find another horse by commanding one of his knights to relinquish his. When the knight refused, Duke William killed him.

It was now two in the afternoon. Both sides had fought each other to a standstill and there was a pause in the fighting.

Torkil addressed his housecarls. "Our numbers are depleted, but we can fight for a stalemate for we will have reinforcements arriving soon. The Normans can only fight to win. They are trapped with dwindling supplies. We must hold the shield wall until nightfall."

The Normans began the attack again by probing the flanks of the defenders' line and, on several occasions, managed to tempt the fyrdsmen to break ranks, only to be turned upon and slaughtered. This gradually, but significantly, depleted the number of defenders on the flanks. At the same time, the attackers discovered that they could approach the Anglo-Saxons on the gently sloping west side of the hill, and began to exploit this route. This meant that the defenders were now facing an enemy coming from two directions, one of which gave the Normans the possibility of charging directly at their enemy's standards. The Anglo-Saxon shield wall began to shorten and, as the defenders were increasingly compacted, William gave orders for his archers to fire high in the air so that their arrows fell on the Anglo-Saxons' heads. While they tried to protect themselves from the missiles with their shields held high, the Normans called up their reserve cavalry to make a charge.

The old Danish warrior was shaken out of his daydreaming by a trumpet blast nearby. He kicked his horse and trotted forward to join his *conroy* in the line of riders to receive orders.

The cavalry marshal cantered to the centre of the line. "You are to canter up the western slope and attack the enemy from that side. It is too long and steep to gallop all the way. There is very close hand-to-hand fighting going on; no room for lances. Use maces or swords. You are our last reserve. The Duke depends on you to bring us victory."

Ivar stabbed his lance into the mud where it was collected by a foot soldier, and unclipped his mace from his belt. The riders spurred their horses, and the line of cavalry leapt immediately into a canter.

Torkil's housecarls were ordered to group in the centre of the line to protect the standards. They moved with difficulty through the furious hand-to-hand fighting, sometimes fighting back-to-back with a comrade against the attackers. The carnage was awful with the dead and the dying everywhere. The cacophony of metal against metal, horses whinnying, wounded men screaming in agony, and foes cursing each other added to the general chaos.

William could now see Harold surrounded by the remaining housecarls, standing by the banners. Any thought of challenging Harold to single combat had long left his head, but he knew that his enemy would have to be killed if he were to achieve victory. He picked four knights: Hugh de Montfort, Walter Giffard, Hugh de Ponthieu and Eustace of Boulogne and tasked them with hunting down King Harold while a general distracting assault was made on the housecarls from the west by his reserve cavalry.

Torkil was standing next to Godric when the cavalry rode towards them from the west side of the battle. The remaining housecarls readied themselves for the assault. In so doing, their attention was taken away from the King who was waiting, sword in hand, by the standards. Torkil glanced round at him and was alarmed to see four horsemen coming from the east side heading directly towards the King. One lowered a lance and thrust it through the King's chest. The knights leapt from their horses and attacked the dying King with their swords, one severing his head.

Whether the distraction of watching the King's death caused him to be less wary than he should have been or whether it would have made no difference does not matter. The leading rider in the cavalry charge swung a spiked mace which struck Torkil on the shoulder. The force of the blow knocked him to the ground, his helmet fell off, and his chain mail hood fell back across his shoulders. The rider dismounted and walked back to Torkil who had by now raised himself to his knees. The cavalryman swung his sword at Torkil's neck. In the late afternoon sunshine, the housecarl saw the flash of the sword and heard the swish as the weapon flew through the air. The power of the blow registered but, beyond that, he felt no pain for the nerves which would have registered such feeling were severed.

The four knights dragged off King Harold's mail shirt, dismembered his body and castrated the corpse before presenting it to William. The fighting continued sporadically, for none of the housecarls asked for quarter, and none was given. Others had already left the field; many fyrdsmen had deserted before the final act. But the Normans had not finished and pursued the fleeing Anglo-Saxons so that the slaughter continued until nightfall. This pursuit was to prove costly for the Normans.

As the Anglo-Saxons fled, they met a strong force of

housecarls, the reinforcements which had just arrived from London. A force which, had they arrived two hours earlier, could have turned the tide of battle. These new troops, together with some fleeing soldiers, formed a strong defensive position to the north of Battle Hill on the edge of a ravine. When the Norman cavalry attacked the new force in the gathering dusk, they were unaware of the precipitous ravine, and many horses and men fell to their deaths.

This setback for the Normans could not change the fact that the Anglo-Saxons had been vanquished, but at huge cost to both sides. Of the fifteen thousand combatants, perhaps six thousand were dead, and more would die of their wounds. The totality of King Harold's defeat was matched only by the enormity of the influence the outcome was to have on the people of his kingdom.

# Chapter 21

## The Aftermath

At first light, Ivar crawled out of his bivouac, a sheet of greased sail cloth propped up with poles, the standard issue for the troops. He shivered although he had his thick sheepskin coat on. His feet felt numb with cold, even though he had slept in his boots. Men were already on the move up the hill, for the prospect of rich pickings overcame the need for rest. After yesterday's exhausting battle, the spoils would be waiting for the victors.

Ivar ached from the exertions of the day before, exertions which twenty years ago would not have caused a twinge. The pain in his body was compounded by the night's uneasy rest on the hard, damp ground. There was a heavy dew on the grass and the indications were that rain might soon add to the dampness.

Ivar looked at the height of the hill and decided that to walk up was the lot of the infantry. He was a cavalryman and would let his horse make the effort. His mount was tethered to a peg which had been hammered into the ground, the neat circle of close-cropped grass showing that the animal had already breakfasted on such forage as was available. Ivar brushed the cobwebs, which had optimistically been woven during the night, off the wet saddle and threw it over the horse's back before reaching under the animal's belly to grasp the girth and latch it tight. After forcing the bit in the unwilling animal's mouth and fastening the throat lash, Ivar took the reins and led it over to his bivouac to reach inside for his sword belt.

The smoke from the cooking fires made patterns in the windless sky behind him as he guided the horse between the obstacles on the slope: piles of byrnies, dead horses, and corpses in ghoulish profusion in the positions the warriors had been in when death overtook them. With the advantage of the speed of the horse even when walking, Ivar was soon ahead of the throng of men labouring up the hill. Nevertheless, there were already some people at the top as he approached. But most of them were not soldiers: there were priests incanting, waggoners piling bodies on to their carts, and some women who were searching for their menfolk's bodies. But even their presence did not deter the carrion hunters. Magpies and crows hopped from body to body defiling the mangled cadavers. The whole area was a jumble of corpses and the detritus of war. Here and there, some of the seemingly dead were moaning in pain. Ivar knew that they would soon receive the attention of the soldiers climbing the hill and the moaning would stop.

The royal standard of the pretender King Harold was gone, as was his body, but it was clear where the last stand had been for there the preponderance of slain were bearded and moustached Anglo-Saxon housecarls.

Ivar was intrigued about the red-haired housecarl he had killed. As the man had been in the royal bodyguard, he must have been a person of some importance. Ivar recalled that, as the Anglo-Saxon had looked up at him, his eyes betraying that he recognised the inevitability of his impending death, there was something about his appearance which reminded Ivar of himself twenty years ago.

He dismounted, tied his horse to a bush and wandered around the site of the climax of the battle. By this time, the crowd of plunderers was beginning to arrive at the top of the hill. The first of them had already started stripping byrnies off the bodies, and any other objects which they could later sell for a good price. It was in front of two men conducting their ghastly business that Ivar found the head with the red hair, a head made redder by the gore of decapitation.

"Leave that body," instructed Ivar to the two soldiers. They could hear from his accent that he was not a Norman and realised that he was a mercenary.

"You can't give us orders. Go back to your own country."

Ivar's sword was in his hand in an instant. "If you want to see your families again then do as I say."

The soldiers looked at each other and let go of the mail shirt they had been pulling off the body. Both knew that they had been lucky to have survived yesterday and did not relish taking risks today.

"What's that in your hand?" demanded Ivar.

"Oh, come on. We are allowed to take what we can find," said one of them. He opened his hand and in it, though partly covered in blood, a silver object glinted.

Ivar, realising that this might be a clue to the man's identity, said, "This is for you. Give me the chain." Ivar threw a silver piece on the ground in front of the soldier.

He scrambled to pick it up and handed the bloody chain to Ivar who wiped it on his jacket and sheathed his sword. At the end of the chain was a bear's claw. It was almost identical to the one on the pommel of his sword.

"How about another silver piece for this?" said the second soldier, holding up a flat package, wrapped in greased cloth, with a leather thong running through it.

"What is it?" asked Ivar.

"Don't know. He was wearing it round his neck."

Ivar reached into his pouch and took out another coin. Sitting on a pile of shields, he carefully tore open the package using his seax. Inside was a piece of folded vellum. The inscription on the page read: *Ego Torkilus tainus Selceefletis Vectis insulae Finni normanni pronepo oro pro remissionem peccatorum. Deus misereatur animae meae.*

One of the two soldiers had been watching Ivar as he opened the package. He came over to where the Dane was sitting and asked, "What does it say?"

With a shocked look on his face, Ivar slowly said, "I, Torkil, thayne of Selceeflet on Vectis, great grandson of Finn the Norseman, pray for forgiveness of my sins and may God have mercy on my soul."

One of the wagons lumbered past where Ivar was sitting. The driver and his boy jumped out and lifted up two bodies to join those already in their load.

"Put this one on too," said Ivar.

"Can't do that. The Duke has ordered that we should pick up the Norman dead and leave the Anglo-Saxons to rot."

Ivar's sword was once more in his hand. "Put him and the head on your cart and bury him with the rest."

They did as they were bid.

# Epilogue

It is a little known fact that a decision made by King Edward at Britford, a short distance from Sarum, in 1065 set in train a series of events which ultimately led to the disaster of the Battle of Hastings. For it was at Britford that Earl Tostig was stripped of his earldom. This led to the bitter feud between Tostig and his brother King Harold which culminated in Tostig persuading Harald Hardrada to invade England. Had that invasion not taken place, King Harold would have had a well prepared, rested military force, which would have included the very best of his housecarls, to meet the Normans.

The 25 September 1066 was one of the most important days in English history, for it was the battle of Stamford which determined the fate of the Anglo-Saxon nation and led to the terrible misfortune of losing the battle of Hastings.

It is said that fortune favours the brave and, in the case of King Harold, this was certainly true at Stamford. The dividing line between audacious and foolhardy is sometimes hard to define, but in the case of the remarkable transport of ultimately fifteen thousand men and their equipment on old worn Roman roads two hundred miles, in at the maximum six days, must be rated as an outstanding military achievement. On arrival in York, the army would inevitably have been tired from the exertion of the forced march. Had they had to face a fully prepared Norwegian force of superior numbers, the outcome of the battle might well have been very different. But Harold had indeed good fortune by springing his surprise attack and catching the great warrior Hardrada, who was famous for his generally cautious nature, totally off guard, unprepared and inadequately armed.

Luck is a fickle mistress, and yet Duke William had it in abundance. He had been very lucky in the internal politics of Normandy prior to the invasion, but his greatest stroke of luck was perhaps that he did not make his invasion attempt in August 1066. Had he done so, his heavily laden open troop and horse transport ships could have run into King Harold's huge fleet of seven hundred ships. The result would have been inevitable. Even if he had managed to get ashore with his army at that time, he would have been met by an Anglo-Saxon force of vastly superior numbers.

His luck held when storms kept him at St Valery in September, because the outcome was that his enemy had to deal with the invasion by the Norsemen before, with depleted numbers, turning their attention to him.

It seemed impossible that Duke William's luck should continue, but it did. The English King, flushed with the scale of his victory in the north, made the impetuous decision to move against the Normans with an ill-prepared, inadequately equipped, tired army. Nevertheless, the Anglo-Saxons fought so bravely that, had they not stopped in their advance down the hill when Earl Leofwine was killed, they would probably have carried the day.

Luck for the Normans was bad luck for the English. Had their reinforcements arrived two hours earlier, it is unlikely that the tired Normans would have had the power to resist the fresh troops.

History would have been very different if Duke William had not been so extremely fortunate. For he might very easily have been driven back into the sea by the Anglo-Saxons where their fleet was waiting to prevent a retreat to Normandy. But there is another scenario. If King Harold's travel-weary army had met the full Norwegian army in a battle-prepared state at

Stamford, the outcome could well have been very different. It is quite likely that it would have been Hardrada's army, together with the reconstituted army of Morcar and Edwin which would have been Duke William's adversary at Hastings. The result of such a battle with far superior numbers against them would surely have been disastrous for the Normans. Such an outcome would have altered the course of world history, and the language spoken by the English people today would inevitably have been very different.

# Map of the route to Miklagård

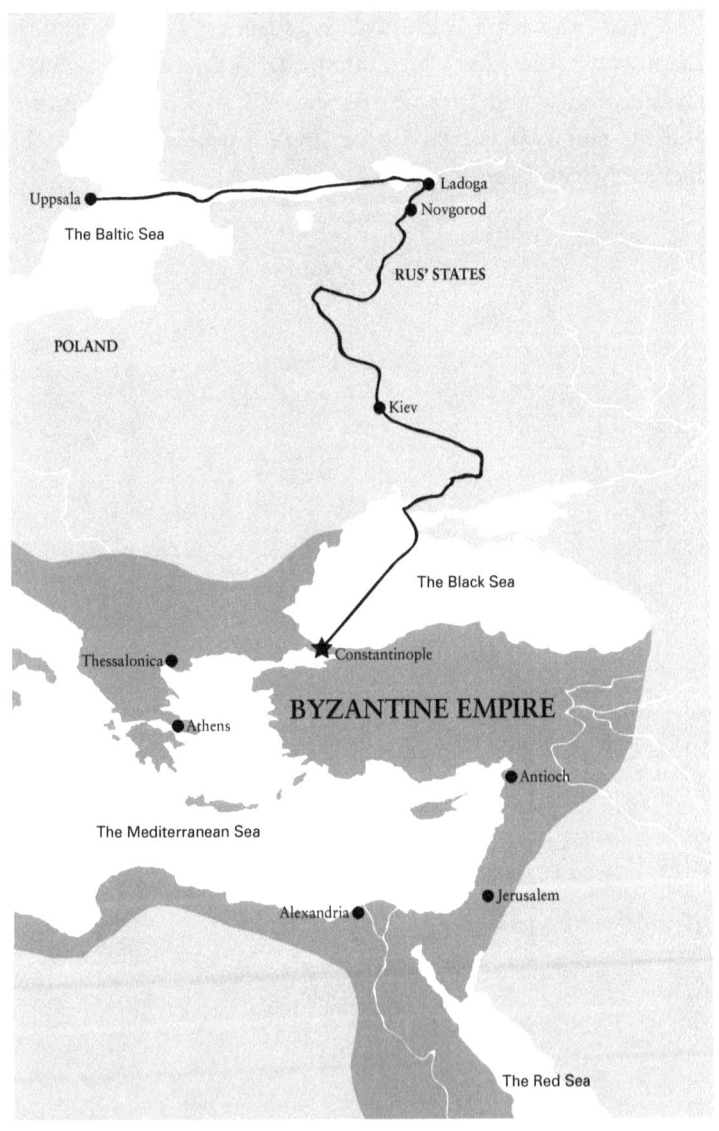

# Bibliography

*Turkey – A Short History*. Roderick H Davison Published by Eothen Press 1988

*The Anglo-Saxons*. James Campbell Published by Penguin Books 1991

*Exploring the World of the Vikings*. Richard Hall Published by Thames and Hudson 2007

*A History of the Swedish People*. Wilhelm Moberg Published by Norstedts 1972

*Story of the Crusades*. Alfred Duggan Published by Faber 1963

*The Penguin Historical Atlas of the Vikings*. John Haywood Published by Penguin 1995

*Harald Hardrada, The Warrior's Way*. John Marsden Published by Sutton Publishing 2007

*Blood Feud*. Rosemary Sutcliff Published by Puffin 1976

*The Anglo-Saxon Chronicle*. Published by Everyman Press 1912

*The Year 1000*. Robert Lacey and Danny Danziger Published by Abacus 2000

*The Godwins*. Frank Barlow Published by Pearson 2003

*1066 The Year of Three Battles*. Frank McLynne Published by Pimlico 1999

*Heimskringla: History of the Kings of Norway*. Snorre Sturluson Published by The University of Texas Press 1991

*Childhood in Anglo-Saxon England*. Sally Crawford Published by Sutton 1999